MW00941072

Portal to the Forgotten

John Gschwend

This book is a work of fiction. The characters, incidents and dialogs are products of the author's imagination and are not to be construed as real.

Copyright @ 2016 by John Gschwend

http://johngschwend.com

Chapter 1

Tyler stumbled over a box turtle. He rolled the turtle onto its belly with his hiking boot. "Sorry, little dude." Tyler rested and rubbed at his burning thighs. They had not ached this much since his football days in high school. He shook his head as he thought of it; that was only two years ago. He had better start exercising more often or forget ever keeping up with Grace.

"Come on Slowpoke," Grace said, as she stopped and turned back. "We can rest at the top of the hill. From there we can look down on all the beautiful, fall colors." She snapped around and started back up the trail.

He smiled and sucked in another deep breath. Looking up at her, he was looking at beauty right now—no need to climb and look back down for it. No pair of cargo pants ever looked better. Her blond hair, tied in a long ponytail, swung back and forth to match the dance of her hips. He would follow her anywhere. He laughed to himself. He had been following her everywhere since he had first met her in his history class at the University of Arkansas. He had followed her to her track meets, her karate tournaments, swimming competitions. Now here he was climbing some steep mountain just to be with her. She was nineteen and had more energy than a sugar-high hummingbird. Yeah, he believed he would continue to follow

3

her.

"Hey, Sweetie, wait just a minute," Tyler said, as he stopped and sat on a big rock. "Come and sit by me for a minute. I've gotta catch my breath."

Grace turned and giggled. "What's the matter, tough guy? You can't hang?" She skipped back to him and kissed him on the forehead. "We can rest a few minutes, but you have to keep the energy up, gotta keep the rush going." She snuggled next to him on the rock. "If you sit still too long, the laziness takes you."

Tyler put his sweaty arm around her. "I thought I was going to have to run you down and kick your butt."

She made a motion toward her waist as she always did to remind him of her black belt. She winked one of those big, blue eyes, and he melted inside all over again. She could have any guy she wanted. She wanted him. He was so extremely lucky to have a beauty that was not hung up on her beauty. She was hung up on living large…and him. He had been sure of it since the day she had carved—*Grace Easton loves Tyler Morgan* on a big oak at the university and faced the consequences straight on as she always faced everything.

"Look!" Grace pointed to an eagle floating overhead. "What a beautiful and graceful bird." She jerked her phone from her pocket and snapped a picture. "Ah, he's too high for a good picture."

Tyler watched it. She was right. A year ago, he may have noticed the eagle, but he would not have appreciated its beauty as he does now. In fact, with it being the middle of October, he would have bow in hand, hunting deer, not hiking and nature watching in the Ozark Mountains. Grace had done that to him. She had drawn him in like a moth to a light. He still loved to hunt, but not as much as he loved being with the ball of energy, Grace.

"Wouldn't it be wonderful to be able to fly?" Grace said as she marveled at the eagle making tight circles overhead. "You could just soar and be free."

Tyler dropped his gaze from the eagle to her. "You probably can. You can do everything else."

She spread her arms and pretended to soar. "It would be heavenly."

He noticed a scratch on her arm. "Hey, Babe, you okay?" He held her arm and inspected it.

"Oh, just a scratch where I scraped a rock down the trail. Don't worry so much."

He dabbed at it with his shirttail. "Maybe we should put something on that when we get back." As he fussed over her, he saw her turn and cock her head; then he heard it—drumming. It was a monotone sound: bum-bum, bum-bum, bum-bum. It grew progressively louder.

"What is that, Tyler?"

He looked in the direction from which it was coming. There was nothing there, just the trail going up the mountain. Suddenly, leaves and debris began moving toward the direction of the sound, as a magnet pulls metal nails. They swirled and seemed to disappear into nothingness on the trail. But there was no wind anywhere else, just there on the trail. The drumming grew louder. Then there were horns—trumpets, maybe.

Grace stood, turned to Tyler. "Did you see that?"

The debris moved as if toward a giant vacuum. The very air seemed to ripple like waves from a stone dropped in a pool. Tyler literally felt his skin crawl as he looked around for the quickest way down the mountain. He pulled at Grace. She pulled back, but he did not let go of her wrist.

"Let's go check it out," she said. Her eyes were wide with excitement as she tucked her phone back into her cargo pants.

"No. I...I don't know."

"There must be a camp or something up the hill. Someone up there has a little band."

Tyler felt his hairs stand on end. He saw Grace's do the same. It was as if a static charge was in the air.

"Come on, let's check it out!" She pulled away from his tight grip and ran toward the sound.

"Grace, wait!" He started after her. "There's something strange going on. I don't like the looks of it."

She ran about twenty yards. Instantly, she was gone! He blinked, could not believe it. She was nowhere in sight. She had disappeared into thin air! Tyler froze. He could not get his legs to work. He could not get his voice to sound. He may just as well have turned to stone.

"Bum-bum, bum-bum, bum-bum." The sound grew softer and softer until it was gone. It was like the music from a convertible's radio as it traveled down the highway. The farther away the car went, the quieter the music became until it was gone altogether.

The leaves stopped swirling. The static charge was gone too.

Tyler closed his eyes and rubbed them with his fists. When he opened them, Grace was still gone. He finally got his legs to work, and he staggered to where he last saw her. He searched in all directions, but found nothing. He sank to his knees. "Grace! Oh, God. Grace!"

The eagle's shadow passed over him as it soared away.

Chapter 2

As the day grew, the autumn chill fled from the sun. A man shielded his eyes from it as he noted it beginning to peek over the trees. He huffed a breath and now it was invisible—not a good sign. He had better get on with it before it grew too warm. He shucked his buckskin jacket and draped it over a log. He then knelt onto one knee and placed his deerskin moccasin onto his fireboard. He spit into his hands, and retrieved a wood drill he had leaned against the log, inspected it, still in good shape. The slender cottonwood stick had served him well many times. He placed the round end of the stick into a small depression on the fireboard and began rotating it between his hands. After a short time, smoke began to rise from where the stick rotated in the depression. As the smoke increased, he rubbed his hands back and forth faster, making the stick spin faster, until smoke rolled from the fireboard. He lifted the stick and a small, orange ember rolled out of a notch he had carved into the depression and onto a leaf that he had placed there to catch it. He carefully lifted the leaf with the ember cradled in it and placed it into a wad of grass and wood shavings, which resembled a bird nest. The bird nest had been situated at the base of a pile of sticks he had arranged for a campfire. He blew at the ember and it flashed bright. He kept blowing and it kept flashing until the bird nest erupted into a ball of fire. He fanned it with his leather hat until the sticks caught as well. He drew in a satisfying breath and smiled as he did every time he started a fire in this manner. He felt a kinship to his ancient ancestors.

Now that the fire was going, he bent over a freshly skinned deer and carved a thin slice of meat from a ham. The sharp, stone flake he used zipped through the meat with great efficiency as such stone tools had done for millennia. After cutting several more slices, he hung them from a rack he had fashioned from green saplings. He watched smoke drift over the meat, keeping flies away and curing it at the same time.

He felt that old pride again knowing he would waste none of the deer he had killed. The meat would be smoked. The tendons would be removed and later dried to be made into bowstrings and to lash stone points and feathers to his arrows. The hide would be brain tanned to make buckskin. The bones would be used to make tools. He knew nature provided all that a man could need.

Soon he had the rack full of meat and the deer processed to the best of his ability with his primitive tools. He sat by the fire and nursed it. He needed the smoke to stay over the meat and do its job. He was grateful for the deer and his own ability to hunt and kill it. He bowed his head, prayed, and gave thanks to the Creator for giving him the ability to hunt and to kill his food. However, more than that, he honored the deer for its sacrifice so the hunter could live.

Slowly, he raised his head to listen, frowned. He heard a sound he dreaded, the sound of wheels on the dirt road behind him. As the sound drew close, he turned to see his ex-wife driving up in her big Expedition, smothering his smoking meat in dust. The moment was spoiled for all time now.

She slid out of the vehicle, her jeans so tight it must have taken her an hour just to get them on. "Hey, Tonto, how's it goin'?" That was probably the only Indian name she knew. She was not known for her brain—he had not married her for it anyway. That is why the marriage had not lasted—nothing at all in common. "I almost forgot how far back in the boonies you live."

He took in a deep breath, had to summon up patience, and placed another stick on the fire.

"I see you done killed another Bambi," she said, as she flung her long brunette hair out of her eyes. She picked his homemade, hickory bow off the picnic table. "You know they make these things now with wheels on them, supposed to make them easier to shoot. It's what they shoot on TV on them hunting shows."

Yes, Chris, compound bows. He thought it, but didn't say it —no need prolonging the unwelcome visit.

"That wouldn't do for you would it, Luke?" She dropped the bow down on the table. "Oh, no. You gotta live like you was in the Stone Age." She rolled her eyes. "Why don't you get a life?"

He let it pass. His days of fighting with her were long over. The heartache was finally gone too.

"I've been trying to call you all week," she said, as she planted her butt on the picnic table. "I'm sure lots a people been trying to call you, but I reckon you left your phone at home again like you always do when you go play Fred Flintstone. You could at least tell folks where you're camping."

"Cut the crap, Chris. What's up?" He got to his feet and dusted off his seat.

"Boy, Luke, you've lost your pot belly." She looked him up and down. "Maybe we could go out sometime."

He had lost weight because of the hard divorce, but he was not going to let her know that. "Come on, Chris; what is it?"

She sighed. "Well, while you was out hunting like a wild Indian, they locked up your cousin, Tyler."

"Tyler! For what?"

She flicked a tiny, rock elm leaf from her sleeve. "They have him for murder or kidnapping or something."

"Murder!" He marched to her and grabbed her arm. "Damn it, Chris, stop goofing around."

9

She pulled free. "He said they had been hiking up at Gentry Knob, him and that girl, Grace Easton, and she just disappeared." She made quotation marks with her fingers as she said, "Disappeared."

"What do you mean, *disappeared?*"

She made the quotation marks again. "Disappeared."

He sat on the table beside her. "You for real?"

"Yeah." She softened. "And, Luke, they say he had her blood on his shirt. They got him at the county."

Luke closed his eyes and tried to calm himself. Tyler was as good a boy as they come. Luke knew he had not harmed anyone, especially his girlfriend—he adored her.

"What do you think?" she said.

He had no watch on, so he looked up at the sun again. It was getting around noon, too late to do anything today after the meat was smoked—it would be a sin against nature to waste it. "Gentry Knob is in my township. I'm going to the county and talk to him tomorrow."

"Are you kiddin'? Sheriff Scott will laugh you out of the jailhouse." She hopped off the table and dusted her butt. "Luke, the people voted you constable as a joke to get rid of that old fart, Mr. Rincon, who had been constable for a hundred years. And who better to put in that position than shy, ole Luke? You were just a stooge. The guys are still laughing down at Jack's Bar."

He knew she was right. He had been the constable for over a year and never really exercised his authority. He was too embarrassed to do anything, but now he had to do something for his cousin.

"If you go over there, the high sheriff might throw you in the pokey." She put her arms around him. "Seriously Luke, they've got him a lawyer from Fayetteville; he's in good hands. There's nothing you can do for him." She saw his mind was made up and dropped her arms from around him. "Look, Luke, it looks bad for him. You remember my friend, Sarah? Well, now she works over there at the jail. She said they all believe he killed the girl."

Luke kicked an acorn with his moccasin. "Thanks for telling me. Now I have to figure what to do. Tyler didn't kill anyone. I'll talk to him tomorrow. I'll take the district attorney with me if I have to, but the sheriff will have to let me talk to him."

She nodded, shrugged her shoulders, and went to her vehicle. "Luke." She hesitated, and then said, "I'm sorry. I hope it works out. I know how freaky you are around people; glad to see a little spunk out of you for a change. Might would still have this if you had been spunky when we was married." She put her hands on her hips and winked. He gave her a half smile. With that, she climbed aboard, wrestled the long SUV around, and drove away.

He added sticks and built the fire back up, crossed his legs and sat beside it. He watched the smoke do its magic on the meat, but his mind was on Tyler. Tomorrow Luke would not be living the old way like his ancient ancestors. He would be back in the modern age. And he would have to be a real constable, not just a title. He was good in the wild, better than anyone he knew, scared of nothing in it. He wished he had that same courage around people; but no matter how hard he tried, he didn't. His skin crawled just thinking about dealing with a lot of people. Tomorrow he would have to face his fears. Tomorrow he had to help Tyler.

Luke parked his pickup in front of the jail. He sat in the truck and stared at the modern detention facility. It seemed out of place in the historic town. It was nothing like the old jail, which was a relic from the Old West. The old jail fit the town better, but it burned to the ground a couple of years ago. Luke sighed thinking about it. He hated seeing historical things disappear. Oh, well, time waits on no one. He looked at the front door and summoned the courage to get out of his pickup and go in. It would not be easy—hell, his heart raced thinking about it. He felt like Gary Cooper in *High Noon* as he reached up and touched the badge pinned to his shirt pocket, never had worn it in public before. He had only put his name on the ballot because his buddies dared him, and he thought it would look good to Chris. He had been a fool for her—she had made a fool of him. "What the hell." He stepped out of the truck.

When he opened the front door, Sarah, sitting at her desk, smiled, said, "Hi, Luke. Chris said you would be comin' today."

Luke noticed a woman with short, red hair sitting in a chair by the wall. Luke nodded at her, turned back to Sarah and smiled. "How are you, Sarah?"

She stood. She had gained a lot of weight since he had last seen her. "Luke, Hon, don't wear that badge in here. You know how the sheriff feels about constables. He threw Ricky Fannon out the other day, said if he came back he'd chunk his fat butt in the jail. I'm sure one of the deputies will let you talk to Tyler, but not with that badge on." She looked past him. "Oh, crap!"

The door swung open and Sheriff Scott stepped in. He was big as a damn Sasquatch. He was so intimidating, no one had run for sheriff against him in years. His eyes fell on Luke's badge right off, then drifted up to Luke's eyes and settled there.

To Luke's surprise, he was not afraid of the big man at all. He was determined. "Sheriff, I need to see Tyler."

"Not with that badge on you're not. No one sees my prisoners unless I say so. This is my jail—the county jail. Go find you a township jail to preside over." He stepped past Luke and dropped a folder on Sarah's desk.

The red-haired woman stood up from the chair. "Sheriff, I've been sitting here all morning, and I was here yesterday. Please just give me a little of your time. Tell me about the girl disappearing."

"I have nothing to say to you, Miss." He turned back to Luke. "I have nothing to say to you either."

Luke pulled the badge from his shirt and dropped it into his pocket. "I need to talk to my cousin."

A wry smile grew on the sheriff's face. He stood there for a long minute saying nothing, then yelled for someone named Rocky.

A skinny deputy came from a small side office. "Yeah, Sheriff?"

"Take Luke Morgan up to see his cousin." The sheriff went into his office, but called out, "Pat him down before he goes in. Arrest him if he has a gun."

Luke thought to himself, *The arrogant ape thinks he is insulting me, but all I want is to see Tyler.*

The deputy let Luke in after a sorry attempt at a pat-down, then locked the door behind him and disappeared down the hall.

Tyler bear-hugged Luke. "Where have you been? They think I killed Grace!"

They sat on the bed. "I was camping in the mountains, deer hunting."

"Luke, she freakin' disappeared. You hear me? Disappeared!"

Luke scratched the back of his neck. He didn't know how to interrogate, but he'd watched enough reruns of *Columbo* to get a general idea. "Start from the top."

Tyler told him the story and Luke just sat there for a time trying to let it register. "You sure she didn't fall or something?"

Tyler stood. "Luke, I've been hunting all my life, just like you. I know my way around the woods almost as good as you do." He walked across the room and turned. "She disappeared. Poof! We heard drumming, and she ran toward it and vanished. I never took my eyes off her. She was there one instant, and the next, she was gone."

"What about the blood, Tyler."

"She had scratched her arm, and I wiped it with my shirttail."

Luke closed his eyes. The story was so far out there. He didn't know what to do. Tyler was as close to him as any brother could be, and he had never been a liar.

Tyler sat back on the bed beside Luke. "Luke, I know how this sounds, but I can only tell the truth." He squeezed Luke's arm. "I've always only told the truth. You know that."

Luke looked squarely in Tyler's face. "I believe you. There has to be an explanation. I'm going up to Gentry Knob when I leave here. What about this drumming?"

Tyler got back up from the bed and paced the small cell. "Yeah. It was weird. Bum-bum, bum-bum and horns too. And there was this strange charge in the air. Our hairs stood out like when you rub a balloon to your head. Leaves seemed to be sucked to the place where she disappeared at. Hell, Luke, it's like she stepped through an invisible crack and disappeared. I was so scared I couldn't get my feet to work. Then, almost immediately the static and drumming was gone."

"And so was Grace," Luke said.

Luke stood, and Tyler buried his face in his shoulder and cried.

When Luke walked by Sarah's desk, she whispered, "I'll watch out for him the best I can."

Luke whispered back, "Thanks, Sarah."

"You bet." She winked. "Don't forget, Luke. I'm available. I don't care if that trashy Chris is my friend. She was so mean to you. It was such a waste of a good man."

Luke felt his face burn red, nodded, and started for the door. The red-haired woman, still in the chair, smiled.

The pickup rocked and jerked as he climbed the narrow mountain road. He did not know the area that well, not a lot of deer up there. Tyler had not known it well, either. That Grace could lead him anywhere—she was always high on adventure. He parked the truck at the trailhead. There was never a lot of traffic there. No one wanted to hike the steep and rugged trail.

He threw his backpack on and headed up. The afternoon sun had warmed up the October day, and spider webs hung across the trail, a sign nothing had used the trail recently. His lungs and legs were thankful he was in good shape because the trail was not for the weak.

He had always been up for exploring, had been exploring the Ozark Mountains since he was a kid. Luke took pride in knowing his great-grandmother was an Osage Indian. His friends said there was no way he had Indian blood in him, with his blond hair and blue eyes, but he felt her blood in his veins, no matter what they said. He felt a kinship to the land, felt more at home in the wild than with people. The Osage once called these very mountains their mountains. Maybe that explained why he felt the way he did when he was in them. From books he had learned to build ancient tools—bows, arrows, knives. That did not matter; he still felt a connection to the ancients of the mountains, as if they had taught him. When he killed a deer with the weapons he had made himself from nature, he felt connected to the natural world. He could never explain it when people asked him why he hunted with them, especially his ex-wife. But when he took his stone-age tools with him, when he wore his buckskins and leather hat, when he left his cell phone at home, it was truly spiritual to him. When Luke killed his prey this way, he believed he felt the way wild predators felt—it was nature.

Luke found the spot where Grace had disappeared. There was yellow police tape strung from trees and rocks—ridiculous. Now Luke didn't feel like such an amateur lawman.

Luke found the big rock Tyler had described, sat on it and imagined what Tyler saw. The trail ahead where Grace was supposed to have disappeared was narrow, with big rocks on both sides. She could not have fallen or even walked off the trail there; she would have had to climb to get off it, and then, she would have had to have a rope. A flat rock on one side of the trail was large—much taller than a person. The other side of the trail was basically the side of the mountain, and it went straight up for twenty feet. It was like a canyon or funnel that ran for about a hundred feet. She would have had to sprint up the trail for a long way before she could have stepped off it. Tyler had said he had never taken his eyes off her.

Luke walked up and down the trail several times. There was no way that girl could have gotten out of Tyler's sight, unless he closed his eyes and counted like he was playing hide-and-go-seek or something.

Luke went back to the big rock and sat on it again. A shadow moved over him, and he looked up to see a bald eagle—not something you see often there. He watched it ride the thermals, just floating above the world. Luke imagined what it must be like to see the world from up there. Eagles and hawks float around on high, scanning below for movement or any sign of prey. It was a vantage point hunters can never have. The closest thing was climbing a tree or sitting in a tree stand. Luke closed his eyes and floated with the eagle. He could almost feel the wind. He could almost—

Suddenly, a feeling came over him—the spirit. At least, that is what he believed it was whenever his skin would begin to tingle and all his senses flared. It would happen when an animal or person was near, but he had not seen it, yet. The spirit was on him now like a sixth sense. He opened his eyes, but did not move a muscle. A bobcat was only a few yards from him and walking up the trail to where Grace was last seen. Luke watched the cat as it eased through the narrow draw. But yet, it did not disappear, just kept going until it rounded a curve in the trail and was lost to Luke's sight.

He stood up from the rock and looked down at the tracks in the dirt. The bobcat had walked right by Luke and had not noticed him. Luke knew it was because its sense of smell was not as good as many other animals. Bobcats depended on sound and sight, and Luke had not moved.

Luke noticed bear tracks in the dirt too. He had not noticed them earlier when he was looking around in the draw. He followed them toward the spot where Grace was last scene. It was a big bear. It was easy to follow with such a big print. This would be a good bear to kill. He could use the hide and meat. He could make oil from the fat. He had done this before. He could fashion a coat... The tracks stopped. They stopped right in the middle of the trail. Luke looked up. It was the spot where Tyler had said Grace had disappeared; yellow tape was tied to a nook in the big rock. He felt a strange chill. There was no mistake; the tracks stopped as surely...as surely as if the bear had vanished into thin air. But Luke had walked through the area several times; nothing had happened to him. Nothing had happened to the bobcat.

Luke pulled the water bottle from his pack and emptied it in just a few gulps. He was immediately hot—immediately cold. He walked backwards a few steps, then turned and started back toward his truck. He took long strides down the hill, sliding, and almost running. He had the sensation that someone was behind him. He was never afraid in the wild, but he was afraid now. This was not nature. This was not natural. That bear did not fly off that trail.

When he made it down to his truck, he turned back and looked at the mountain. Usually when he came back to his truck, it meant he was back in the modern world, and he felt a little depressed. Now he felt relief. He also felt shame.

What was he going to do? He could not tell the sheriff about the bear disappearing. Hell, he could not tell anyone—they'd think him crazy or a liar...just like Tyler. He got in the truck and laid his head on the steering wheel. He would go home and build a fire outside. This was how he always worked out his problems. He started the truck and wheeled it around. He would need a big fire.

Chapter 3

When Luke pulled up at his log cabin, a Ford Focus was there. He didn't know how the little car had traversed the rough road, but there it sat like a big, blue bug. His cabin door swung open, and a red-haired woman stepped out onto the porch, waved at him as if she were an old friend stopping by for a visit. He recognized her; it was the woman from the jail, the red-haired reporter.

Luke felt his face burn. Here was a total stranger coming out of his home without being invited into his home. But at the same time, he was curious why she had come and how she had found the place. He drew in a breath to calm himself.

When Luke stepped out of the truck, she leaned on a porch column. "I'm sorry to go in your home without being invited, but I had to use the little girl's room."

"Did you find it okay?"

"Yes, thank you."

As Luke walked toward the porch, she went out to meet him. Extending her hand, she said, "Hello, I'm Moon."

He shook her hand. "Moon?"

"Yes. Moon Serling."

"Like *The Twilight Zone* Serling?"

She smiled. "The same spelling."

Her smile lit her up, changed her as the tail fan changes a bland peacock. Her dark, rusty hair just touched her shoulders and curled up just a little like *That Girl*. She was short, maybe five feet, and for some reason, he had always been attracted to short women. Her eyes were as blue as a baby-doll's eyes. She would have been extremely pretty, except for the stud sticking to the side of her nose like a BB—he was not into that. She had no makeup and he liked that. Luke caught himself. His ex-wife had said all men always judge women by their looks. He had to stop if for nothing else but proving her wrong.

"Alright, Miss *'Twilight Zone*,' why are you snooping around my cabin?" Luke opened the door and went into the cabin before she could answer. He scanned around; everything seemed to be in place. He had nothing there of value to anyone, but him.

She followed him in. "It's Moon, and I wasn't snooping around. I told you; I had to use the bathroom."

He struck a match, bent, and started a fire in the potbelly, wood stove in the center of the cabin. "Have a seat." She sat on a bench at the kitchen table.

He took the blue coffee pot off the stove, lifted the lid and inspected the inside. Then he took it to the sink and placed it under the hand-pump. He poured a little water from a jar down the pump and began working the handle. Soon he had it primed and water spilling out and into the coffee pot.

"You don't have running water?"

He filled the pot, poured coffee in the top of it, and placed it on top of the stove. He turned to her. She sat at the table in the middle of a two-room log cabin and was as out of place as a Cadillac in a cornfield. Everything about her said "city girl." He shook his head. "No running water."

"I can assume, then, your toilet is outside." She grew sheepish.

"That would be a correct assumption." He sat across the table from her.

She let out a long sigh and sank in her chair.

"Want to tell me why you're here and snooping around?"

"I wasn't really snooping." She sat up straight and placed her hands on the table, palms down. "Constable, I saw you at the sheriff's office. I know you interviewed the man who was with the girl who disappeared."

"How did you find out where I live, and what do you want?"

"That receptionist, Sarah, likes to talk." She winked. "And she's hot for you."

Luke blushed—he always had a problem with turning red for no reason. "Well, what do you want?"

"I work for the *Arkansas Daily*. I'm doing a piece on people vanishing. That mean ole sheriff wouldn't let me talk to Tyler."

"Miss, you talk as if people vanish into thin air every day."

"There are more instances of it than you would believe. There was an old man recently in Kentuck—"

"Look, I'm sure you are a nice enough girl and all, but I have nothing to say on the matter." Luke didn't know why it disturbed him so, but he didn't want to talk about it. He had not come to grips with the disappearing bear tracks, yet—not to mention Grace. Now, here was this strange girl with this ridiculous notion. On top of that, he didn't believe she was a reporter.

"Did you go up there?" she said.

He got up from the table. "Ma'am, I have nothing else to say." He reached up on a shelf and retrieved his bow drill kit. "Now, I'm not going to be rude, but I'm going outside and start a fire."

She stood. I guess I'm wasting my time here."

"I'm sorry."

She followed him out the door and stood by her car.

Luke went around to his backyard fire pit. He soon had a fire started with his bow drill. He could have lit a match or brought fire from the stove, but that was not how he started his fires when he wanted to relax and meditate. When he would sit by the fire, he would imagine going back in time. Starting the fire like the ancients primed him for the journey.

He went back to the house to pour a cup of coffee to drink by the fire. She was sitting on the porch. He wondered why she had not left.

He stepped up to her. She was wiping tears. She said, "I'm sorry, but I just don't know what to do."

Luke ran his fingers through his hair. "You drink coffee?"

She wiped her eyes again. "Sure."

"I only make it black."

"Black is fine."

"I've started a fire around the back. You go on around there, and I will bring the coffee."

"Sure. Thanks."

He poured the coffee and thought how strange the situation was. Here was a pretty girl at his house and he wanted her to leave. She was here because she wanted a story about people disappearing. It was a very strange day. What was next—Big Foot coming to visit?

She was sitting on a stick of firewood when he went around there. He handed her the coffee and then sat flat on the ground by the fire. She got off the firewood and sat beside him—a little too close.

"When I was in your house, I saw you have a lot of primitive weapons," she said, then blew on the coffee.

"You mean when you were snooping."

She smiled and then slowly nodded.

"They're not weapons. They're tools." He sipped his coffee. "It's a passion of mine to live as simple as I can, to make my own tools for hunting and fishing and stuff."

"Cool."

The more he looked at her, the prettier he found her, BB and all. She smiled at him, and he felt his face turn red and a flutter flared inside like when he was a teenager.

"You have a great place here, way back by yourself and all."

"Moon, what are you doing here? What do you want to know?"

She perked up. "I just want to know what happened. The

sheriff's department said Tyler said the girl just disappeared. It's the making of an interesting story."

"Interesting is not the word. I believe tragic is better. I knew Grace. I mean, know Grace."

She bit her bottom lip. "I'm sorry. You're right." She picked up a stick and stuck it in the fire. "Constable, did you go up there?"

"Luke. The name is Luke."

"Okay, Luke, did you go up there?"

He put his own stick in the fire. "Yeah, I went up there."

"Well, what did you find?"

"Nothing." He saw no reason to tell her about the bear tracks. In fact, he was starting to believe there had to be an explanation. Maybe the wind blew the tracks away or something. There had to be something. Things just don't disappear.

"Will you take me to the place? The sheriff's department would not even tell me where it is."

"Look Moon, people don't disappear into the blue." He stirred in the fire with a big stick. "I don't know what happened, yet, but people just don't up and disappear."

"Yes, they do. They have been disappearing into thin air as long as there has been history."

"Bull! It's just a modern bunch of crap. They show all that UFO stuff on TV, and people will believe anything. It's all the rage with vampires, werewolves, spacemen; you name it."

"It's not new, Luke." She pulled a few sheets of paper from her small purse. "In fact, here is the story that got me into this stuff." She handed him the papers.

He unfolded them. They were worn from many foldings. "What is it?"

"Please read it, if you don't mind."

He smoothed the papers and began to read. "*One morning in July, 1854, a planter named Orion Williamson, living six miles from Selma, Alabama, was sitting with his wife and a child on the veranda of his dwelling. Immediately in front of the house was a lawn, perhaps fifty*

22

yards in extent between the house and public road, or, as it was called, the "pike." Beyond this road lay a close-cropped pasture of some ten acres, level and without a tree, rock, or any natural or artificial object on its surface. At the time there was not even a domestic animal in the field. In another field, beyond the pasture, a dozen slaves were at work under an overseer.

Throwing away the stump of a cigar, the planter rose, saying: "I forgot to tell Andrew about those horses." Andrew was the overseer.

Williamson strolled leisurely down the gravel walk, plucking a flower as he went, passed across the road and into the pasture, pausing a moment as he closed the gate leading into it, to greet a passing neighbor, Armour Wren, who lived on an adjoining plantation. Mr. Wren was in an open carriage with his son James, a lad of thirteen. When he had driven some two hundred yards from the point of meeting, Mr. Wren said to his son: "I forgot to tell Mr. Williamson about those horses."

Mr. Wren had sold to Mr. Williamson some horses, which were to have been sent for that day, but for some reason not now remembered it would be inconvenient to deliver them until the morrow. The coachman was directed to drive back, and as the vehicle turned Williamson was seen by all three, walking leisurely across the pasture. At that moment one of the coach horses stumbled and came near falling. It had no more than fairly recovered itself when James Wren cried: "Why, father, what has become of Mr. Williamson?"

It is not the purpose of this narrative to answer that question.

Mr. Wren's strange account of the matter, given under oath in the course of legal proceedings relating to the Williamson estate, here follows:

"My son's exclamation caused me to look toward the spot where I had seen the deceased [sic] an instant before, but he was not there, nor was he anywhere visible. I cannot say that at the moment I was greatly startled, or realized the gravity of the occurrence, though I thought it singular. My son, however, was greatly astonished and kept repeating his question in different forms until we arrived at the gate. My black boy Sam was similarly affected, even in a greater degree, but I reckon more by my son's manner than by anything he had himself observed. [This sentence in the testimony was stricken out.] As we got out of the carriage at the gate of the field, and while Sam was hanging [sic] the team to the fence, Mrs.

Williamson, with her child in her arms and followed by several servants, came running down the walk in great excitement, crying: 'He is gone, he is gone! O God! what an awful thing!' and many other such exclamations, which I do not distinctly recollect. I got from them the impression that they related to something more--than the mere disappearance of her husband, even if that had occurred before her eyes. Her manner was wild, but not more so, I think, than was natural under the circumstances. I have no reason to think she had at that time lost her mind. I have never since seen nor heard of Mr. Williamson."

This testimony, as might have been expected, was corroborated in almost every particular by the only other eye-witness (if that is a proper term)--the lad James. Mrs. Williamson had lost her reason and the servants were, of course, not competent to testify. The boy James Wren had declared at first that he SAW the disappearance, but there is nothing of this in his testimony given in court. None of the field hands working in the field to which Williamson was going had seen him at all, and the most rigorous search of the entire plantation and adjoining country failed to supply a clew. The most monstrous and grotesque fictions, originating with the blacks, were current in that part of the State for many years, and probably are to this day; but what has been here related is all that is certainly known of the matter. The courts decided that Williamson was dead, and his estate was distributed according to law."

Luke smiled and nodded. "Okay. It's a pretty weird story. Who wrote it?" He handed it back to her.

"A writer named Ambrose Bierce."

Luke stood and dusted his pants. "Are you kidding me? I ain't no country bumpkin. I know Bierce was a famous writer in the 1800s. One of his short stories is my favorite, *An Occurrence at Owl Creek Bridge*."

She stood too. "Yeah, but he wrote this as a newspaper article. He went there and interviewed people and everything."

Luke looked down at her. She was excited with the story. If she were not so damned cute, he would have run her off for screwing up his meditation. But she was cute. She did seem to be in earnest. He smiled. "You hungry?"

She looked toward the house, then back toward him. "Sure. I

24

guess." She stuffed the papers back into her purse.

"You like deer meat."

"Never had it."

Luke had not made a fire in the fireplace in a long time—the wood stove was much more efficient. Yet, here he was now sipping wine in front of it with a pretty, but strange girl he had just met. Homemade wine was no champagne, but he didn't know if this was going to be a romantic evening or not. The whole situation was odd.

Moon crossed her legs as she sat in the homemade oak chair, sipping the wine from a peanut butter jar. "What sort of grapes are these?"

Luke sat in a mating chair beside her. "Muscadine. They grow wild around here." He wanted to say something else, but he didn't know what to say. He felt as if he were on his first date all over again. He watched her from the corners of his eyes as she looked around the room.

"This is a very cozy place you have here, but don't you miss modern things? You have no television, no Internet, no running water."

He looked around the room, too, as if he had just noticed. "Well, I do have electricity and I have a cell phone."

She turned toward him. She was a little too close. "What are you doing out here all alone. You're way too cute for that."

He felt his face immediately flush red again. He went to the fireplace and placed a couple of sticks of wood on the fire. He wished and prayed to God that he would not blush so easily; but he always had and he reckoned he always would.

Moon giggled. "I'm sorry. I didn't mean to make you uncomfortable in your own house."

He took a deep breath and went back to the chair. He forced himself to look at her. He knew his face was still glowing. "I like being out here alone and depending only on myself and what I can make myself."

"Well, it's a waste."

It was impossible for him to turn redder. He looked into the fire, not knowing what to say or do. The crackling fire was the only sound for a while.

She broke the silence. "Luke, again, that venison was delicious. I loved the biscuits and gravy too."

"I'm glad you enjoyed it." He found himself smiling. "One reason I have electricity is for the freezer for all my game."

They sat there for a very long time not saying anything. Finally, Luke said, "Look, I'm sorry I wasn't as nice to you as I should have been. This whole thing has been strange and taxing to me. I mean, my cousin's in jail, and a friend has disappeared. You know?"

She nodded and smiled. "Luke, you don't look like the lawman type. What made you want to be a constable?"

Luke poured more wine into their glasses from a big mason jar. "I got laid off from the shoe factory and had time on my hands, going through a divorce. Some buddies kinda talked me into running for office. It was like a joke. Around here constables really don't do much, don't get paid." He looked at her. "I've held the office for over a year, and I haven't really done a thing. I guess this is the first time I took the position seriously. To tell you the truth, I just stay here in the woods."

"I noticed the sheriff doesn't think much of you."

"Naw. I've known the sheriff all my life. It's not me; it's the position of constable. He let me know that right off."

She turned in the chair. "Why did you take off the badge in front of the sheriff?"

"I wanted to see Tyler."

She kept looking at Luke, but said nothing, wanting more.

Luke set his glass on a small table beside him. "Moon, me and my older brother fought all the time. We were known to get into trouble for it. That's why I know the sheriff so well. My brother joined the service—Special Forces. He later taught me better—never fight a fight that doesn't have to be fought." Luke thought of his brother—missed him so much. "I admired him for joining the Seals. I should have joined the service."

"Why didn't you?"

"James—my brother—said both of us shouldn't be in at the same time, said we shouldn't do that to Mom."

"He still in?"

Luke looked at the floor. "He was killed in Afghanistan."

"I'm sorry, Luke."

Luke poured more wine. "He did his duty. Tomorrow I will do mine. I'm only a constable; but I still have a duty and it holds as much weight as the High Sheriff. I've got to find out what happened to Grace."

"Luke, let me float with you. I won't be in the way. I mean go with you."

He cut his eyes toward her. The homemade wine was a little much for her. That's the thing about homemade wine—it sneaks up on you.

But he thought about her request. What would it hurt? He was liking the way he felt around her anyway. The BB on her nose was looking more attractive all the time.

She stood, albeit a little wobbly. "I have to pee." She started toward the door. Luke noticed she was a little rubber-legged.

"Need help?"

"No. I'm good."

He handed her a flashlight. "The toilet is just behind the house."

She went out the door like her feet were tender. Yeah, muscadine wine was no grape soda.

Luke watched her go out the door. She had a fine body, and she turned out to have a nice personality—a great combination. He grinned and shook his head. You never know what turn of events will happen. Where had this strange girl come from?

Then he thought of Grace. He had run it through his mind a thousand times. People just do not disappear. There was no way Tyler harmed her, and Tyler was no liar. He had said she vanished. And what about the bear tracks? There was no wind that could do that. They came to a sudden stop, just as if the bear had vanished.

He put the dishes in the sink and poured in hot water from a pot off the wood stove. As he washed, he figured on what he would do tomorrow. He would start from where the bear tracks disappeared and work a circle from there. He would make the circle bigger as he looked. There must be a cave or something the other searchers had missed. That made the most sense. He had to find out something. He had to get Tyler out of that jail. When he finished the last dish, he grew concerned for Moon. She had been gone for a long time.

He found her halfway between the toilet and the house. She lay on the ground passed out. He forced himself not to gawk at her nakedness. Her pants and panties were left just in front of the toilet. He picked her up and took her to his bed. He took off her shirt and pulled the covers over her. He wanted to kiss her, but that was wrong, too. Her red hair fanned out on the pillow, and he felt an old familiar warmth in his heart that he hadn't felt in a long time. He also felt guilty for giving her such strong spirits.

He grabbed a pillow and heavy quilt and went outside to the fire. As he went out the door, he was greeted by coyotes singing. He admired them—the smartest wild animals in the woods. He soon had the fire blazing, and he positioned the quilt next to the fire as he had done many nights before. Soon he was on his back looking at the stars. Orion was his favorite constellation. Luke had always thought it looked more like a kite, than a hunter. Many of the ancient civilizations believed their origins were from there. As he admired it, he thought of Moon's story of the disappearing farmer, Orion Williamson. People don't really disappear—or do they? It was the last thing running through his mind as the howling coyotes sang him to sleep.

When he pulled up at the trailhead, that strange feeling came over him again. He wanted to think it was not fear, but it was, sure it was. He didn't bring his pistol, didn't need it for what he was afraid of. He looked out the windshield and up toward the mountain. What was going on up there?

"We going to get out?" Moon said. She was not trying to be cute. He knew she could clearly see the apprehension all over him.

He pushed the door open and slid out of the truck. It was like jumping into cold water, may as well hit it and get it over with. Moon did the same.

They were early and the sun was just beginning to appear over the eastern mountains.

He looked at Moon as she came around the front of the truck. She had her hair in a short ponytail. She wore a leather jacket, cargo pants, and hiking boots. She appeared different from yesterday. The BB was even missing from her nose. The little purse had been traded for a small backpack. He was glad he decided to let her go. He was glad to see she could also be embarrassed as she had been when she awoke without any clothes.

"You got your camera in the backpack?" Luke said.

"Yeah. I've got everything I need in there." She smiled. "Shall we head up?"

Luke grabbed his backpack from the bed of the truck. He kept it packed with wilderness stuff. Yet, the only thing in it that would be of any use today was the water bottle. He slung the pack over his shoulder and started up the trail.

As they arrived at the scene, Moon said, "All of this yellow tape is ridiculous." She snooped around like a beagle trying to catch a scent. "Did Tyler say anything about feeling a charge in the air, or anything like that?"

"Yes, he did."

"Now tell me again what Tyler told you." Luke told her again.

"Moon, don't you think you should take pictures for your story?"

"Yeah. I guess I'm so excited I forgot." She pulled the pack from her back and dug out the camera. She began snapping shots, but Luke saw she was not good at it. She was no photographer. She appeared not to be interested in pictures in the least.

After a while Luke sat on the big rock he had sat on the day before. The eagle was back. Its shadow fell over him again as it had yesterday. He looked up at it as he thought how he had climbed over and looked under every rock and stump in the area. He didn't know what else to do.

Moon sat beside him. "You said Tyler had heard drums?"

"Yeah. That's what he said. He said it was just a bum-bum, bum-bum sound. He said he heard trumpets too"

Moon scratched her head. "What time of day did this happen?"

"Morning. I don't know what time." Luke noted she asked questions like a reporter, but she took no notes. She didn't have a recorder either.

Luke felt his skin begin to tingle, heard crackling noises. He looked at Moon; he could tell she had heard it too. "What is it?" Luke said.

Moon said nothing as she scanned in every direction. Slowly her hair rose as if it were charged with electricity.

Luke felt his own hair do the same. The crackling grew louder.

"Bum-bum, bum-bum, bum-bum..." The sound was faint and far away at first, but then it grew louder.

"The drums!" Moon said. "Where's it coming from?"

Luke shot to his feet. He closed his eyes and listened as he always did while hunting, to focus all his senses to his ears. "Coming from the direction of the police tape."

"Bum-bum, bum-bum, bum-bum..." The sound grew louder. Luke thought it sounded like a Tarzan movie. Now he also heard the horns.

Luke was as afraid as he had ever been, but something compelled him to walk toward the sound. He was there to investigate, after all. He walked past Moon, her eyes glued on the direction of the sound. Luke fought his fear. He had to find Grace. The air developed ripples. Luke could see them as plain

30

as if they were in water. The air appeared refracted. He saw the beginnings of a faint vortex.

Luke felt a sharp pain in the back of the head, and he sank to his knees. His world spun. He grabbed the back of his head and looked up to see Moon running toward the sound with a pistol in her hands. She held it commando style, in front and ready. He realized she had hit him with it. In an instant, she was gone. He shook his head and looked again. She was not there. She had disappeared. Luke struggled to his feet and staggered toward the place he had last seen her, toward the ripples. The drums grew louder. Some kind of force was pulling him. He fought it. It was not like a vacuum—more like an electrical field, a magnet.

There were gunshots. Fear corkscrewed through his body as he clawed air to stop, but he could not. He tried to turn as leaves and sticks flew by him. He tried to stop, but...

Chapter 4

In an instant, he found himself in some kind of village. It could have been in Africa or South America or something on National Geographic. It was all strange. Where did it all come from? There were giant orange-feathered—

Something slammed Luke to the ground and pinned him to the dirt. He fought to free himself, but soon realized he was trapped by a tangle of vines or ropes. No—it was a big net. He struggled and fought against it, but it was no use. He was caught like an animal. He screamed out in fear and rage. Someone jumped on him and pounded him. He tried to swing. He tried to fight, but it was useless. Then another piled on, then more, seeming to come from everywhere. They had big sticks and they beat him. It was a whirl of confusion. They kicked him. He tried to swing again, but the best he could manage to do was squirm.

"Bum-bum, bum-bum, bum-bum..." The drums beat and the horns continued.

He struggled, but the net tightened. He saw green faces, orange faces, white hair. It was the nightmare of all nightmares, but it was no dream; it was real. As he struggled and fought, he saw one with a green face beside him dead with blood draining from his head—bullet hole Luke instantly figured. The drums echoed in his brain. He tried to tuck his head under his arms, but it did no good. The beating continued. He screamed out, but the pain screamed back. He saw blue lights in his head, then nothing.

Luke blinked his eyes. He drew in several stuttered breaths and tried to clear his head—it hurt. He sat up and tried to collect himself and figure out where he was. He was now alone. He was bruised and scratched all over his body as if he had been dragged through rocks and brambles behind a mule team. He inspected his limbs; nothing seemed to be broken, but he was as naked as day one. Everything was crazy. He staggered to his feet. Pain immediately rushed to his head, found a goose egg on the back of it. "Thanks, Moon," he groaned. He remembered her hitting him with the pistol—or he thought she had. He discovered that he was in some kind of cage like a gorilla at the zoo. It was solid too. Posts were driven deeply, and he was not going to budge them. It had a door, but it was tied shut with a big rope. The ends of the rope were tied to more posts away from the cage, which Luke could not reach. There was nothing but a jungle outside of the cage. He found a fur rug on the cage floor. Closer inspection found it to be some kind of robe. He put it on and tied it with a cord that was hanging from the cage. He didn't recognize the animal that had been sacrificed to make it—not anything from Arkansas anyway.

He was trying to convince himself he was dreaming. Maybe it was some kind of stupid joke. He was still trying to figure it out when an orange-faced man approached the cage. The man had long, white-blond hair and wore deerskin or some other animal's fur. As the man stuck his face close to the cage, Luke saw the orange color was paint—like an Indian or something.

Luke grabbed the cage and shook it. "What the hell is going on? It ain't funny. I'm a law officer and I will arrest everyone responsible."

The man jerked up a long, pointed stick, which Luke had not

seen, and stabbed Luke's hand. Luke recoiled and looked at the wound. Blood dripped from his hand, but it was just a scratch. He was lucky—the man intended it to be more.

Luke backed away from the edge of the cage and that sharp stick. He didn't understand what was happening, but it was real.

The man spoke some words Luke had never heard before, and it sure was not English. In fact, it didn't sound like anything on National Geographic either. The words seemed to buzz or vibrate. He pointed the stick at Luke, and Luke got the man's meaning sure enough. The man hit the cage with the stick, then turned and walked back into the forest.

Luke wiped the blood onto the robe. Fear came over him in a warm wave. It was almost funny—almost. It was like the fear he felt when he was only six, and he had lost sight of his mother at the county fair—fear of being alone among strangers. But the people at the fair weren't this strange, and they damn sure didn't beat on him and poke him.

He took stock of his situation. The first thing he had to do was escape from the cage, get back to his truck, and find help. These people were probably some kind of cult. They pulled some kind of trick and made it look like those girls disappeared. Now, he was finally thinking straight. Now, everything was starting to make a little sense. People just don't really disappear. Magicians could make elephants and airplanes *seem* to disappear. However, it was all a trick.

Two women carrying some sort of skins came to the cage. Both women wore furs, too, and they had the same white-blond hair, and they had green painted faces. They stuck the skins through the posts of the cage and backed away.

"I'm a law officer," Luke said. "You better let me out of here. They will come looking for me anyway."

One of the women pointed at the skins and said something in the buzzing language.

"Let me out of here, dammit!"

They turned and went back into the forest from where they had come.

Luke looked after them, wondered why the manhunt for Grace had not found this cult. They had flown over in planes and choppers. They even had bloodhounds. The hot fear came over him again. He shook the cage again, but the wooden posts were solid as steel.

He looked down at the skins. They were bundles of something. He picked one of them up and unwrapped it. It contained what looked to be a rabbit that had been cooked over a fire. He dropped the bundle. For all he knew, it was poison.

"Luke," came a whisper at the edge of the forest.

"Moon?"

Moon eased out of the forest with her pistol at the ready. She didn't seem at all like the innocent reporter Luke had met. She moved deliberately like a Navy Seal or something.

She pulled a knife from her boot and tossed it to Luke, never taking her eyes off the forest. "Cut that rope and stay right on my tail. Be as quiet as you can."

Luke began sawing at the big rope. "Moon, who are you? What's going on?"

"Just cut the rope. Do it quickly. Trust me."

"Trust you? You're no more a reporter—"

Three orange-faced men charged out of the forest with spears raised. Moon dropped them with three quick shots. "Hurry, Luke!"

Luke sawed so fast, that his hand was a blur. The door swung open as four more men ran from the forest. Moon dropped them with precision.

Moon took the knife from Luke and started around behind the cage. "Stay with me, Luke!"

Luke sprinted to catch her, but one of the strange, blond-headed men tackled him. Moon ran back and shot the man in the head.

"Let's go!" she said as she pulled Luke to his feet.

A spear swooshed and stuck in the ground by their feet. Moon shot the blue-faced man who had thrown it.

They ran through the forest like deer. It was no doubt to

35

Luke that Moon had picked the escape route before she came after him. After what seemed to be a mile or so, they slowed to a jog, but never stopped. They ran in a shallow creek for a long distance. He figured she was trying to hide their tracks. He looked back. No one was following. He was glad he was in good shape because Moon was a machine. She was no reporter.

The robe came untied and his naked body was revealed as the fur fanned back like a cape. He didn't care. He just wanted to get away from whatever those people were. He knew he had to stay up with Moon—she had the gun. She knew more about what was going on than he did. Hell, he didn't have a clue what was going on.

Moon jumped out of the creek and ran toward a rocky hill. "Come on, Luke."

Luke's feet were killing him; he looked down and saw blood. He wasn't going to stop even if his feet fell off. He stayed right on Moon's heels. She climbed to a rock ledge and pulled herself over. He grabbed the ledge, and Moon helped him over too. He tumbled onto his back and the robe fell open. Moon quickly looked away.

Luke pulled the robe closed and stood. "Where are we?" He wanted to know the answer, but he was just saying something to hide his embarrassment.

"We're safe here for a time," Moon said.

Luke did a quick scan of the area. They were on a round, flat hilltop, about the size of a basketball court. They had a perfect view in all directions. There were a couple of trees that cast good shade. She had chosen the spot well.

Moon went to the base of one of the trees and picked up something. Luke saw it was his backpack. She had his boots and clothes too. "How did you get that?" Luke said.

"I caught 'em napping."

He took them from her, and she turned her back as he put his clothes on. "What's going on Moon? Who are these people?"

She turned back. "Why did you follow me?"

36

"You told me to."

"No. I mean when we heard the drums, back
tape."

"Why did you hit me on the head?" His hand went to his
head. It was throbbing. Hell, he hurt all over from the
pounding he had taken while under the net, not to mention his
feet—he would need to inspect them later for thorns and such.

She sighed.

Luke looked straight into her eyes, and with a slow measured
voice said, "Who are you?"

She sat at the base of one of the trees. "Damn it, Luke."

Luke thought of the painted-face men and looked down the
hill.

"They won't come," Moon said. "We are too far from the
village now."

Luke looked down at her. "We're not in Arkansas anymore
are we?" He had not even considered saying that, but his
subconscious brought it to the front.

She slowly shook her head.

He dropped down beside her. He felt he would throw up.
He wasn't just afraid—he was confused. He felt lost.

She pulled her pistol from her pocket and put fresh rounds
in it. Luke could see it was a 9 mm. "Luke, we have fallen down
a rabbit hole, and we are now in Wonderland." She put the
pistol back into her pocket and turned toward him. "But I'm
not Alice, and there is no rabbit."

He studied her face—she wasn't joking. He wanted to say
something, but could only stare at her.

She stood. "You should have stayed on the ground when I
hit you."

He suddenly felt thirsty. He pulled the water bottle from the
backpack and took a big pull. He had roamed the wilderness all
of his life and had never been lost—never been afraid, but this
was something totally different. He felt clammy. His stomach
churned.

She squatted down beside him in a catcher's stance.

"Remember Orion Williamson?"

He remembered the unbelievable story—not so unbelievable now.

"Orion stepped through a wormhole. Now, so have you."

Luke sat the backpack down. He closed his eyes. "You mean we are in outer space or something?" He opened his eyes to see she was smiling. He saw nothing funny at all.

She stood. "No, Luke. We are still on earth."

Luke shot to his feet. "What the hell are you talking about? Cut to the chase! Where are we?"

She looked past him and shaded her eyes with her hand. He looked where she was looking, saw smoke. "They will be hunting us tomorrow," she said.

"Who?" Luke watched the smoke. It looked like Indian smoke signals from an old western. "You said we were too far from the village."

She watched the smoke like she was reading it. "The ones with the painted faces are the Chooners. They are somewhat like helper bees. They don't get too far from home, not too much to them." She scratched her head and looked at Luke. "The hunters, the warriors, are called Scrains. They will hunt us until they kill us...or we kill them."

Luke felt the fear shoot up his back like an electrical charge. He didn't know how she knew all this, but he believed her.

She bent and tightened her boots. "I've got to check our perimeter, set a few traps. You stay right here." She looked at the western sky. "It will be dark in a couple of hours. I doubt they will be here tonight—they don't like darkness, but I'm not taking a chance."

He said nothing. He found it hard to regulate his breathing. He didn't know what he should do. He didn't know which way to turn.

She took his hands. "Luke, I'll be back before dark. Don't leave this spot." She smiled again. "Make us a little camp and make a big fire. There's a little food in my pack."

"But they will see our fire."

"I've read their smoke. They already know where we are." She slid over the ledge, but stopped at the edge. "I'll be back. You'll be safe." With that, she smiled and dropped out of sight.

He sat with his back against the tree; his eyes closed, and he tried to understand what was going on. He shook all over, felt like a rabbit or quail with a hawk circling, helpless and vulnerable, afraid to move. He looked at his hands shaking, clasped them together and squeezed them to stop the trembling. He pulled them up to his face and prayed as he had never prayed before—surely the Good Lord was here too. He squeezed his hands so tightly blood dripped from the spear wound and ran onto his lips and into his mouth.

The taste awakened a long forgotten memory. It kindled in his brain like the first ember of a fire. He licked the blood as he fanned the memory. As a young teen, first learning to knap flint and make stone tools, he had cut a gash in his finger on the sharp stone. He had no water to wash the fine shavings of stone from the wound, so he sucked at it to clean it. Now he looked at the scar as he remembered. He was now an expert at fashioning stone tools. He hunted with them almost exclusively. He had always prided himself as a hunter, like the ancients, even when everyone made fun of his foolish and prehistoric weapons.

He stood, instantly felt ashamed like a slap to the face. He was not prey. He was a hunter—a predator. And he was good at it; some say the best. He wiped his face and noticed the orange sun in the west. He clinched his fists and felt the blood swoosh through his veins. But this time the fear was not as strong as he remembered who he was—what he was. The fear was still there, but he had it identified now. Now he only had to control it.

Luke hid among the bushes and watched as Moon climbed over the ledge. She scanned, but could not find him. She pulled the pistol from a deep pocket—she went into commando mode. He remained silent, motionless, in the recesses of the

39

brush as he had done countless times before as a hunter. He was slowly growing back to his old self. Now he wanted to see exactly what she was.

She bent to one knee and inspected where he had sat by the tree. She looked at the fire, which was still blazing strong—she would know he was still close. She looked to the sky. The sun was down, but still a little light left. She tried to pick up his tracks, but he had brushed them away. He saw a smile cross her face. She had recognized what he had done. She put the pistol back in her pocket. "Okay, Luke. They won't come for you tonight."

Luke examined her. Oh, how wrong he had been about her. That cute innocent redhead had tricked him well—not anymore. He had no idea if she were friend or foe. If he wanted, and had a weapon, he would be in control of the situation, but he only had a rock. He stepped from the brush, dropped the stone. "Let's talk."

She nodded and sat by the fire. "Alright, Constable. Since we are now in this together, that's a good idea."

"Should I expect the truth from you?" He sat across the fire from her.

She picked up a stick and tossed it into the blaze. "I guess I had that coming." She looked at him. "Luke, we will need each other now." She shook her head. "I won't deceive you anymore."

"Who are you? What are you?"

She nodded. "I work for the government, but I can't tell you more than that." She looked away for a second and then turned back. "Moon Serling is my real name as I told you before."

"Where are we, Moon?"

"We went through a wormhole. We are in another dimension, in a place called Thoria."

Luke blew out a breath. "I find that hard to believe. Oh, something strange is going on, but I don't know about all this other dimension crap."

"This is not science fiction."

Luke shot back. "You seem to know a whole lot about it." Luke stood. "How do you know so much about these painted-faced demons?" He pointed his finger at her. "How did you get away from the net? How did you get my clothes? How did you know about this spot? You didn't have enough time to scope it out."

"Sit back down, Luke." After a minute he did. "I knew they would be waiting when I went through the portal. They have a ritual. When the portal opens, they have a net waiting for anything that may come through—birds, rabbits, deer, whatever. Usually nothing comes."

"Come on, Moon; you expect me to believe this mess?"

"Don't be stupid, Constable. You still have the bruises as proof."

Luke's hand went to the stab wound. He was being stupid. He realized he needed to keep his cool and learn what he could from her. "Okay, Moon."

She untied her ponytail and let her red hair fan over her shoulders. Luke was taken back by the change. He felt his breath stutter.

"Constable, I promise I will only tell you the truth." The firelight flickered over her face and enhanced her beauty.

"I will shut up and listen."

She smiled. "Those people are called the Florians. They somehow found this wormhole—something we are just beginning to study. Either someone opens it for them, or they know when it is going to open on its own. We don't know."

"We?" Luke said.

"My organization."

"How do y'all know this stuff and what is your organization?"

"I told you. I'm not saying anything about the organization."

Luke threw his hands up. "Okay. Keep going."

"When they trap something in the net, which isn't very often, they put it in a cage for a few days; then sacrifice it to their gods."

"Grace!" Luke's heart dropped as he thought of Grace going through the portal. "Did you see Grace? Do you know what happened to her?"

Moon slowly shook her head. "I don't know. I..." She looked away.

"What, Moon?" Luke moved around the fire next to Moon. He took her hands in his. "Tell me what you know." He squeezed her hands. "Please!"

She turned back to him; her blue eyes slowly looked up and looked into his. "I found her boots." She looked down. "And her clothes."

"What does it mean? Maybe they gave her skins like they did me."

"Luke, they give skins to be sacrificed in. You would have been sacrificed tomorrow when the Scrains returned."

Luke let go of Moon's hands and sank to the ground. He could see Grace's pretty face in his mind, felt a sharp pain in his heart. He thought of Tyler in jail being held for a crime that he had nothing to do with.

"Luke, I'm sorry."

He nodded.

"We have to think of tomorrow."

Luke looked up. "Can we get back to our own dimension?"

Moon said nothing.

"Then what is there to think of?"

"We have to get out of this valley. Across the mountain are friendly people."

"People! Do they paint up like savages too? Do they sacrifice innocent girls?"

Moon shook her head. "We will be safe there."

Luke only thought of finding a way home now. If Grace was dead, why worry about anything else.

"We must sleep," Moon said. "We have to be on the move before first light. We will have to be sharp. The Scrains are great hunters and warriors. Luke, we will be lucky to get out of this valley alive."

Luke nodded absently, but he was thinking of Grace. He knew it was all out of his control, but he felt responsible for her death. He felt responsible for Tyler spending the rest of his life in jail. Now he was going to be hunted like a deer.

A switch snapped in his brain as he thought about being hunted. He thought the hell with that—he had to find a weapon. "Do you have another gun?"

"No. And I'm low on ammo."

He knew he should not try to take her gun. She was an expert with it, and she could do the most damage. She would not give it up anyway, probably kick his butt too.

"Good night, Luke." Moon rolled over on her side and made a pillow of her pack. "Tomorrow will be an adventure."

Luke looked at her form in the firelight. In another situation, he would have found her irresistible, but tonight his mind was on tomorrow. Luke reached his pack and found a length of paracord and his Swiss Army knife. He felt the adrenaline rising in his blood. Tomorrow will be different from today. Tomorrow he will be the hunter again.

Chapter 5

Luke awoke to the chitter of a bird he had never heard before. It was strange. He knew the call of every species of bird in Arkansas—not this one. Then he remembered his situation. No wonder he didn't know the bird. He sat up and rubbed his face to get the blood flowing. It was still dark. Moon lay on the ground by the coals of the spent fire, but he knew she was awake. "Morning," he said.

She sat up and smoothed her hair. "Ready to run?"

"Run?"

Moon stood, stretched. "Yeah. At first light, the Scrains will descend on this place like mosquitoes on a naked butt. We want to be long gone."

Luke looked to the east. The sky was barely turning pink. The stars were fading. "What if we run into them?"

"We will run into some of them. We will kill them." She threw her pack onto her back. "You ever killed a person, Constable?"

The thought bore into him like a hot iron. "No."

She picked up his pack and helped him put it on. "Think of a nasty cottonmouth snake, ready to strike. You strike him first. After the deed is done, you don't think of it anymore, because there will always be more snakes ready to strike if you let your guard down."

He took her advice to heart—she was the expert in that field. He would try to think of bad snakes. He reached down and picked up his weapon.

"What is that?" Moon said.

He held it up for her to see. He had found a wedge-shaped stone and had lashed it to a stick with paracord that he kept in his pack, making a primitive ax. "My weapon until I can do better."

"I heard you doing something last night. I figured you were preparing." She smiled and looked at it. The smile morphed into admiration. "I've studied all manner of weapons." She looked up at him. "You know what you're doing, don't you? You're good at this."

He nodded. "I've been making stone tools since I was a kid."

"This is not just a tool, Constable. This is a weapon. Can you use it?"

A smile slowly grew on his face.

She nodded, tied up her ponytail, and then began throwing sticks on the coals. "Make the flames big. They will be licking their chops like hounds. We want them excited as all hell for the hunt. We want them to charge this hill."

Luke picked up a small log and dropped it onto the fire. "Yeah. They won't be expecting us to hunt them."

Now it was her turn to smile. Luke could grow to love that smile.

She went to the ledge and turned back toward him. "Luke, we must kill these people or they will certainly kill us. You fully understand this, don't you?" Her eyes reflected the growing firelight.

"I thought on it all night. I made my peace with it. I'm prepared to do what I have to do. They're just bad snakes."

"Well, then, may God be with us," she said.

"If praying helps Him to be with us, I did my share last night."

She smiled, nodded, and dropped over the ledge.

45

Luke stayed right on Moon's tail. She never looked back; she knew he was there. Luke felt the excitement of the hunt as he had never felt it before. He had never hunted such a predator before, never hunted grizzly bears or mountain lions either—he had now skipped over those for the ultimate predator. He had psyched himself up for the chase, tried not thinking about them hunting him. The ax felt strong in his hand. It was not the best weapon, but it would do for now.

They ran through a dark forest of giant trees; he had never seen trees so large. It was starting to get light, and the only plan they had seemed to be to just run like a deer through the woods. They stopped for a quick breather and Luke asked, "What's the plan?" He waved his arm in an arc. "It's growing light."

"Just stay with me. I do have a plan." Before he could reply, she was on her way again. It was his cue and he was right behind her.

They came to a line of steep ridges that spanned the horizon. Moon pointed toward them. "See that cut through the ridges?"

"I see it." It was a narrow canyon with steep walls.

"The first bunch of Scrain that had been following us has probably attacked our camp by now only to find our campfire. When the sun breaks the horizon, the next bunch will leave their camp by the river to join up with them."

"How do you know they are camped by a river?"

She hesitated and cut her eyes toward Luke. "I know." She pointed toward the canyon again. "They will have to come through there. We will ambush them when they stream through the cut." She didn't wait for a reply and ran for the ridge.

He followed her as they climbed the steep hill. At the top they had a commanding position. From there Luke could see the worn trail below, about a hundred feet long from entrance to exit of the ridge. "How are we going to ambush them?"

She rolled her pack off her back, reached in and pulled out

two black grenades. "You know how to use these?"

A lump grew in Luke's throat. He shook his head. What was she doing with grenades?

She demonstrated: "Pull this pin. Then toss it down on them below." She handed him both grenades. "It's that simple."

"Why are you giving them to me?" he said as he took them. He held them as if they were eggs.

"I'm going down below to stop them. When I stop them, you drop the grenades. Don't miss or this adventure will be over. You understand?"

She was red with excitement. "Luke, do you understand?"

He nodded. "But how will you stop them?"

"They will stop right under you. Wait for them to bunch up, then drop the grenades." She smiled. "Good luck and be strong." With that she was gone.

He laid the grenades and his ax on the ground in front of him. Looking down at the trail below, it was like being in a deer stand above a game trail. He prayed for strength to be with him when he needed it. He didn't feel as strong as he had earlier. He didn't want to admit it to himself, but he knew it was because Moon had left him alone. It was easy to be strong when she was near.

The grenades sat there like coiled snakes. He took in quick breaths—almost hyperventilating. "This is not real. This is not real." Moon had been gone for five minutes, and he had no idea where she had gone. He tried to summon up the predator instinct, but his main concern was not letting Moon down, and, of course, staying alive. He found he admired her, probably more than anyone he knew.

There was movement on the trail. He hunkered down. He felt that old excitement grow deep within his soul. If he had a tail, it would be twirling like a lion's tail, a lion ready to spring after a zebra. The fear was gone. The apprehension was gone. He waited patiently as he had done so many times before. His measured breathing increased. All his senses were at peak. His springs tightened. He waited, knew Moon was doing the same.

They were like wolves waiting for the other to make the first move.

The blond men entered the cut, all carrying spears. They looked like cavemen on the cover of some novel, all with fur robes, some with fur hats. They were talking. The buzzing carried through the canyon.

Luke glanced at the grenades. In his mind he rehearsed the procedure for activating them. He wanted to do it fast, but he didn't want to be the one blown up.

They moved closer; soon they would be thirty feet right under him.

Luke's heart raced like an engine, his breathing short and rapid, but now controlled. His hands were only inches from the grenades and ready for service.

Where was Moon?

The group moved through the cut like a snake. He counted maybe a dozen—maybe more.

How was Moon going to stop them? Luke wished she had said.

Back down the cut, there were five more coming. The two groups were too far apart. They needed to be bunched together for the best advantage. The first group was now directly under Luke.

Luke whispered, "Where the hell is—"

"Hey, Blondie!" Moon was standing in the exit of the cut.

The first group stopped right under Luke, but the second group was still too far. Luke reached for the grenades, but hesitated.

Moon began walking toward the stalled group under Luke, her hands at her side. The group at the entrance kept walking toward the middle group. What was Moon doing?

Luke picked up one of the grenades, but waited.

The Scrains began chanting and buzzing. They suddenly started running toward Moon. She pulled her pistol and shot the first one. The shot echoed through the little canyon. The rest stopped like stunned geese.

Out of reflex, Luke pulled the pin on the grenade. He fumbled it and dropped it. It rolled, bounced and careened down the canyon wall. It hit the trail about ten feet in front of the warriors. One went to pick it up. It exploded, carrying half the group away in chunks. The other half turned and fled back down the path.

The pistol opened up.

Luke snatched up the other grenade and heaved it at the running men. He hit the last one on the head, knocking him to the ground. The grenade exploded, killing all but two of the remaining men. As the two sprinted from the canyon, Luke noticed that one wore a white robe. For some stupid reason, Luke reckoned the fur must be from an albino deer.

Moon put the pistol back into her pocket. She looked up at Luke and gave him a thumbs up, cool and dry as Clint Eastwood. She surveyed the carnage, and she simply turned and went back out the canyon.

Luke's chest heaved like a bellows. He looked down at the body parts. He had only seen something like that when a big truck once mowed over a pack of dogs. He wheeled around and sat flat on his butt. He raised his trembling hands to his face. He knew why he had fumbled the grenade—buck fever. It had happened to him before while deer hunting—get too excited and the body gets out of sync with the brain. He had better control it, or he would not live long here. He squeezed his eyes shut and held his head in his hands, had better come to grips. He had to be strong. Soldiers had been killing like this since the beginning of man. He thought of his own brother, the Navy Seal. He took a deep breath and stared up at the sky, not looking for anything, but not knowing where else to look. He drew in a few more breaths, and the excitement and fear mellowed a bit, just a small but noticeable bit. The sky was as blue as he had ever seen it. There were no clouds, nothing but blue. Something was missing, though, but he couldn't put his finger on it. He found himself searching the sky, briefly forgetting the terrible incident that had just happened.

"They're not there." Luke jumped and looked around to see Moon coming up the ridge.

"What's not there?" he said.

She came closer and sat beside him. "Contrails."

He looked back up at the sky. Of course. No lines in the sky.

"There are no vapor trails because there are no planes." She looked the sky over as if she were looking for the lost planes. "The only things up there are birds."

Luke nodded and said, "And God, I hope. I need something familiar here."

She looked over at him and smiled.

"Haaa!"

Luke spun around to see a man bearing down on him with a spear. Luke shot to his feet and grabbed the spear with his left hand as the man lunged it at Moon. Luke whirled full around, pulling the spear from the man's hand and with his right hand, he smashed the man's face with the stone ax. The man melted to the ground.

"Yaaa!" Another man charged from the trees.

Luke threw the ax. It found its mark between the warrior's eyes. Luke recognized the albino deer robe. These were the two who had run out of the canyon.

"I guess I don't need this," Luke heard Moon say. He turned to see her putting the pistol back into her pocket.

Luke looked at the two men he had just killed. One of them had a crushed skull with part of the bloody brain oozing out. He had done that. He turned and puked. Today he learned a hard truth—he could kill a human if he had to. He wiped his mouth and slowly faced Moon.

"A bad snake," Moon said. "Just a bad snake."

Luke glared at his boots as he trudged behind Moon. He hoped the boots lasted longer than any other pair he had ever owned. He had never considered such a worry before. If they wore out, he would normally go to the store and get another pair. Yeah, that ain't happening here. The miles they had walked today through forests, savannas, and small prairies had made him realize he had better consider building moccasins at the first opportunity.

At least the country was beautiful and pristine. It reminded him of descriptions in historical journals from people like Thomas Nuttall. Animals abound—birds of all types, deer, rabbits, and some creatures Luke had never seen before. The sweet smell of wilderness permeated the air; some smells he knew, some he didn't.

They stopped at a small pine forest for a breather. There, Luke inspected and then pulled dried sap from the side of a pine tree.

"I know what that's for," Moon said.

"Nature's glue," he said, as he placed it in his pack. "This will do until I can make it by Walmart."

In the late afternoon, they stopped to rest at a creek meandering through a small prairie. A narrow, white rock ridge protruded from the ground like a razorback. From there they could see for miles and would be safe from surprise attack.

Luke bent to fill his water bottle. The water was clear with shiny minnows darting around in it. Pretty, colored rocks formed the streambed. One caught Luke's attention—he knew it. He reached down and dug out a flat, white stone about the size of a plate. He examined it, and then looked at the white ridge beside the stream.

Moon bent to fill her water bottle. "Whatcha got there?"

Luke didn't answer. He reached in the water and fished out another stone. This one was gray and shaped like a potato. He struck the edge of the white, flat rock with the potato rock and sheared off a sharp flake. He smiled. Oh, yes.

Moon capped her water bottle and put it back into her pack. "What is it?"

"It's novaculite, a flint that I can make tools and weapons with."

She grinned and nodded. "Then that's more precious than gold here."

Luke picked up one of the spears he had taken from the dead Scrain warriors, studied it. "Why do they not use stone points?" He looked over at Moon. "They only have sharpened sticks."

"As far as I know, this world has not discovered flint knapping. They use rocks, but just for hammering. Well, they use stone flakes for knives and such, but they don't make arrowheads."

Luke set the stick down and stared at Moon.

She noticed. "What?"

"You said you could not tell me about your organization, and I will respect that, but you sure know a lot about this world. If you know so much, I suspect you know how to get home."

She turned from him and looked across the prairie. "Luke, if I could get you back to Arkansas, I would." She turned back to him. "I would do it right now." A tear ran down her cheek.

Luke relaxed and his heart melted. He took her hand. "I'm sorry. You are all I have in this world." He immediately realized how stupid it sounded. They both laughed.

From far across the prairie, strange trumpets sounded. He let go of her hand and climbed the ridge. He could not believe it. He pointed. "Elephants." There were thirty or more in the distance headed their way.

Moon climbed beside him. "No, Luke. They are mammoths."

Luke hesitated, wasn't sure he had heard her correctly. He looked hard at the large animals on the distant prairie; then slowly turned to her. "Wooley mammoths?"

"Columbian mammoths." She smiled as Luke looked back at the herd. "There are many more animals here that have gone extinct in your dimension."

Luke thought *our* dimension—his and hers, but he was too excited about the herd to go into that.

The wind came from the direction of the mammoths, and their smell drifted over Luke. He inhaled deep and slow. It reminded him of the smell of the zoo. But these weren't elephants or giraffes. They came within one hundred yards, but they continued past, slow and smooth and large. Luke wiped his eyes to keep tears from coming. Mammoths. Real live mammoths. A low rumble came from them, just like elephants on TV. It vibrated in his own chest. He watched them for over thirty minutes, until they were mere dots in the distance as they traveled their grass highway.

He hadn't noticed, but Moon had climbed down from the ledge and had skewered a trout with one of the spears. It was still stuck to the spear lying in the grass. She was gathering drift and grass to build a fire.

"If we build a fire, won't the Scrains see it and come after us?"

"They know where we're at already, but they are afraid of the mammoths, think they're demons or something. With them on the prairie, we are safe."

Luke picked up a few sticks from the edge of the stream. "I thought early man hunted mammoths to extinction."

Moon dropped her sticks on the ground and turned to Luke. "Dorothy, we're not in Kansas anymore." She smiled and flashed her pretty teeth. "Now, let's have this ready for a fire tonight. We will need it to keep the animals away and to let the Scrains know we are still here."

Luke worked by the moon and firelight, chipping away at the flint, making arrowheads and spear points. No two points were alike—they were all originals. They were tools and weapons, for sure, but they were art also. It took talent, a talent few people possessed, but he had it; and he was proud of it and thankful for it. He usually used copper and deer antlers to chip away at the flint, but the potato rock and his pocket knife worked well enough.

He gathered a few stalks of cane from the river's edge, stripped them down, and cut them off to around three feet long. He turned to Moon, who had been silently watching. "Cane makes great arrows."

"Too bad you don't have a bow to shoot them with."

He smiled and continued to work with the arrows. He pulled a short length of paracord from his bag, stripped it to the nylon center, and then pulled the nylon center into strands of string. Next, he placed a flat rock next to the fire. When it grew hot, he put a piece of dried pine sap on it. When it began to melt, he took a small stick and mixed ashes with it.

"Glue?" Moon said.

"Glue," Luke said as he placed one of the stone points on a cane shaft. He had cut a slit in the end of it and dabbed a bit of pine pitch into it. The point fit perfectly—he knew it would, had done it hundreds of times. He straightened the point quickly before the glue could set. Then he took the nylon string and bound the head tightly to the shaft. When he was satisfied with the point, he put more glue over the string to hold it all in place. "All I need now are a few feathers."

Moon pulled her pack to her and reached inside. "I have something here." She pulled out a wad of colorful feathers.

"What do you have?" Luke said as he took the wad.

"They look like parrot feathers attached to a string. That last warrior you clubbed had them hanging from his wrist. I don't know... Something told me to get it. I'm sorta ashamed now, but I guess it was a trophy."

Luke untangled the little bundle. It was a type of bracelet made of bones and feathers. The feathers were not very strong, but they would do for now. Luke tied them on the shaft as best he could and dabbed a little glue on. But pine pitch was not the glue he needed for that—he needed hide glue. That would have to wait for another time when he could boil animal hides down to make the glue.

"All that is needed now is a bow." Moon said as she took a nibble of the fish.

Luke picked up one of the spears. It was about six feet long. "My bow."

"That thing won't bend."

He put his knife to work shaving on one side of the spear.

"That will take all night," Moon said as she placed a piece of fish into Luke's mouth.

He swallowed the fish. "It's hard for sure—hickory." Luke sharpened his knife on a flat piece of novaculite and began shaving wood.

"While you are whittling on that, I'm going to bathe." She stood. "I trust you won't look."

Luke immediately turned red. He hated himself for it.

"That is so cute."

He turned redder and scraped harder and faster, wished she would just go bathe. He heard her behind him taking her clothes off. He was tempted to look, but he was too embarrassed to say anything, much less turn around.

She stepped into the stream. "This is cold!"

He thought, *Of course it is; it's the middle of October.*

"But it feels so good to get some of this filth off me."

Luke kept his eyes on the bow as she splashed around in the stream, but his mind was more on the splashing now than the bow.

Soon she got out of the water. "Luke, close your eyes. I have to stand by the fire to put my clothes on. I'm freezing."

Luke did as he was told, wishing he had the nerve to look. No one could say Luke was not a first rate gentleman—or chicken.

"Luke."

Luke still had his eyes closed. "What?" He could hear her pulling on her cloths.

"I think you are a good constable. Okay, you can look now."

Luke opened his eyes. She was putting her jacket on. Her red hair was wild as she fluffed it. He believed he was actually falling in love with her. Yet, he had never even touched her.

"But you don't look the lawman type," she said as she sat by the fire.

"You don't look the government agent type."

"Fair enough," she said as she pulled at her wet hair.

Luke placed the center of the bow over his knee and pulled on both ends. "This is coming along nicely."

"I have to tell you, I'm impressed."

Luke scraped on it for about another thirty minutes, flexing it over his knee often. Then he pulled another length of paracord from his pack. He bent the bow and tied it on. He pulled the string back. "Lucky day. I'd say it's about fifty pounds. Plenty enough strength to kill anything. Well, maybe not a mammoth."

He looked across the fire. Moon was asleep. He had been so busy with the bow, he didn't even know she had lain down. He was tempted to lie beside her, but he didn't have the nerve.

He gathered his arrows and placed them by the bow and a tomahawk he had fashioned to replace the ax. He looked at Moon and thought about her great ability with the pistol. Tomorrow she would see what he could do.

Chapter 6

The ground was like a stone mattress, but Luke somehow managed to fall asleep with the sounds of coyotes yipping across the prairie—the sounds of home, a little familiarity and comfort. He even dreamed all night—weird dreams. Now he was hunting dinosaurs—dreams are funny that way. In the dream a herd of Gallimimuses was charging toward him like the scene in Jurassic Park. He had his homemade bow ready, but he doubted his arrows would penetrate their hard skin. As they grew closer, the ground quaked. He staggered like a drunk trying to keep his balance, and it was almost impossible to draw his bow.

"Luke!"

Moon called, but he couldn't find her. All he could see were dinosaurs as they darted around him like speeding cars.

"Luke!" He awoke from the dream with Moon shaking him and yelling. It was breaking daylight, the ground still shaking. "Get up! Buffalo!"

He shot to his feet. Bison appeared to be everywhere. He was immediately afraid he would be trampled, but at the same time, he felt the adrenaline—the rush of being alive. He grabbed his pack and his weapons. "Climb the ridge!" he yelled above the stampede.

Moon shimmied up the little ridge like a bear cub and then reached down and helped him up.

There were thousands of them. They thundered across the prairie like a story from the Old West. They crashed across the creek and trampled the ground where Luke and Moon had just slept. The smell was immediate and strong. On and on they came, kicking up dust and grass.

Moon squeezed Luke's arm. "What a sight."

Luke held his breath until he remembered to breathe. He knew the history of the American bison before the hunters had slaughtered the great herds. He smiled and shook his head—what a sight! In his mind's eye, he could see the Indians on horseback pursuing the great herd. He could see the village where the buffalo would be processed, every bit of the animal used. There would be a great celebration. "Unbelievable!"

"Believe it," Moon said. "They still exist here in abundance, not like back in your world." She smiled as she took in the magnificent scene.

Luke's smile dropped. She was right. This was another place and not the American West. There were no Indians here. That time in his country's history was gone, never to return. His kind had been cruel and wasteful. For the next twenty minutes, the herd stampeded by, but Luke's smile was gone.

When the last animals thundered past, Luke and Moon slid down from the ridge, dusted themselves, and headed across the prairie, wading bison manure. The ground was rutted and hard to walk on. A great dirt swath, like a wide snake, slithered across the prairie as far as they could see. No one would have a difficult task following a large herd of bison.

As they walked along, Luke took his mind off home as he practiced with his bow. He shot at grass stalks, grasshoppers, bison turds, anything, just to get the feel of the new bow. They had found a dead crow, and Luke collected the wing feathers for his arrows. Now living off the land was real, not just a hobby as it had been back home in the Ozarks. He now knew he would have to collect or make everything he needed to survive—or kill what he needed. He was now a real hunter-gatherer.

The large, golden prairie slowly changed to a savanna. A few miles farther, and they were in a forest again, where Luke found a pecan grove. "We better fill our pockets with these," Luke said. "We shouldn't pass up food." He began stuffing his pack with the pecans. He was made for this. He had played this game for years. Back home he collected pecans, hickory nuts, persimmons, and all other manner of nuts and fruits from the wild. But, it was only play. He could always go to the store in his truck any time he wanted—not now.

Moon picked up a few, then stopped and looked at Luke. "I have to tell you something."

Luke stopped picking up the nuts and turned to her. Her beautiful auburn hair floated with the wind. He couldn't help himself from swallowing hard. "What is it?"

Before Moon said another word, a spear flew from the sky and stabbed in the dirt between them. Moon went for her pistol, but another spear sliced her arm, sending the gun careening to the ground.

Luke spotted a Scrain in the pecan tree. He put an arrow in the man's chest in an instant. It was automatic. The man tumbled from the tree like a stunt man in an action movie. Luke crammed another arrow on the bow and wheeled around in time to see another charging. He shot him in the face. The man's feet ran out from under him, and he slammed on his back, dead.

"Look out!" Moon yelled.

Luke turned just as another Scrain lunged his spear at him. Luke deflected it with his bow. The man grabbed Luke around the neck and drove him to the ground. Luke's face hit the dirt hard, and he saw flashes in his head. The man grabbed Luke's hair and slammed his face into the dirt. Luke elbowed the man in the side, pulled his new tomahawk from his belt, and drove it into the man's throat. The man gurgled and fell dead.

Luke turned in time to see Moon kick a Scrain in the face

with her boot. He heard the dull crunch and knew the man was dead when he hit the ground.

Moon picked the pistol up from the ground, was ready for the next one. But, there were no more.

It happened fast—too fast. They had been careless, but they had been lucky. They had not seen them on the prairie and mistakenly thought they were safe—they were wrong. Luke could not know back then that all of those years of practicing and shooting running rabbits with primitive weapons would some day save his life. Now it had, and he was sure he would need that training again.

He looked around and saw Moon holding her arm, her sleeve soaked with blood. "Moon!" He ran to her. "How bad is it?"

"Help me get my jacket off," she said.

Luke eased the bloody jacket off, and she removed her shirt —she wore nothing under it. The spear had scraped a large gash in her forearm.

"I've got a first-aid kit in my pack." Luke fumbled around in his pack and pulled it out. He had to slow down and take a breath. He knew he had to be cool. Getting in a panic would help nothing. He slowly wrapped a bandage around her arm. He felt her looking at him.

"You did well, Constable." She dabbed at Luke's bleeding lip —luckily, the only sign of the pounding he had just taken.

He finished taping the bandage and slowly raised his eyes to hers. In his peripheral vision, he could see her naked body. His heart raced and it wasn't from the fight.

"Thank you, Luke." She smiled.

"You're welcome." His eyes stayed locked on hers. They were perfect eyes.

"But now I'm getting cold," she said.

Luke grinned, and this time he didn't turn red. He helped her get her shirt back on, being careful around the wound. "It's a good gash, but you'll be fine."

"Thank you, Doctor."

Luke looked the dead men over, seeing if he could find anything of use. The men were young, twenty or so. The Scrains' faces were not painted solid like the Chooners, but they wore painted stripes and swirls. To Luke they looked like blond Vikings. Some had bones pierced through their skins. Others had scars on their faces that resembled birds.

"Let's head out," Moon said.

"We had better be more careful. There may be more ahead," Luke said.

"No. We are getting out of their territory."

Luke picked up his bow. "How can you possibly know that?" He reached down and wiped the blood from his tomahawk onto a clump of grass.

A horn echoed through the woods; it sounded like a bull's horn he had heard coon hunters use to call in the dogs.

Moon stood. "Yes!"

"What is it?" Luke said.

"Come on, let's go," Moon said as she took off toward the sound.

"Moon, wait!" It was no use.

They jogged through the forest and soon stepped out into a large opening. It was a village. There were long huts made of logs and sticks. There were also round houses made from all types of stones. They looked like igloos. In the center of the village was a large flat-topped pyramid made of stones with steps ascending all four sides, sort of like what the Mayans had, but on a much smaller and cruder scale.

Moreover, there were people—a lot of them. They were all looking at Luke and Moon. They were not moving, just staring. There was something strange about them. They were white people, but they reminded him of American Indians. Then Luke realized what was so strange—they all had red hair.

Luke slowly turned to Moon. She was smiling with tears running down her cheeks..

"These are my people, Luke. We are safe." She stepped forward and spoke words that sounded like some sort of

American Indian language and in a loud voice with exaggerated hand gestures. The people cheered and a man in a buffalo robe with a strange, skinned hat walked toward them.

"What did you say, Moon?" Luke took her arm. "What do you mean, these are your people?"

The man walked to within ten feet of them. He looked to be around sixty or so; tears were running down his face, too. "Sha-She?" the man said softly.

Luke laid his hand on his tomahawk.

"Sha-She?" the man said again, but a little louder.

Moon nodded. "Da." She ran to the man, and they embraced for a long spell.

The man turned, raised Moon's hand high in the air, and yelled, "Sha-She!"

The horns suddenly sounded out in every direction. The people all descended on Moon in high jubilee. They pulled at her clothes and laughed. They jabbered in that strange language. Moon laughed with them. She hugged many of them in turn. Yes, she knew them.

They started toward the center of the village, but Moon stopped as she remembered Luke. She said something to the older man and walked back to Luke. "Luke, you stand right here. Don't move."

"Stay here?"

"I will be back soon."

"I'm not gonna stand right here." Look took a step forward. "What do you mean—"

Moon put her hand up. "Stop, Luke!"

Luke stopped as if he had been slapped. He was confused.

"I'm going to ask you to trust me again." She lowered her hand. "Now, I will come back shortly and explain everything. But right now you have to stand right there and not move."

Luke didn't have too many choices. He looked around. Nope —not too many choices at all.

He watched Moon disappear into the crowd with the rest of the red-haired people as they went toward the center of the village and into a long hut. Luke reckoned it was some kind of meeting hall.

All at once he was alone again. As he took stock of his situation and looked around, he realized he was wrong—he was definitely not alone. There were lookouts in the trees and they were watching him. They had long pointy sticks just like the Scrains. No wonder Moon didn't want him to move. Luke backed up to a tree and sat down. He sat there for hours. He finally fell asleep leaning on the tree.

"Who are you?"

Luke awoke with a start. He looked up to see a tall young man.

"Why you here?" the man said.

Luke scrambled to his feet. At first, he thought he was dreaming again; then he realized where he was.

"Talk!" the man said as he hit the butt of his spear on the ground.

Luke reached for his tomahawk, but the man was faster and quickly had the point of his spear inches from Luke's face.

Luke dropped his hand away from the tomahawk. With a sigh he said, "My name is Luke." He looked at the man. He was just as primitive looking as the rest. "How do you know English?"

The man lowered the spear. "Don't know English."

Luke realized he wasn't being understood. "How can you speak to me in my words?"

The man ignored the question. "Where you come from?" He pointed his finger at Luke. "You come from Orion's place?"

Luke had read somewhere that some ancient cultures worshiped the star constellation Orion. He wondered how this man knew the name. How the hell could he speak English? Who were these people? Who was Moon and how did she know these people?

The man reached down and picked up Luke's pack. "From Orion's place?"

Luke pulled the pack from the man. "I come from Arkansas. You ever heard of that? You know, the Razorbacks. Wooo Pig Sooie."

The man tugged at Luke's shirt. "Orion?"

"No, Red. Not Orion. I come from Arkansas, the United States of America."

"We go to Orion," the man said and pulled at Luke's shirt.

Luke pulled back. "You got a rocket-ship?" He threw his pack onto his back. "Just drop me off in the Ozark Mountains on your way."

The horns sounded again and Luke turned to see Moon coming alone. She had colorful feathers arranged on her head like a laurel wreath an Ancient Roman or Greek might wear. She still had on her hiking clothes, but she also had a spotted, fawn skin cape over her shoulders.

Luke looked around and the man was gone. Luke turned and looked in all directions, but he was gone. The lookouts were still in the trees, but the "Orion" man seemed to have disappeared.

Moon took Luke's hands in hers. "I know you have many questions, and I will answer them soon; but right now, you have to come with me. Be cool and don't go for your weapons."

"Don't go for my weapons!"

"Leave them all right here with your pack. They will still be here when you return. I promise."

She had a *Mona Lisa* smile on her lips. There was nothing to do but trust her. As he dropped his pack from his back, he said, "We going to see the Mad Hatter or the Queen of Hearts?"

"We're going to see the Wizard of Oz." She laughed. "No Luke, we're going to see the king of Frelonna"

Luke placed his bow and arrows across his pack. "I always wanted to see a king."

Moon pointed to his tomahawk. Luke dropped it beside the pack, and they headed to see the king.

They entered a big log cabin. There was a large fire pit in the middle and a hole in the center of the roof that allowed the smoke to escape, just like a tepee. Large windows let light in, revealing drawings of stick men and stick animals painted on the walls. People sat on logs draped with animal furs. The king sat on a throne made of mammoth tusks and big furs. Luke thought of the mammoths out on the prairie—it was probably their cousin's carcass he was sitting on.

The king had graying, red hair. He had no bones sticking from him like many of the other men in the large house, but his face had scars on both sides. It was no doubt to Luke, some big animal had once clamped its jaws around the king's face.

Moon pulled Luke down onto a log directly in front of the king. The king sat there like a big toad with his eyes closed— maybe he was asleep. If that was the case, he could sleep through a bomb attack.

There were about fifty people—mostly men—in the cabin, and they were humming a monotonous seesaw tune. It was starting to get on Luke's nerves like fingernails on a chalkboard when suddenly they began ramping it up. The few women began whistling bird sounds. The men kept up the seesaw tune, but louder and louder. Moon squeezed Luke's hand. The sound grew. It sounded like a forest full of birds being hummed at by strange men.

Luke needed a cold beer. The weird was getting weirder. He knew he would wake up from this crazy dream any time now.

They stopped all at one time as if someone had pulled a plug or flipped a switch.

The king's eyes flashed open—one of them was whited over.

Now Luke squeezed Moon's hand and jerked back as if he had been slapped. He hoped this wasn't like an old Tarzan movie where he would be burned at the stake or pulled apart by the natives.

The king stared straight into Luke's eyes with his one good eye. He raised his left hand and said some mumbo-jumbo, and a half-naked woman came in with a fur robe and draped it over Luke's shoulders.

Luke nodded at the woman and the king. "Thank you. Thank you."

The woman went out the door and another appeared with a spear. She handed it to Luke. It was made of ivory with carvings along the length of it. No doubt, it was from a mammoth.

"Thanks." Luke inspected the spear. It was a work of art. He wondered how they carved the designs in it. He started to ask Moon, but another woman came in with a shield.

She held the hide-covered shield over her head, spun around and did a little dance. Her breasts were bare, and Luke blushed. Moon giggled as Luke took the shield from the dancing beauty.

Luke turned to Moon. "Why are they giving me presents?"

"Because you brought the king's daughter home."

"King's daughter? Home?"

"Luke!" the king's voice boomed, and it startled Luke. Then he began a long speech with many gestures. Luke didn't have a clue what he was saying, but he listened intently. Then the king stopped suddenly, nodded, and grunted. One by one, the women began the whistling again, soon followed by the men humming. The king stood and smiled down at Luke. Then he turned and went out of the building. The rest of the people stood and followed him out. And just like that, Luke and Moon were left alone.

Luke tried to make sense of what had just happened. He definitely was not in Arkansas anymore. He would not be surprised one bit to see the Scarecrow or the Tin Man at any second.

Moon took his hand. "Well, Constable, you received some nice gifts."

Luke looked at the gifts again, then back up at Moon. This was all too much to digest. It was really a bad dream. Nothing else could explain it. First, he was fighting blond Norsemen, next he was sitting by "Maureen O'Hara" and being showered with prehistoric gifts from the original red-haired "Celtic-Indians." All in all, it wasn't too bad for a shy boy who spent most of his time in the backwoods hiding from strange things.

Luke took the robe off and set the spear and shield on the floor. He turned back to Moon. "What is going on?" He ran his fingers through his hair and looked squarely into Moon's eyes. "Who are you? You're more than a government agent."

Moon smiled. She got up from the log and sat on the throne. "Okay, Luke, I will tell you what I can. I am a princess. My real name is Sha-She. I've been called Moon so long that you can keep calling me that."

Luke shook his head and shrugged his shoulders. Where was Alice and that cat?

"Look, Luke, I'm going to give you a brief synopsis. They are preparing a feast for us, and we don't want to keep them waiting."

"I'm all ears."

"This is my home. When I was twelve, I was kidnapped by the Scrain. They were going to sacrifice me at the big wind—"

"Big wind?"

"Yes. It's how you and I got here, the portal. I escaped through the portal before they could kill me. I wound up in your world. You can imagine how lost and confused I was. I stumbled along scared and lost until I came upon a colony of free-thinking people, and they took me in."

"Free-thinking? You mean, like hippies?"

Moon laughed. "I guess you could call them that. They were smoking weed and strung out on other drugs all the time. There was a full moon that night, so that's how I got my name."

"They taught you how to speak English?"

"Yeah, but I was only with them a couple of years. They were killed by a drug dealer. Then I became a ward of the great state of California.

"California? But we came through the portal from Arkansas."

"I know that, Luke. Let me finish my story. I went from foster home to foster home until I was taken in by a very special couple."

"They adopted you?"

"No. They trained me."

"Trained you?"

"First, they studied me, then they trained me."

"Moon, what are you talking about? Who were these people?"

"Luke, I had told everyone who would listen who I was and where I was from. Everyone just thought I was a kid with a big imagination, you know. This couple heard about me and took me in. They sought me out."

"Who were these people?"

"They were scientists. They worked for the government."

"What sort of scientists?"

"They were studying UFOs."

"They thought you were an ET?"

"At first they did. But eventually they believed I came through a wormhole."

Luke stood. "And they were right."

Moon nodded. "At first they looked to the stars, but soon they became obsessed with transversable wormholes, portals between different dimensions. They studied about them and looked for them." She rubbed her hands together. "Luke, these people weren't nuts. They had the ear of people in very high places. They were given the money to pursue this. It was top secret from on high."

"Moon—Sha-She—this is extremely hard to believe."

"I told you, call me Moon. It's the truth, Luke. For goodness sake, look around at where you are."

"If it was all top secret, why are you telling me?"

"Who can you tell?"

Luke sank back down to the log. Her words were like lead. He felt an immediate sinking feeling in his belly.

"I'm sorry, Luke."

Luke nodded and waved it away. "Did they ever find this transversable wormhole?"

"No. They were killed in a car accident."

Luke was numbed by the story. He sat there for a few minutes not saying anything, just letting it all process. Moon said nothing. After a while, Luke looked at her. "Moon, what government do you work for?"

She climbed down from the throne and went toward the door. "Come on, Luke; we are guests for the feast, and we don't won't to keep them waiting. I love smoked buffalo, don't you?"

Luke stood, but did not follow.

Moon stopped at the door and turned back to Luke. Her smile slowly melted away. "I'm sorry that I lied to you."

"Who are you?"

"I've already told you. I'm Sha-She, princess of Frelonna."

Luke bowed. "I understand who you are here, Your Highness. But who are you in my world?"

Moon looked into Luke's eyes for a long time, and then said, "I am Special Agent Moon Serling. I work for the government of the United States Of America."

Luke nodded. "Special Agent, what was your mission when you found me?"

Moon just stood there for a minute and then said softly, "To find my way back home."

Chapter 7

The king asked Luke—no, ordered him— to stay that night in a cabin with six other men. Moon winked at him as she followed a few women to some other place in the village. The men picked and laughed at Luke into the wee hours of the night, talking in a peculiar language that he had given up trying to understand. They tugged at his clothes and pointed at his odd, sandy-blond hair. At first he was angry with Moon for leaving him in such company, but later he reckoned it wasn't her choice. The men finally grew tired of the fun and fell asleep on their stinking, animal-hide mats.

Luke tried to rest, but he could forget about sleep; a couple of the men fired up chainsaws. He lay there like a dog trying to find just the right spot to get comfortable, thinking of the lice waiting to take up lodging on his body. He scratched at imaginary bugs and maybe some that weren't so imaginary. After about thirty minutes of suffering and listening to the loudest snoring he had ever heard, he went outside to get fresh air and quiet.

He found a log bench in the central plaza and parked there. He looked up to see the closest lookout in his perch. The man waved his horn at Luke. Luke waved back. The camp was quiet except for an occasional cough or snore that hit a particular high note and escaped through the walls of the cabin.

As the night closed around Luke, the weight of the last couple of days settled over him like lead. A few tears escaped his control and traveled down his dirty face—he didn't bother to wipe them. This all cannot be real. This had to be an awful dream, and soon he would wake up in his own cabin deep in the woods of the Ozark Mountains of Arkansas. There will be no Agent Moon, no strange, blond people, no village of red-haired people, no other dimension.

A soft, deep rumble started somewhere in the distance and rolled through the village. It vibrated in his chest. And then came the trumpet of an elephant. Mammoth. Luke squeezed his eyes closed and fought for control. It was almost impossible to think about it. This couldn't be real.

Luke dropped his face into his hands. How could this be true? Was he really in another world? He recalled how he had shunned many modern technologies. He had moved deep into the woods, hunted with primitive tools. He never used a GPS or compass to navigate the woods, only the sun and stars and moss on the north side of the trees. Oh, what he would give now just to have a radio, just to know there were other people —his own people—out there somewhere.

He wiped his eyes, remembered his phone in his pocket. He pulled it out and powered it on. There were no bars—not one. Of course not—there were no cell towers. There was no electricity, no modern anything. He had thought it was the way he always wanted to live, and now here it was. Here he was.

He smeared his runny nose on his sleeve. There was no use crying, no use in self-pity. What would be the point? He gazed around at the sleeping village and then turned to the speckled sky. The stars were brighter than they ever were on the darkest night in the Ozarks. He studied the heavens—the stars were the same as back home. He was in the northern hemisphere alright. He found the Big Dipper and Little Dipper. He found the North Star. How many nights had he slept under God's diamond-filled sky? How many times had he wished to live in the times before flight, before blinking lights of planes trespassed on the beauty of the twinkling stars? There were no lights here. There were no vapor trails during the day. The sky was pristine. The only movement in the dark heaven was an occasional shooting star with all its splendor.

Gradually, he felt an appreciation for what he was seeing. Man had not screwed it up, yet. Luke was still seeing nature in charge. Man was not altering the course of nature here, not conquering it as he tried to back home.

All of a sudden strange feeling corkscrewed up Luke's back. There was something behind him. He didn't have to see it—he felt it. His weapons were fifty yards away by the cabin door. He eased his hand into his pocket for his Swiss army knife; not the best weapon, but better than nothing.

"No! Don't do it," came a hard whisper from behind. It was the man who had spoken about Orion.

Luke pulled his hand from his pocket as the man sat down beside him. "Who are you?" Luke said.

The young man looked Luke up and down in the dim light. He ran his hands over Luke's clothes. He yanked Luke's badge from his shirt.

"Damn it!" Luke grabbed the man's arm, but it was like grabbing steel. He let the man have the badge.

The man turned the badge to try to find enough light to inspect it. He soon gave up and gave it back to Luke. "We go."

Luke put the badge in his shirt pocket. "Go where?"

"Orion."

"What do you mean?" Luke stood and pointed toward the constellation. "That Orion?"

The man didn't look at the constellation, only at Luke. "Get your things. We go."

Luke looked up toward the lookout. He wasn't there.

"Go now before he wakes up," the man said as he placed his fist at his own jaw in a punching motion.

Luke looked around for anyone else.

"Get your things." The man pointed toward Luke's weapons.

"We go to Orion."

Luke hesitated. But here was a man that spoke his language. If he wanted to do Luke harm, he could have already. Instead, he was telling him to get his weapons and go with him. "What the hell." Luke grabbed up his stuff. "I'll at least look at your starship."

The man moved through the darkness quiet as an animal, and Luke tailed him like his shadow. Luke had developed his "night eyes" and could have followed the well-worn trail through the forest on his own.

After a little ways, Luke stopped and looked back toward the village. He only knew two people in this world—he hoped Grace was still alive somewhere. Moon was asleep back there, and he felt as if he were betraying her. But then, he thought how she had lied to him. She was really an agent for the government, not some innocent local newspaper reporter. And there was no telling what branch she worked for, probably some shady organization. But he still felt as if—

"Come. We go now," the man said.

Luke turned back toward him. "I'm going no farther until I at least know your name."

The man stamped the butt of his spear in the ground and stood erect. "I am Adam."

"Adam?" Luke was surprised. He was expecting some name he couldn't pronounce.

Adam stepped closer and placed his hand to his own chest. "Like Adam in the Bible."

Luke felt a sudden hope that he had found a way home. If this man knew about the Bible, there had to be a connection to home. There must be some kind of communication to Luke's world.

"Now we go." Adam turned and started back down the trail.

Luke tightened his pack on his back and shoved his tomahawk into his belt. Now he felt hope as he followed Adam through the dark woods and prairies. He imagined some crevice or canyon through a mountain that was lost to his world, but known to this one. It would lead him back home. He smiled. He dreamed up ways he would tell the people back home about this world, how he would convince the sheriff to bring his posse here to look for Grace.

Grace. Poor Grace. Where was she? They would find her. They would come back with bloodhounds. Hell, they would come back with helicopters and state of the art electronics to find her. And so he walked most of the night blindly following Adam and anticipating a way home and a plan to find Grace.

At daybreak, they were trekking across a prairie when he spotted a mountain range rising in the west. It looked like the Ozarks and he was giddy. Of course, they were the Ozarks and the path would be there. The canyon would be there. He was practically home. He pumped his fist in the air. "Yes!"

They climbed the path through the foothills, and everything looked so familiar. It was almost as if he could remember some long ago hunt there. As he ascended, relief came over him like a sudden rush of air from a held breath, like waking from a nightmare and realizing it was a nightmare.

Luke called ahead to Adam, "Where is the canyon that will lead us back to my world?"

Adam stopped and turned. He realized what Luke was feeling. Luke could see it on his face. Adam slowly shook his head. "No canyon. No *your world*." He turned and pointed to an outcropping with a cave behind it. In front of it stood a man with a long stick. He was a spitting image of Charlton Heston's Moses. "Orion," Adam said.

Luke's heart dropped like a stone as he followed a narrow path up to the man.

Moses rushed to Luke and took both his hands. "Welcome! Welcome! Adam told me he would bring you. Now please say some English words so I know this is no dream."

Luke looked the man up and down. He wore a buffalo robe and rawhide sandals. He had long gray hair and he looked like something from out of the Old Testament. "Who are you?"

The old man let go of Luke's hands, raised his own hands as he turned in a circle. "Oh, Heavenly Father, thank you for answering my prayers."

Adam said, "This is Orion."

"What?" He had thought Adam was speaking of the constellation.

Orion took Luke's hand. "Come, come; let us go into my abode." He pulled Luke toward the large cave. "I haven't talked to anyone except Adam that could talk good English in over fifty years."

The cave was the size of a small house with a stone fireplace just under the outer ledge of the huge opening. Along the back wall were two beds made of logs with animal hides stretched across them. There was a table with benches just in front of it. There were chairs made of oak slats like Luke had made for his own cabin. On the table were clay plates and bowls. A crude desk sat between the beds.

Orion sat at the table. "You and Adam sit with me. Please do. Please do."

Luke parked himself in one of the chairs and drew it up to the table. He examined the cave further. There was a large curtain against the cave wall made of sticks tied together with some type of vine or chord. Luke figured it was a wall to stretch over the huge opening during bad weather.

"I brought the man like Orion wished," Adam said.

"You done good, Adam. You done real good."

Adam smiled and nodded like a child.

Orion stared at Luke with a grin spread across his face.

The smile was contagious and Luke couldn't help but smile back. "Mr. Orion, where are you from?"

"Oh, I love to hear the sweet sound of my own language." Orion shook his head. "Music. Music, indeed." He took a long breath. "I come from Alabama. And where you from?"

"Arkansas."

"Another Southerner—I knew it. I knew it. You didn't have no accent."

The gears in Luke's brain came to a screeching halt. His mind reached back for something scratching to get out. Where had he heard Orion and Alabama together? It hit him. "Selma! You're from Selma, Alabama."

"Why, yes. Nation! How did you guess that?"

"Your name is Orion Williamson."

Orion slapped the table. "That's me. You a medicine man or something?"

Luke tried to remember the rest of the story from the newspaper article.

"I ain't good on guessing, so you're gonna have to tell me who you are," Orion said.

The wind dropped from Luke's sails. He realized this wasn't his way home. In fact, it was the nail that pinned the door shut. If Orion had really disappeared from that field in 1854, he had been here for a long time. But he only looked to be about eighty or so, not one hundred sixty.

"Well, man, you gonna tell me?"

Luke sighed. "Luke Morgan."

"A fine name, a fine name, indeed." Orion said.

"Luke, good name," Adam said.

"Adam, get us wine from the shelf," Orion said. "Please do fetch it."

Adam retrieved a jug and three cups. They looked like something made in junior high art class. He placed the cups on the table and poured the wine all around. The sweet aroma was strong.

Orion raised his cup. "To Luke, my new friend."

They all drank the wine in a few gulps. It was pretty good to Luke, but he would rather have had a good cup of coffee, maybe a little whiskey in it.

"Mr. Orion—"

"Just Orion, my new friend."

"Okay then. Orion, how long have you been here?"

Orion got up from the table and walked to a wall. There were a good many chalk marks on it. "This is my crude calendar. I've been here about fifty-four years." He looked at the marks and sat back down.

"Do you remember how you got here?" Luke said.

The smile finally left Orion's face, and he looked down at his cup. "How could I ever forget?"

"I guess that was a stupid question," Luke said.

"I had just stepped off my porch to go tell my overseer something when there kicked up a drumming sound and a swoosh of air." He looked up. "The next thing I knew I was under a net and being beaten by these savages with big sticks. I was confused, to say the least."

Luke nodded. "How did you get away?"

"In them years, the red-heads and the white-heads was in a war. I managed to get away before they could put me in that cage when the red-heads came a stormin' through the village."

"Have other people come in through that portal?"

"Through what?"

"The portal. You know, the way you got here."

"I've snuck back to the white-head village several times when the drums was a beatin,' hoping to get back home, but they ain't no use; you can't get out it. I've seen all kinds of animals come in, but no people. Mostly nothin' comes in, just every now and then. I ain't been back there in years. Damn near got caught the last time—too old now. I just don't have the key to get out so why bother."

Luke rubbed his face and nodded. Yeah, a key would be nice. He hadn't heard anything yet that was encouraging. Everything was crazy. That portal must pluck things from different times. In this world it plucked Orion about fifty years ago; but back home, it was before the Civil War.

Luke placed his head in his hands and thought for a spell; something had to make sense. He looked up. "Are there other people besides the red-heads and the white-heads?"

"There are others."

"Are they more modern? Do they have cars, planes, and such?"

Orion scratched his head. "Do they have what? You mean rail cars?"

Luke realized Orion had never seen such things. "Do they have guns? Do they have wagons?"

"Luke, the red-heads and the white-heads make their weapons from bone and wood. They don't even use stone. Well, some, but not like the Indians back home. They ain't even got a bow and arrow. And I ain't showin' 'em either."

"Why not?" Luke said.

"I don't want to give them any advantage over me." Orion pointed to a bow hanging from an outcropping on the cave wall.

"I guess I understand that," Luke said.

Orion reached across the table and squeezed Luke's arm. "It's more to it than that. My adopted grandmother was a Creek Indian. She told me stories of when she was a little girl. White man changed all that. I want to leave these people as they have always been. This ain't America, but The All Mighty created it all the same, and I ain't gonna change it."

Luke understood. But he was surprised to hear someone from Orion's time being concerned about Native Americans. Luke had always suspected our understanding of all history was only a skeleton of the truth. Parts of history will always be lost.

Orion got up from the table. "Adam, let's feast. Get two chickens from the pen and clean them. I will build up the fire."

Luke wanted to know more about *the others*, but he would ask later.

Adam dutifully disappeared from the cave, and Orion stoked the coals in his round fireplace. After placing sticks on the fire, he soon had a blaze going.

After a time, Adam came in with two skinned creatures that resembled small dogs.

Luke looked at Orion. "Chickens?"

Orion laughed. "They're possums. I've built a pen that I keep them in. Me and Adam catch 'em and throw 'em in there and keep 'em like chickens. I purge 'em out with persimmons or wild grapes, what have you. It sweetens 'em up a bit."

Soon the table was spread with roasted possum, roasted pecans, cattail stew, and some type of grain kernels in possum broth. It was all cooked over the fire with spits and soapstone pots. Luke not only found it edible, he found it all delicious. Who needed fast foods? The plates and bowls ranged from wooden to a red clay. The forks and knives were made of ivory and bone, and they all functioned as good as any silverware.

Luke had lived off the land before back home in Arkansas, but he had still used modern knives, forks, and cast iron cookware. He knew if he didn't find a way back home soon, the modern things he had with him now would soon be lost or used up. But he wasn't afraid of that—other things, but not that. He found it comforting to know he could survive. He even found the thought exciting.

That night he lay in the cave listening to Orion snore. He listened to wolves and night critters off in the distance and thought of home. He missed his mother and sister, but he really had no one else back there. He had always been a loner. He was always shy and reclusive. But when he thought of his cousin locked up in the jailhouse, Luke knew he had to get back somehow if only to free him.

He got up from the bed and walked to the opening of the cave. The stars' impact on him was immediate again. He just couldn't get over how clear they were. They had never seemed so bright as here. They had never seemed... They had never seemed so relevant as now. They had never seemed so important.

He heard shuffling behind him; then Orion joined him. They stood there together for a time not saying anything.

Luke finally said, "These stars are not as bright in my world."

Orion studied the stars. "What is your world, Luke?"

Luke thought about it and knew Orion wouldn't understand. Luke was proud of his world, but ashamed too. Man had achieved so much, yet, wasted so much. He turned to Orion. "Same as yours. I reckon Arkansas ain't much different from

Alabama.

Orion looked at Luke, and Luke knew Orion didn't believe him. They both just let it pass.

Orion looked back up to the heavens. "I think on home sometimes: my wife, daughter, my slaves. My daughter is grown now; my wife remarried, surely. My slaves all belong to someone else. I hope they are all happy. Actually, I hope my slaves have been freed. He looked at Luke. As a fellow Southerner, I reckon you find that strange. Living back here all these years has given me time to think on a lot of things."

Luke shook his head. "No, Mr. Orion, I don't think it strange at all. One of these days I bet all slaves in America will be free."

They stood there silently for a time. A shooting star streamed across the sky like a flare. They both pointed at it and smiled.

"Adam tells me you showed up with his king's lost daughter," Orion said.

Luke turned to Orion and nodded.

Orion sat on the cave floor and Luke joined him. "I remember the girl disappearing, but everyone thought she was dead. She was captured by the white-heads." He turned to Luke. "She must have found a way out through the gateway there."

"Then, I must go back there to get out," Luke said.

"They will kill you if they catch you."

"Then they won't catch me."

Orion sighed. "Luke, I feel I should tell you a little about me. I took up with one of the red-haired women years ago. I'm gonna make this short because I don't like talkin' on it. While she was with me out on the prairie huntin' buffalo, we was caught. What they did to her I will never talk about." He turned to Luke and patted his arm. "Don't let them catch you. They hate the red-heads, and by now, they know you have been among them."

"How did you get away?"

"Me and the boy escaped when she allowed herself to be captured." He looked toward Adam.

"Adam is your son?"

Orion nodded. "His mother sacrificed herself so we would live. We ran toward a herd of the big elephants." He took one of Luke's hands. "Remember, the red-heads and white-heads are afraid of the big elephants. They worship them. They collect their bones and tusks, but they are scared to death of the big beasts."

As if on cue, Luke felt the vibration in his chest again as the low growls of the mammoths echoed through the mountains.

"They like to gather at the foothills and caves down there. It's why I took up residence here. I'm as safe as if I was on the moon while they're down there."

Orion patted Luke's arm again. "I'm turning in. I'll see you in the morning."

Luke nodded and watched Orion disappear back into the cave. Luke stood there for a spell, felt restless, wasn't ready for sleep. He walked down the trail to the foothills. He came to a ledge, and he could see the vast prairie spread out before him. Though it was dark, he could still make out the silhouettes of about twenty big mammoths standing in the grass. The big beasts were extinct back home in his world for whatever reason. In this world they ruled. For some reason he couldn't explain to himself, it brought a smile to his lips. This was now his world, for better or worse, and he was more and more coming to realize it.

He thought of Moon. She would wonder what had happened to him. He had been wrong to just strike out and not tell her. Besides all that, he missed her. Tomorrow he would consider getting Adam to lead him back to her.

He found a big rock to sit on. For now, he just sat and took in the night sounds. There were many, and many he didn't know. Tomorrow he would change his focus. He would begin in earnest to learn his new world. He would study every advantage to survive in it. He knew Orion would be a big instrument in that study.

He had to respect a man such as Orion. He had learned to

live in another world and had survived in it for a long time. Moon had known that when she shoved that paper about Orion in Luke's hands back at the cabin. Luke suspected she knew even more than she had told.

Luke dusted his pants off and headed back to the cave. Tomorrow would be the first day in the rest of his life, a life so very different than he could have ever dreamed of only a few days ago.

Luke awoke to the smell of something inviting. He sat up. Orion and Adam were next to the fire. They had something brewing. It wasn't coffee, but it still smelled good with a nutty aroma.

"Well, Luke, glad to see you awake," Orion said. Adam nodded.

Luke rubbed his face and climbed out of the cot. "What you got brewing there?"

Orion poured a black brew from the clay pot. "I call it coffee." He handed it to Luke. "To tell you the truth, I don't know what the plant is, but the locals drink it; and it hasn't killed them or me yet."

Luke blew the steam off it and took a drink. It sure wasn't coffee, had a taste somewhere between pecans, chocolate and mint. "Whew, they could make a killing off this at Starbucks."

"What is Starbucks?" Orion said.

Luke grinned. "A store back home."

Adam handed Luke a bowl containing dried fruit. "Good food."

Luke bit into one. "Mmm. Dried persimmons. This honey on them?" Luke put a handful into his mouth.

While Luke was eating, Orion retrieved a handful of things from deep in the cave and spread them out before Luke on the floor. "I was looking at your hunting things and reckoned you could use some of this.

Luke finished his drink and examined the stuff on the floor. He found turkey feathers, pieces of cane, deer sinew, pieces of flint and flint tools. There were pieces of horns and antlers for knapping the flint. It was a toolbox for a primitive hunter.

"I looked your hunting equipment over while you slept," Orion said. "But I could tell it was all built in a hurry. Your cane's not dry good—arrows are too flimsy. Use whatever you want here until you can gather your own. I don't know what your bowstring's made out of, but it sure is tough."

"Made from a strange plant we have back home." Luke lied. He knew Orion wouldn't understand about nylon.

Luke spent the rest of the morning building arrows. He tuned them until they flew as they should—correct spine, straight and true. He replaced the colorful feathers with good, stout turkey feathers. He tied them on with sinew and glue made from animal hides and used the antler tools to knock away flakes from his flint to make points. They were sharp enough to shave hair.

He found a ragged piece of deerskin in the pile and fashioned a quiver to carry the arrows. When he finished, he walked down to the prairie and practiced shooting.

Orion and Adam had followed him down.

After a while Orion said, "You shoot better than anyone I ever saw. How did you learn to shoot so good?"

"These are the instruments I hunt with back home." Luke shot again and hit a tuft of grass dead center.

Orion laughed. "They don't have guns in Arkansas?"

Luke propped up on the bow and thought how amazed Orion would be at the modern guns—or compound bows, for that matter. He said, "I just choose to hunt this way for the challenge."

Orion took the bow from Luke. "Well, you have no choice in the matter now." He placed an arrow on the bow and let it fly. His arrow hit right beside Luke's arrow. "My adopted Creek grandfather taught me to shoot."

Luke spent the rest of the day with Orion and Adam, learning the ways of this new world. He learned new plants to eat. He learned what animals to hunt and the ones to avoid. He was told of the water courses. He was instructed where to find fruit trees, which fruits to eat, which not to eat.

Orion gave Luke a crude map. It was made from some sort of paint on an animal skin. "Luke, this is most of the world I know here."

Luke stretched it out on the desk. He identified the Florian village and the village. He saw something strange written on a location beyond the mountains. Luke put his finger on the spot. "Does this say *giants?*"

Orion nodded.

"You don't really mean giants, do you?"

"Of course."

"Right," Luke said as he folded the map and put it in his pack. He turned to Orion. "Did you see these giants?"

"I saw them."

"How tall are they—twenty, thirty feet, big as an oak tree?"

Orion frowned. "You mock me, Luke."

Luke patted Orion's arm. "I'm sorry. It's just so hard to believe...all of this."

"I reckon I understand. But giants are in the Bible." Orion closed his eyes and began to recite: "There were giants on the earth in those days; and also after that, when the sons of God came in unto the daughters of men, and they bare children to them, the same became mighty men which were of old, men of renown."

"Genesis," Luke said.

Orion nodded. "The giants I speak of are around eight to ten feet tall."

"Are they warriors? Did you see them?"

"Don't go across the mountain, Luke." He took Luke's hand. "They are evil, fallen angels or worse. You have no reason to go there."

Luke felt the immediate change in Orion's demeanor.

"Hear me good on that, Luke."

"I understand."

Luke had enough on his plate without worrying about giants, which were probably just bogeymen anyway. Luke already knew the Florians were a warrior tribe, and they were intent on doing him harm; but now he knew that may be the only possible way home. They had the *door* between the two dimensions. Luke hoped it swung both ways. He had to find out, no matter the dangers.

The Frelonnians were Moon's people. Orion had said they had been tolerant of him because of Adam, but they didn't want him among them. Adam lived with them but often visited his father. They were warriors, too, and they could be just as vicious as the Florians.

The next morning Luke packed his things for the trip back. He had to find Moon. He should not have left without telling her. And he found he missed her.

Orion walked down to the prairie with Luke and Adam. "Luke, if you don't find the way back to Arkansas, you are welcome here." He offered his hand and Luke shook it.

"Mr. Williamson, I appreciate your offer, and I thank you for all this." Luke raised his quiver.

Orion looked across the prairie and then back at Luke. "If you find a way back, will you travel to Alabama and tell my family that you found me?" He handed Luke a little carving. It was a mammoth fashioned from ivory. "Give this to my daughter if you do. It's very important to me that she receive it." Orion rubbed his great beard. "If not her, maybe a grandchild—some descendant. Tell them it is the key."

"The key?"

Orion patted Luke's hand. "Just humor an old man."

Luke placed the carving in his pack. If he went through the portal, he hoped he didn't wind up in the 1850s. "I will be glad to deliver it."

"It's very important to me."

"I promise. If I make it back, your descendant will get it."

Luke and Adam started across the prairie. A small herd of

85

wild horses mingled with a few mammoths. It was a moving sight. He turned back to see Orion going back up the trail. He did look like Moses.

Chapter 8

They came to a small river where Adam had left a dugout canoe. Luke ran his hands across it. Black char came off on his fingers from where it had been burned out. Days had gone in to making it—burning it out and chopping away the wood. Seeing it meant more to Luke than admiring a fine new car. He had always wanted to build one—it would have been the ultimate challenge in bushcraft, but there was little need for it in the Ozarks. Luke finally got his fill admiring it and boarded it with Adam. They started down the lazy river.

"Why are we going back a different way from the way we had come?" Luke said.

"This will be faster," Adam said. "This river goes downstream to the village."

"Why didn't we just take this way in the first place?"

Adam grinned. "Did you have a canoe at the village?"

"I take your point." He turned back toward the front and stroked the water with his paddle.

The river was fresh and pristine. It was like traveling through a Bierstadt painting, with the broken golden prairie, red and yellow trees along the river's edge, and snow-capped mountains in the distance. Luke spotted birds in the trees along the bank that he knew well, but he also saw some he didn't know. There were pigeons and big woodpeckers and unique-looking sparrows. He saw birds with long tails and some with fat beaks. It truly was a naturalist's dream. A birder would be in heaven. Luke pulled his binoculars from his pack. It was simply amazing. Everything his binoculars fell on was beyond belief.

"What's that?" Adam pointed toward the binoculars.

Luke handed them back to him. "Don't drop them. It will be a surprise when you look through them."

Adam nodded as he took the binoculars. He did almost drop them. He looked at Luke wide-eyed. "Make things come close." He put them back to his eyes and tried to look at everything.

"They are called binoculars."

Adam handed them back to Luke. "Good. Good binoculars."

Luke laughed and Adam laughed back as they rounded a bend. At the same time, they spotted a big, bull mammoth standing in the middle of the narrow river. They quickly paddled backwards, but they were too near for the large animal's comfort and most certainly their own. He raised his trunk and bugled, and then he charged them, just as Luke had seen elephants do on TV. Luke grabbed an overhanging limb at river's edge and held it. They were getting ready to exit the canoe when the giant beast stopped about twenty yards away, making a big wave and spraying water. Luke felt he had to keep his mouth shut to keep his heart from leaping out. The bull trumpeted again and then slowly turned, climbed out of the river and started across the prairie.

Luke turned to Adam and let go of the limb. "Whew, that was close."

Adam laughed and made a motion with his arm, simulating the mammoth's trunk.

Luke watched as the mammoth went through the tall grass. Beyond, he saw smoke rising over the prairie. Adam stopped paddling—he had spotted it too. There was something familiar, but strange, about the smoke. Then Luke realized what it was. It was smoke signals.

Adam turned in the canoe. "Meat camp. We go help."

"Help do what?"

"Help with meat."

"I don't know, Adam. I think we should get back to the village. Moon will be looking for me."

Adam pulled the canoe to shore. "We leave it here; come back to it later."

"You know what. On second thought," Luke said. "I think it would be a grand idea to go traipsing across the prairie. If we're lucky, we could be eaten by a dinosaur."

"A what?"

"Never mind."

They cleared the tall rushes and trees at the edge of the river and entered the prairie, but the smoke was farther than it appeared from behind the trees—a lot farther.

They struck out toward the smoke. Luke didn't know what was about to happen, but he had no choice but to go along. He had no idea where he was, nor how to get back to the village and Moon.

Adam climbed a hill and motioned for Luke to follow. When they made it to the top, the vista spread for miles. The prairie ran to the ends of sight. It was like two prairies, a high one and a low one. Where the high one ended, there were canyons and cuts. After that, the lower canyon picked up again and ran until it touched the sky. A picture or a painting could never do the scene justice.

Luke pulled his binoculars from his pack again. In one of the canyons, the Frelonnians had made a camp at the entrance of it. There were fires burning and people milling around like they were having a cookout or picnic. Then Luke scanned to the base of the canyon cliff. There were bison lying scattered among the rocks with people walking among the dead animals.

Adam tapped Luke's shoulder. "Good! Many buffalo."

Luke understood now. He had read about this. The American Indians would drive the bison over the steep cliffs to their deaths. That is exactly what had happened here. Now these people were butchering and processing the dead animals.

Adam started down the hill and toward the mouth of the canyon. Luke followed.

Adam walked into the camp with his hands high into the air, chanting and yelling. The people looked up from their work and yelled back. Adam pulled his bone knife from his belt and joined in the butchering.

The process was like a factory. The men butchered the animals with tools made of bones, antlers, and even sharp rocks they had picked up from the ground. A modern butcher with his steel knives could not have been more efficient.

The women cut the meat up further and placed it on smoke racks as Luke himself had done many times. They scraped the meat from the buffalo hides and bones. This was not a hobby —it was existence.

Luke walked up to one of the fires to find kids cooking pieces of meat stuck on the ends of sticks. A pretty girl of about twelve offered Luke a piece of meat. He started to decline, but being hungry, he took it. It was a piece of tongue. Luke hesitated, but then crammed it into his mouth. It was good, but needed a little salt.

Luke walked among the people. He recognized some from the village. He watched them as they worked. Luke had played the game of being primitive; now here he was in a real world of primitive. These people could not put away their simple tools and animal-skin clothes when they were tired of them and then put on their slippers, get their remote control and watch the television. They couldn't get the bologna from the fridge and make a late night sandwich. This was it. This was everything.

Luke stood over a young man skinning a big bull. The man had a long flake of flint. Luke had never seen anyone skin an animal as fast as this man was doing. And he was efficient too. There were no holes in the hide. It would be used for clothes or shelter. The man sliced the meat into thin strips and laid them on the skin. Young boys and girls gathered the meat from the skin and took it to one of the smoking racks. This was a factory.

The butchering went on into the night. Not all the meat was used; too many animals had been driven off the cliff. Soon the wolves were circling the camp, and guards were positioned to keep the beasts away. It was an awful sound when they did get to one of the buffaloes that the people had not butchered. The movie sound effects had wolves all wrong. They were much more gruesome. There were no wolves in the modern Ozarks, only coyotes; and now being near them, Luke had a sudden appreciation for the danger. He strung his bow.

The next morning Luke and Adam were back on the river. If Luke ever made it back home to Arkansas, he would never forget the experience at the canyon. He would use what he had learned there. If he were stranded in this world for all time, he would have to use it here, no other choice.

The river carried them along at a good clip, and soon they were back at the village. Luke waited at the river as Adam went to retrieve Moon. Luke was worried about going into the village without her. He didn't know if it would be safe.

He sat at the river's edge, skipping flat rocks across the surface of the river, thinking about all that had transpired. He had always wondered what it would be like to go back in time and live like prehistoric man with his primitive weapons and tools. Now he knew. Now he knew for sure. It was almost as he had imagined. Almost. He had always been able to use modern things when he grew tired of playing prehistoric. Now it was real—real all the time.

Adam came back. "Sha-She gone."

Luke stood. "Gone?" He looked toward the village. "Where?"

"Sha-She just gone. Not say where."

Luke sat down on a rock. What was he going to do now? Where was he going now? He suddenly felt alone, like the last man on earth. He looked up at Adam. At least he had Adam and Orion.

Adam took Luke's hand and pulled him from the rock. "We go find Sha-She."

Luke felt hope. "You can find her?"

Adam looked at him as if he had said the most stupid thing ever.

"How can you find her?"

Adam smiled and pointed to Luke's feet.

At first Luke didn't understand, but then he got it. "Boots. We are the only ones around with boots. You can track her. Of course you can."

Adam climbed back into the canoe. "We go."

Luke looked around, then back to Adam. "How can you track Moon's boots if you are in a canoe?"

Adam laughed and shook his head. "You are funny, Luke."

Luke didn't see anything funny. Nevertheless, he climbed into the canoe; he had no other options.

The river widened beyond the village and moved smooth as a painter's brush stroke. The ride and the natural world around Luke took his mind from his predicament, if only for a brief time. Otters swam and played in the river like rascals. All manner of waterfowl flushed from the water's edge.

Luke, in the front of the canoe, stroked the water with his paddle, thinking of the pristine world around him. He couldn't help it. It moved him to the depth of his soul just to be in this unique world. He could survive here—he could thrive here. This was the place of his dreams. This was the playground he pretended to be in while roaming the Ozark Mountains. How many nights had he lain on his wool blanket—not some modern hi-tech sleeping bag—by a small fire, looking up at the stars and wishing for such a place? How many times had he fallen asleep by that fire and dreamed of such a river?

Luke slowly scanned his surroundings. He was here. He was actually here, but it was so very hard to comprehend. He had won the lottery. The smell of fall hardwoods and falling leaves filled the air as the river entered a beautiful forest.

A sweet, soothing melody drifted from the back of the canoe. Luke turned to see Adam whistling. It was such a soothing tune, a strange deep whistle, not at all a high, tinny sound. It almost seemed to be coming from a wooden or bamboo flute. Adam smiled. His teeth were white as if he had just come from the dentist's office. His long auburn hair flowed down to his strong shoulders. He looked like something off the cover of a paperback novel. He resumed the whistling as he stroked the paddle through the water. Luke wondered what Adam would think of his world. What would he think of cars and planes? Of course, he would not like it. How could he? This world was so much better.

Luke turned and pulled at the paddle. He drew in a deep breath and took the time to appreciate it. The air was sweet and clean. He would never be able to describe it to anyone who had never breathed it. But then, he thought, he may never have the chance to try. He was torn. Was that a good thing or bad?

"Sha-She's tracks will be there," Adam said as he pointed ahead.

The canoe's bottom began bumping the river bottom and then came to a stop on a shallow shoal. Adam jumped out and pulled the dugout to the shore.

"How do you know her tracks will be here?"

Adam pointed to boot tracks in the mud. "There."

Luke smiled. Of course. This was the first shallow ford in the river. If she were going to cross, it would be here.

Adam tapped Luke's shoulder with his fist. "We follow?"

"Let's go," Luke said as he began following the tracks.

Adam grabbed Luke's arm. Luke turned to see Adam looking down the riverbank. There were tracks in the mud—bare feet.

"Scrain," Adam said.

They ran back to the canoe and gathered their weapons. It didn't take Adam long to pick up the trail like a hound. He was soon running, and Luke raced just to keep up. Adam reminded Luke of one of those African trackers he had seen on television.

Luke fell in with Adam's rhythm, letting him find the sign. Luke was too busy worrying that the Scrain would catch up to Moon before they could save her. He was all screwed up inside —scared, anxious, and angry.

A small prairie bordered the river, but it soon bumped up to a thick forest. Adam never checked up, but Luke felt as if the trees were closing in on them. He remembered the Scrain hiding in the pecan trees, and he didn't want to be surprised again.

Finally, Luke had to stop; he was out of breath. Adam ran ahead a ways before he realized Luke wasn't behind him. As Adam walked back, Luke panted and said, "I have to rest a few minutes."

"Maybe I should keep going," Adam said.

"No. Give me just a minute." Luke leaned on his longbow and took slower and deeper breaths. "I may not be able to find you."

Adam nodded. He wasn't breathing hard at all. He picked a stone off the ground and scraped at the point of his spear. He touched the point with his finger. It was sharp.

Luke wondered if Adam had killed before. But he knew the answer. This was a wild place, and you had to do what was needed to survive in it.

Adam tossed the stone. "We go now?"

Luke took one more deep breath. "We go."

A little piece farther they came to a small creek, and Adam bent to examine tracks. Luke immediately saw bare feet tracks on top of the boot tracks. They jumped the little creek and continued, but Adam put his arm out and stopped Luke.

"What?" Luke said, but then saw a Scrain coming down the trail toward them.

Luke and Adam leaped from the trail and prepared to ambush the man. But the man began staggering and then fell before he got to them.

Adam turned to Luke. "You stay." Before Luke could protest, Adam was sneaking down the trail with his spear at the ready. When he moved up to the man, he raised the spear to strike, but he let the spear down.

Luke went to Adam. Adam turned to him with a look of disbelief.

Luke looked down at the Scrain. He was cut up like a jigsaw puzzle. One of his ears was cut off and an eye was butchered out. Luke turned and threw up.

Adam stared up the trail, saying nothing. He was like a statue.

Luke wiped his mouth. "What is this? What does it mean?" He was more afraid for Moon than ever. He was afraid for himself.

Finally, Adam looked back down at the Scrain. "We move slower now." With that, he stepped over the Scrain and started up the trail.

Luke looked back down at the dead man. No, he damn sure wasn't in Arkansas anymore.

Adam moved ahead like a marine on point. Luke stepped around the man and followed.

After a short time, they came to some small, rocky hills. Lying at the base of one of the hills was another Scrain. They walked up to him together. Adam scanned the area like a soldier waiting to be ambushed.

"My god!" Luke said. The Scrain was cut up like the other, but this one had his privates cut off and placed on his chest.

Adam looked around the immediate area. "This is where they fought."

Luke saw what he was talking about. The area was scuffed up with boot and bare feet tracks. A horrible feeling ran down Luke's spine.

Adam drew a circle around one of the boot tracks with the point of his spear. "Sha-She like a panther." He fashioned his hand in the shape of a claw.

Luke felt numb. He had never experienced anything like this before. He thought of Moon in the chair at the jail. She had seemed so fragile and innocent. But he had seen her at work before this. This was different. This was like an animal.

Adam squeezed Luke's shoulder. "We be careful of the panther."

"Why did she do this?" Luke said. "Why did she cut them up so? Why not just kill them and be done with it?"

Adam made a scratching motion on his spear. "She's marking her territory. She trying to frighten the Scrain."

Hell, it should work, Luke thought. He was damn sure frightened.

Adam looked toward the closest hill. "You stay." With that, he sprinted to the hill and climbed up. He scanned around and then motioned for Luke to climb it.

When Luke got to the summit, he spotted her. She was in a flat, rocky area a few hundred yards below, in the open where no one could sneak up on her. He pulled out his binoculars. She was picking up rocks from the ground and putting them in her bag. Slowly she turned and looked straight at them. Luke was immediately afraid. She waved. Luke slowly waved back.

"What is she doing?" Luke said.

"Diamonds," Adam said. "Orion calls the shiny stones she's picking up diamonds."

Diamonds? Did she come back to this world for diamonds? She didn't waste any time coming after them.

She started toward the hill.

Adam turned to Luke. "How good you know Sha-She?"

Luke thought about it. He really didn't know her at all. She was beautiful. She was some kind of government agent. She was a liar. She was a killer.

"You stay here," Luke said as he started down the hill without looking at Adam. He watched Moon get closer, carrying her backpack in her hand. She appeared like a different person than he had left in the village, but she was the same. He was the one different—educated. It seemed every day—every minute—there was something new to learn.

They met at the base of the hill.

"Where did you go?" Moon said. She smiled. "They told me you had left in the night."

Luke didn't smile. "Why did you put his balls on his chest?"

Moon stepped back a step as if she had been slapped. The smile vanished. "Remember, Constable, we aren't in Arkansas now."

He said nothing.

She threw the pack onto her back. "Luke, the Scrain are cold-blooded killers. They are like wolves; when they sense weakness, they move in for the kill. They will see no weakness."

"This seems over the top."

"Damn it, Luke! This is who I am. This is what I do. Now you have gotten your ass mixed up in it." She pointed up the hill toward Adam. "Maybe you should go live with your new friend because I don't think you can handle what I do."

Her scolding didn't faze him. He believed he was beginning to get calloused to it all.

He turned toward Adam. "His name is Adam." He turned back toward her. "His father is Orion."

Her anger fell like a stone as she looked up the hill. "I knew him when we were little."

"When you gave me the story about Orion, you didn't tell me you knew him."

She looked into Luke's eyes but said nothing.

Luke touched her bag. "Why are you collecting diamonds? Did you lie to me about knowing how to get home?"

Adam ran down the hill toward them. "We go. Scrain coming. We go now and beat them to the river."

"How many?" Moon said.

"Six or seven."

"Did they see you on the hill?" Luke said.

"No, but they will come down this trail."

"Adam, you two go first. I will follow and slow them down if they get too close," Moon said.

Adam grabbed Moon's wrist in his strong hand. "Sha-She come quick. Adam won't wait for you to butcher Scrain. Sha-She understand?"

She pulled free. "Weya na kayeeya!"

Adam stepped back from her and then bowed his head. He turned to Luke, grabbed his shirt. "We go." With that, he sprinted back down the trail.

Luke looked at Moon.

"Go!" She said.

"Are you right behind me?"

"On your ass." Moon smiled.

Luke hesitated just long enough to take her measure and then darted after Adam.

Adam was shoving the canoe into the river when Luke emerged from the edge of the forest. He had hoped Adam would not leave them. He looked back toward the woods, but did not see Moon. A gunshot boomed through the forest. He considered going back. He looked toward the river and saw Adam waving for him to come. He ran to him and fell into the river.

Adam helped him up and said, "What's that noise."

"It's Moon's weapon."

"Weapon?"

"Trust me, Adam. It is the most powerful weapon in this world."

Six more shots echoed across the river.

Luke put an arrow on the string. His blood swooshed in his veins. He looked at Adam. He was cool and firm.

If they came, Luke was well prepared to get as many arrows off as he could before they got close enough to use the spears. He was nervous, but he was prepared. It came to him that it was like hunting and waiting for that big buck to get into range —the heart racing, the heavy breathing, the anticipation.

Adam slowly reached into the canoe and grabbed his spear, never taking his eyes from the direction of the shots. Luke could see the anticipation in him as well.

Luke could not wait much longer. He was ready for the Scrain to come, and the smart thing to do was wait, but he was concerned for Moon. Sure, she was a killer—and good at it, but she was still only one person against a half dozen or so.

She had fired a total of seven shots. What did it mean? Did she run out of bullets? Was she fighting them hand to hand this very second? Was she struggling for her life?

Adam said, "The panther."

Moon stepped out of the woods with her bag over her shoulder. She was as cool as if she were a birdwatcher on a Sunday afternoon. He knew what the seven shots meant. They were the claws of the panther.

Chapter 9

The village was nestled along the river like a scene of an Indian village from some old western. People busied themselves with basket making, fashioning weapons, building fishing nets, and such. Smoke drifted up from small fires, children chased a puppy, and a handful of teen boys had fun practicing with newly built spears, throwing them at a gourd hanging from a paw paw tree.

When Adam landed the canoe, Moon giggled, climbed out, and went to the children chasing the puppy. She laughed and joined in with a mock chase. It was an extreme contrast from their recent adventure. Moon had been a stranger to Luke just a few days ago. After today, she was more of one.

Luke pulled his things from the canoe. Where did he go from here? He looked around the village. A few of the men waved at him, so he must still be in good standing with the tribe. But, whom did he trust? Who was his friend?

He heard a whacking noise and then heard the boys cheer as one of them hit the gourd with the spear. It broke his train of thought—a pleasant reprieve. He had nowhere else to go, so he moved toward them. They saw him coming, offered him the spear, and pointed to the gourd. He set his things down and took the spear. It was about six feet long and much heavier than it had first appeared—hickory, probably. They laughed and pumped their fists in the air and made strange "La La" cheering sounds. Luke smiled and tried to make the same sound. They laughed harder and "La Laed" harder.

Luke turned to the gourd. He could still hear the fun going on around him as he concentrated on the gourd, but the zone slowly came over him. It happened every time before the shot. The gourd narrowed in his vision. The surrounding sounds and happenings faded in his brain—they were still there, but moved to an unimportant level in his senses. The gourd centered in his vision; everything else faded to gray. He found a black speck in the center of the gourd. Now, that was the only thing in his world. He focused his whole concentration on the speck. He was moving to the speck in his mind. It was everything now— the only thing now. Instantly, there was a loud crack and the gourd exploded into pieces. The world came back to Luke in a rush. It always happened that way when he shot a bow or threw a horseshoe.

The boys seemed stunned. They slowly turned to Luke. He smiled. They ran to the gourd and picked up the pieces. They began chanting and holding the pieces over their head.

"Looks like you have made an impression." Luke turned to find Moon standing behind him.

He nodded. "I'm sure they've seen better."

Moon stared at him for a long spell. "You don't get it, Constable." She took the spear from one of the boys. Took a stance beside Luke and gave it a toss to another gourd on the ground. She was close, but still a miss. The boys laughed. "At this, you are good. At this, you are the best. I've watched you shoot that bow and throw that hatchet."

"I wouldn't say—"

"Luke, I'm not trying to flatter you." She pulled the pistol from her pants and aimed it at the boys. They looked at it with curiosity, not knowing what the device was.

"What the hell—" Luke started.

"Bang! Bang! Bang! Bang!" she said as she pointed to each

101

boy in turn.

"Put that damn thing away," Luke said.

She deposited it back into her pants pocket. "I could have given each one of them a new eye hole if I had wanted. I'm that good, and I know it. You are that good with primitive weapons and don't know it." She retrieved her bag from the ground and turned back to Luke. "You better learn to know it. There is no 911 here." She turned and walked toward her father's lodge.

Luke watched her go. She was more of a mystery than ever. Who was she? What was she? What were her plans for tomorrow and the next day and the next? He knew he had better get to understand her. He needed to know her as best he could. She was everything to him now. Whatever he had to do from this moment forward, she held the key. But wait, there were still Orion and Adam. Luke looked toward the river. The canoe was gone. Adam was gone.

Like a heavy pack, the weight came again. The lonely, lost feelings settled into his soul again. He felt the fear of not being in Arkansas again. He took a deep and shivered breath—like you take when you emerge from cold water. He trembled. His very soul trembled. The cold blanket of self-pity draped over him as it had during the divorce. Even his teeth began to chatter.

"Luke! Luke! Luke!"

He shook his soul from the despair before it took him totally, turned to see the boys pointing at a new gourd hanging. They chanted his name as if he were a big baseball hitter coming in to win the game.

One of the boys grabbed the new gourd hanging and made it swing. They all laughed, pointed, and chanted, "Luke!" One of them handed him the spear.

Behind him, he heard someone say the name, *Grace*. He turned to find women making baskets. They had not said it. But he had heard it. And then he heard it, yet, again. But there was no one speaking. It had to be in his head. Of course, it was. It was his subconscious. It was his inner self. It was the dark part of the brain that most people never use—most people don't even know it's there. He had been so worried for himself; he had not done all he could to look for Grace. It was his reason for being in this world. It was his duty.

"Luke! Luke! Luke!"

The boys chanting brought Luke back to the now. He felt the solid, heavy weight of the spear in his hand.

"Luke! Luke! Luke!"

He turned toward the gourd. His eyes found a small dent in the center of it. He followed its swing. The narrowing of concentration began again. That mysterious part of his brain took over again. Some shooters call it instinct. He didn't know what you called it—he didn't care. He knew it was real. It was like magic. The autopilot took the controls. The gourd rang out again as it was impaled and disappeared in the bushes, riding on the spear.

The boys threw their hands up in amazement and ran to find the spear.

Moon was right. He was good. He was extremely good. And now, he had better control himself. He would need everything he had to survive. He would have to rely on that inner magic more. It was just a game in Arkansas. It was real here. It was real, Grace was real, and he was going to find her.

The fire crackled, and orange and red sparks floated up into the black night and disappeared among the white stars. Four turkey halves roasted over a wooden grate just out of range of the licking flames. The smell of the sizzling birds, the sound of the singing fire, and the sight of the dancing shadows calmed Luke as no bourbon ever could. He poked a big oak stick into the fire and sat back on his log. One of the four men tending the birds nodded his approval. He heard women, another fire over, laughing among themselves as they tended something cooking in stone pots.

He found himself in the company of the king's guards and

their families. There were ten men in charge of the king's protection. They were always close by, as they were now. The king was in his lodge, and the guards were stationed around it. Their small cabins surrounded his.

Moon appeared and sat beside him. He hadn't spoken to her since they had watched the boys throw the spear. He had seen her around the village, but that was all. It didn't appear she was avoiding him, but she hadn't sought him out either. He was sure she was the one who arranged his present company. Luke reckoned she was trying to get him established into her father's inner circle.

"You good?" she said, patting Luke's leg.

"Yeah. In fact, this is a very good atmosphere. I've even learned a few words: "Coola and Roara.""

Moon smiled and nodded. "Turkey and Fire."

"Not bad, uh?"

Moon moved closer to Luke. "Tell you the truth, there are a good many words I don't remember, but they are coming back in spurts." She turned back to the fire and slowly the smile faded. She sat saying nothing for a long time. She finally said, "Luke, I don't necessarily like what I am."

Luke studied her face in the firelight, but said nothing. He didn't know what to say anyway. Hell, he really didn't fully understand what she was to start with.

A few long minutes passed and Moon turned to Luke. She forced a smile, but it couldn't hold, and it dropped.

He clasped her hands between his. They were small, but not fragile.

The women laughed at the other fire. An owl screamed out by the river. One of the men came and rotated the turkey halves, placed a couple of sticks on the fire, and disappeared into the king's lodge.

"I've killed too many people to count, Luke." A tear ran down her face, and she wiped at it. I've seen many of my fellow agents killed—tortured." She bit at her lip. "I am very good at what I do. It's why I am still alive. But I hate what I do." She turned back to the fire. "It would be good to stop killing—to stop looking over my shoulder."

"Your fellow agents are not in this world. Your government is not in this world."

She stared into the fire. "Does it matter, Luke? Even here, I have to kill. Even here, you have to kill."

Luke slowly nodded. She was right. He didn't know what to tell her. He reached around and pulled her close. She put her arms around him. She felt so weak. She felt so vulnerable. She felt as if she needed his protection. But he knew none of this was true. It didn't matter. Right now, he wanted to hold her, and he felt she wanted him to hold her. Maybe tomorrow they could start over. Maybe they could grow a trust. Maybe he could give in to his feelings for her. He wanted to so badly—it was like a cable pulling at his heart. But not yet—not quite yet.

Luke awoke with a start—another bad dream. He opened his eyes and in the dark he saw the limbs of the persimmon tree overhead, its limbs crooked and gnarly like a monster's arms. He heard a crackle from the dying fire and turned toward the sound. It was not a dream. He was really in this place. He sat up and stretched. He was stiff from lying on the hard, bare ground, but it was better than lying on one of the bug-infested skins in the cabin. He would have to make him some sort of tent or shelter of his own.

A man appeared at the fire and nursed it until he had a good flame. Two more joined him. Luke recognized them as three of the king's guards. They ate pieces of the leftover turkey, talked in muffled voices, pointing into the darkness as they ate.

Luke went to the fire and pulled him a piece of turkey from the rack. "Morning," he whispered.

One of the men patted him on the shoulder and whispered something back.

The biggest man—Luke remembered his name as Kreecuk —held up a spear and made out as if he were throwing it at something. He said something and made running motions with his hands, and then he pretended he was throwing his spear again. He saw Luke didn't understand, so he went to Luke's bow and held it up and pointed to the turkey.

Luke understood. "You are going hunting." Luke drew his finger across his throat like a knife cutting.

They laughed and nodded.

Luke grinned. "Hunting!" He made a shooting motion with his bow and nodded that he wanted to go.

Kreecuk muttered around and finally spit out, "Hunting." He bit into a turkey leg and said again, "Hunting."

As the dawn crept in, Luke found himself following Kreecuk along the edge of a cane thicket. The other two men had a shaggy dog and were in the brush stomping and shaking the cane. They were beaters, and they were trying to drive something out for Luke and Kreecuk. In this world, Luke didn't know what to expect, anything from an armadillo to a Tyrannosaurus Rex. The area reminded Luke of a swampy place he knew back in Arkansas, and he had hunted rabbits there just as he was doing now.

The dog began yipping. Luke knew what it meant, reminded him of an old beagle he once had. A rabbit leaped out of the cane and darted in front of Kreecuk. He threw the spear and missed the rabbit clean. The rabbit zigged and zagged like a drunken roadrunner and made a quick turn back into the cane. Kreecuk turned, shrugged his shoulders, and smiled. He motioned for Luke to take the lead and get the next shot.

Luke knocked an arrow and took up the position. They eased along the edge of the brush, the men in the bushes shaking and thrashing the cane, the dog barking and whining. A rabbit squirted from the cane about fifteen yards ahead. Luke drew the bow on the way up and let the arrow fly before the bow stopped rising. The arrow caught the rabbit in the neck, and it was instantly over for the rabbit as it spun circles on the arrow and died. Luke pulled the arrow from the rabbit and held the rabbit for the beaters to see. They all whooped with delight, and the dog jumped up for the animal as Luke held him high until Kreecuk slapped the dog and sent him back to the cane.

They hunted until late morning and had fourteen rabbits; Luke had killed nine of them and had become their good hunting buddy. They marveled at his shooting and tried the bow for themselves, but they gave it up for their familiar spears. Luke was glad of it; he remembered Orion not wanting them to have the technology.

They built a fire by a creek and roasted five of the rabbits. This life was perfect. It was the life Luke had always dreamed of, living off the land. There were no electronics here, no metal weapons, no gunpowder, no gas stove. It was just a few hunting buddies out on a hunt. But this was different from back home. Here you hunted to eat, hunted to live. This was perfect.

The men lounged around the fire and nursed the cooking rabbits. The natives laughed and made motions simulating hunting, no doubt reliving the day's hunt or past hunts. Luke wished he could understand, wished he could join in the camaraderie. He was picking up a few words, but he just wasn't sure of them yet. But he would learn. He would join right in there with them.

The men grew quiet and all stared at Luke. Luke shrugged his shoulders. "What?"

One of the men spewed out a fast sentence, and, of course, Luke had no idea what he was saying, except he heard "Sha-She."

Another man, rubbing the dog behind the ears, stood and made an obscene motion with his hips. "Sha-She?"

Luke grew red and poked into the fire.

The three men laughed and pointed at him, but Kreecuk scolded them and motioned toward the rabbits cooking. "Reedu." With that, the other two men each pulled a rabbit from its stick and began eating. Kreecuk gave Luke one of them. "Reedu."

Luke took the rabbit. "Thank you."

Kreecuk nodded and fetched the last rabbit for himself. He

sat down and pulled his rabbit from the stick. He nudged Luke's shoulder. When Luke looked, he made a nasty motion with his rabbit's hindquarters. "Sha-She." All four of the natives exploded with laughter.

Luke felt his face burn fire-red. But he couldn't help himself. He laughed too, but managed, "No Sha-She."

The rest of the men began manipulating their rabbits into vulgar positions. But they appeared ridiculous since the men had eaten most of the hind quarters. Luke pointed at their ridiculous puppetry and laughed the loudest. Yes, it was just like hunting buddies back home.

When Luke arrived back to the village, he was in high spirit. He had enjoyed himself on the hunt. It was what he was made for. It was who he was. After dressing the rest of the rabbits and replaying the hunt with his friends for the tenth time, he looked for Moon.

The king stopped him in front of his big lodge. He held up his hand and in it was what appeared to be a large diamond the size of a golf ball. "Sha-She." He threw the diamond to the ground and began a tirade of words that were filled with venom.

Luke felt as out of place and vulnerable as a black spider on a white wall. He couldn't communicate, but he well understood that the king was pissed at his own daughter, and it had something to do with that diamond or whatever that shiny rock was. All his guards kept their heads lowered and slowly shook them from side to side. And it was odd, but they were crying. The king ranted and ranted, and it could have been Greek or French or Ancient Hebrew, but it damn sure wasn't English. But there was one word the king kept saying all through the rant: "Nephilim."

Luke didn't know if he was supposed to bow or run away, but he had to know if the word meant what he thought it meant. He raised his hand high like you do when you want to indicate something is tall. "Nephilim?" he said.

A few of the guards noticed—no one else was there with the king but guards—and looked shocked that someone would address the king when he was flying off the handle like he was.

The king suddenly stopped his tirade and stared at Luke for a long spell. Tears slowly tracked down his face, and he raised his hand half-high. "Nephilim."

Luke felt a weight. He whispered, "Giant. It was as Orion had said."

The king slowly turned and headed back toward his lodge.

One of the guards grabbed up a spear and shield and pointed toward the south. He rattled off something about "Sha-She" and "Nephilim."

The king turned, shook his head no, and pulled the shield from the man's hand, throwing it to the ground. He looked back at Luke, turned, and went back to his Lodge. The guards took up their posts around the lodge as if nothing had happened.

Luke looked for Moon, but she was not in the village. He went back to the area where he had slept the night before and piled down on the ground. What had just happened? What did the diamond mean? Why was the king so angry? Why was he crying? Why did the guard grab a spear and shield? Luke wished he could speak the language—he would try harder to learn it.

What did he know? He knew Moon was gone. He knew Moon had been after the diamonds. He knew the king was upset about the diamonds. And he knew the king had said, "Nephilim." Luke knew that in the Bible, Nephilim were giants. This all added up to something bad. Was this why Moon came back here? Did the diamonds and the giants have something to do with it?

Luke shook his head and said, "Nephilim."

A shadow fell over him, and he covered his eyes and looked up. It was Adam.

"Where did you go?" Luke said as he got to his feet. "I needed you here to translate some of this crap they have been saying. Moon has disappeared and the king is upset about—"

"Sha-She is trouble."

Luke had to agree with that statement.

"Is Luke trouble like Sha-She? You came back with her."

It was fair. Adam didn't know him from—well—Adam.

Luke put his hand on Adam's shoulder. "Adam, I am lost. I am from another place as Orion is. I don't really know Sha-She. I am here searching for Grace."

Adam, stone faced, said nothing.

"I need your help, Adam. I know nothing of this world."

Adam reached down and picked up Luke's bow. "We go help Sha-She."

"What do you mean?"

Adam turned and started toward the river.

Luke caught up to him and grabbed his shoulder. "What do you mean, and why bother if she is such trouble?"

Adam looked toward the king's lodge. "She is Kayeeya." He turned and looked at Luke. "She will be our queen."

"I see."

"You help me find Sha-She; I help you find your Grace."

Luke perked up. "You think she is still alive?"

"We find her either way." Adam turned and went to the canoe.

That took the wind from Luke's sails. But he had no other plans, no other choices. He followed Adam to the canoe. "What do you know about the Nephilim?"

Adam stopped, slowly turned. "I know."

Luke's heart raced and he mysteriously felt a strange nervousness. "Are they really giants?"

Adam turned and shoved the canoe from the bank. "Get in."

"Are they giants, Adam?"

"Get in, Luke."

Luke climbed into the front of the canoe, and Adam pushed it into the current. He settled into the back and was soon digging in with the paddle.

Luke turned and faced Adam. "I have to know. Are they real

giants?"

"Never good when Nephilim around. Orion say stay away. Now, you me help paddle."

"You're a grown man. Can't you make your own decisions?"

Adam smiled. "Orion's a smart man. It's why I am a grown man."

From the first time he met Adam, Luke considered himself the most intelligent of the two. Now he had just been served a lesson in reality. He was humbled and a little embarrassed for being so arrogant, which he normally wasn't. He turned back in his seat and began paddling. He would learn from this lesson— he would spend time with Orion.

Chapter 10

When they arrived at the cave, it was empty except for a big, black crow on the table eating pecans from a bowl. The crow flew off with a ruckus. Adam went first to the fireplace, knelt down, and started a fire from a tiny ember that had survived in the recesses of the cold logs. Orion was not there. Luke wondered where the elderly man had gone alone. He had to be too old to hunt.

Adam pointed to a stack of firewood. "Bring more wood for the fire."

He grabbed up a few sticks and placed them by Adam, who soon had a pretty fire dancing. Adam reached into the cupboard, retrieved big roots, different type nuts, and other vegetable-looking things, and dropped them in the big stone pot. He poured water in from a big gourd—he was making a soup. He worked at it for a time, adding some type of ground up seasoning, and lastly, a few pieces of dried meat.

"What are you brewing up there?" Luke said as he examined it.

Adam slid it close to the fire. "Orion calls it dump soup."

Luke laughed. "Because you dump everything into it?"

Adam smiled and shrugged his shoulders.

Luke placed his quiver on the table and pulled out his

arrows. He inspected each one and arranged them on the table in accordance with the work they needed. A couple needed the stone points sharpened. Another needed a new feather, and so on. He chipped at the points and had them razor-sharp in short order. He pulled a piece of sinew string from his pack and placed in into his mouth. He chewed on it to moisten and soften it, and then he wrapped it around the feathers, to which he had added a new one to replace a ragged one. He busied himself with this chore for a time until he had his kit back in top order.

He turned toward Adam. "Do you have a…"

The cave was empty. No Adam. The fire blazed at a good level for cooking and coals and been shored around the bottom of the pot. But Adam was gone. Luke went to the opening and looked out at the area below. There was nothing but one lone crow circling, obviously wanting Luke to leave so he could get back to the pecans. The joke was on him because Adam had put them in the soup.

Luke stood there bewildered. Why did Adam leave him? He began to feel trapped. After all, he really didn't know Adam or Orion before a few days ago. Yet, it was ridiculous to think that way—they were the only things that linked him to home. However, he sure didn't want to be surprised again. Luke didn't even know when Adam left or how long he had been gone.

Well, they would be back some time, and there was nothing to do but wait. Luke went to one of the beds and reclined on it, his fingers clasped behind his head, and he stared at the cave ceiling. The ceiling was black from years of smoke. There was a trail where it rolled out to the opening and into the sky, as it was doing now.

Luke's imagination ran like water through a brook. He could see Orion as a younger man first coming upon this cave. He probably would have still been afraid of being lost in this land. He would have had no one to talk to. He would have missed his family, his wife and daughter. He had nothing with him when he disappeared, no weapons, no tools, nothing. He would have

113

had to start from scratch. He would have been banged up inside and out from fighting with the Scrain. He had not starved; he had not died from the elements. He was resourceful. He met another woman here and fell in love. He must have still missed his family back home. Luke found it hard to keep his eyes open as he thought about Orion. Orion had raised a son here. He had...

Luke stirred from his sleep when he heard liquid pouring into a container. He eased his eyes open, just slits, to find Orion ladling soup from the soapstone pot with a gourd-half and pouring it into a bowl. Luke did not move, but watched the old man arrange things on the table. Orion had his hair tied into a long queue, which hung down his back like a long, white snake. When everything was arranged to suit him, he turned to Luke. Luke snapped his eyes closed.

"You can get up now, Possum." Orion said.

Luke smiled and sat up on the bed. "How did you know I was awake?

Orion laughed. "You must not be a father. I reckon kids playing possum is as old as time."

They sat at the table, and Luke said, "No, Sir, not a father, yet."

Orion smiled. "Let's thank The Almighty for our blessings." He prayed as pretty a prayer as Luke had ever heard. But of late, Luke had been tardy when it came to church and prayer.

Luke smelled the soup and realized that he was extremely hungry. The last thing he had eaten was some hard jerky Adam had given him. He blew on his spoon and then shoveled it in. It was the absolute best thing he had ever eaten. If he had the recipe, he could make a killing with it at an exotic restaurant. "Mmm!" He couldn't get the spoon to his mouth fast enough on the return. Oh, yes; people would pay top dollar for this concoction. "Adam said you call this dump soup?" Luke said between spoonfuls.

"Correct."

No, it would have to have a better name than that. Luke thought for a few minutes, never ceasing on the shoveling it to his mouth. Traveler's Soup or Soup Of Another World or The Soup From Beyond. Yeah, one of those would be better than Dump Soup. He would call his restaurant Portal to the Forgotten Dimension. He didn't know where he pulled that from, but it surely fit the bill. His waiters would wear animal skins. The entrance to his restaurant would have a long tunnel and—

"Slow down there, Luke. We have plenty."

"Sorry." Luke returned the spoon to the bowl at a reduced speed, but he still scooped it in. "I know this has a lot of stuff in it, but what is that unique and distinct taste, the delicious overtone."

"That's what gives it the name, Dump Soup."

Luke's spoon involuntarily began moving much slower. "I figured the name came about because you dumped everything in it; thus, Dump Soup."

The natives call it Shook Avure."

Luke put the spoon down. "And that means?"

Orion sipped a big spoonful and placed his spoon back in the bowl. "To put it nicely, poop soup."

Luke felt the soup grow heavy in his stomach.

"The natives collect the elephant droppings and dry it. Then they smash it up and store it. It is used as widely as we use salt to flavor back in America. But there is one thing, though; it has to have a certain fuzzy mold growing on it first or the flavor is too bland."

Luke knew his face was turning green—it had to be. He pulled a piece from the bread loaf and crammed it into his mouth. With a mouthful, he said, "Any manure in this bread?"

"No, Luke. It is almost like you would get back home." Orion pulled him a piece. "Almost." He smiled.

Luke had a sudden thought: there was no bread here when he fell asleep. There was no oven. He looked at it. It was bread, a little sweet, but it was yeast-bread. He held his piece up.

"Where did this come from?"

Orion smiled large. "I know I'm way out here alone, but I have my ways."

"Am I to believe it's magic? You pull it out of mid air?"

"Nomads."

Luke took another bite of the bread. "Uh?"

"Yes. They travel all over the plains and forests, not unlike some of the Indians back home. They are called Reeze."

No nomadic Indians anymore, Luke thought. What would Orion think of reservations?

"They trade with me at intervals. They are great bread bakers."

"What? Do they carry ovens with them on their travels? Do they have wagons or something?"

"They have them scattered, as they have watering holes, and supplies. You know—caches."

It came to Luke that these would be the people most likely to have seen Grace. If they were nomads and traveled a lot, it would make the most sense that they would see more.

Orion scooted his chair from the table and dragged it to the cave opening. "Here, Luke, bring your chair beside me." Luke did as instructed. "I've a little after-dinner refreshment." Orion pulled a lopsided jug from the shelf. "I made this since I last saw you." He grabbed two mugs from the shelf and handed them both to Luke, and Luke held them while Orion poured. As Orion sat down beside him, Luke took a sip. It was the sweet, muscadine wine. He smiled and nodded his approval.

Luke heard the rumble and trumpet of the mammoths on the prairie. He looked out across the plain and saw them moving in his direction. The sight of the giant beasts moved him more than anything else in this strange dream he was living. Hollywood had tried to portray them, but they always got it wrong. They moved somewhat like elephants, yet they did not. They moved in a smoother motion, and these appeared to glide across the land, bathed in the warm light of the setting sun.

"They're coming in to roost," Orion said. "Tonight you will be able to smell them when you sleep."

This was so unreal. It was better than winning the lottery.

Orion patted Luke's leg. "You know it is a great comfort with them down below my home, knowing almost everyone in this place is afraid of them."

Luke sniffed the air—yes, you could certainly smell them. Slowly it sunk in what Orion had said, "Almost everyone." He started to ask about that, but Orion stood. "Look. There comes Adam."

Adam's long, red hair whipped and trailed behind him like a horse's tail. It was no doubt to Luke if Adam were in his world he would be a model or movie star. He did not detour; he walked with the giant beasts, paying them no mind as he marched across the plain and toward his father's home. Where had he been? What makes Adam's world turn?

Adam ate the soup with more manners than anyone else in his tribe would have. His father had trained him well. Orion rubbed Adam's back as he ate. Luke appreciated the love. And he appreciated Adam's loyalty to his father—it was true and solid. Yet, there was something going on here that they were keeping from Luke. He felt it more than he knew it with evidence, but it was there. Where had Adam been all day anyway? He came back with no game or edibles. And when he entered the cave, there was a slight nod of the head to Orion. It was very subtle, but Luke had noticed it. These two had more going on than he had originally thought. Of course, they did. They weren't just surviving in this place; they were mastering it.

"Me and Luke had wine. Want some?" Orion said as he sat in the chair beside Adam. Adam waved it off as he pulled another piece of bread.

"That was the best soup ever, Son."

Adam smiled. "Orion's the best teacher on cooking."

Luke laughed as he pushed the chair from the table. "Dump Soup." He shook his head and walked to the cave entrance. The beasts had all gathered at the foothills below, about twenty or thirty, maybe more. The light was fading, but he watched a young one nurse and butt at his mother. Unbelievable. Simply, unbelievable. A lone coyote sang out across the prairie, followed by more. He thought of home. How many times had he heard that song? He was torn. This was the life he had longed for. This was the life he lived every chance he could steal away to the woods. But he was missing home, missing Arkansas.

"Luke." Orion said. He turned to see both Orion and Adam standing. "Do you still have the map I gave you?"

"Of course. It's in my bag." Luke dug it out and handed it to Orion. They were both looking at him with what appeared to be pity.

Orion rolled it out on the table. "We know where to find Sha-She." Luke moved around so he could see the map better. Orion put his finger on the map. "She's there."

Luke looked up at Orion. "How do you know she's there?" He turned to Adam. "Where did you go today? You sure the hell couldn't have traveled that far. That's a good day's hike if this damn map is accurate." Luke felt mistrust creeping in like smoke. "What are y'all pull—"

"Luke!" Orion squeezed Luke's arm. "I know you don't know us, but we are friends. If you don't trust us, who can you trust?"

Luke looked at Orion, then to Adam. He was right. Trusting Moon wasn't working out so well, so he knew he had better cool it, at least find out the story. He nodded. "Okay."

"Good. Good then." Orion nodded toward Adam.

Adam traced a path on the map with his finger. "Reeze see her here at waterhole." He moved his finger farther. "Reeze see her here on trail." He tapped his finger at another spot. "Reeze say she slept here." He swiped his finger from the first location, through the other two, and stopped at the spot that said *GIANTS*.

Luke felt as if a heavy stone had settled at the pit of his

stomach—it was not the soup. He turned to Orion, the wise old man. "Why?"

"Adam said she collected diamonds," Orion said.

Luke looked toward Adam, and then back to Orion. "Yeah. So what does that have—"

"They aren't really diamonds."

Luke crossed his arms. "Mr. Orion, I wish you would spill the beans. I don't know what you're talking about."

"I don't know what the stones really are, but they aren't diamonds. The giants collect them occasionally. The Reeze carry the stones to the giants to keep giants from coming here. All tribes pay the Reeze to do this." Luke waited for more, but it was not making sense. "A few months ago the giants and their army came across the mountains to retrieve the bell, and they slaughtered everyone they—"

"Wait—wait—wait a minute. A bell? You mean like ding dong bell?"

"It looked to be a bell. It was silver. I don't know how it got there. Everyone went to see it. Metal objects are rare in this part of the world. It stayed on the prairie for about a week before the giants showed up." Luke lowered his head and shook it. "I know, Luke, but I assure you it is all true."

"Orion only speaks the truth," Adam said.

Orion continued: "The giants sent out messengers to the tribes and said if the stones continued to be delivered on regular intervals, they would not return. So far, they have not."

Luke went back to the cave entrance. Bats were darting around chasing moths. What had he gotten himself into? Hell, it was worse than the rabbit hole. He heard the coyotes again. "Shut up!" he shouted. "Shut the hell up! You are not real! This place is not real!" A mammoth trumpeted down below. "Shut up!" He put his hands over his ears. He just wanted it to all go away. He just wanted to be back at his cabin. No giants! No mammoths! No Orion! No Moon! No Gra— He dropped his hands from his ears. Grace. That's the reason he was here. He slowly turned. The two men were watching him. "What about

Grace?" Luke said softly. "Have the Reeze seen Grace?"

Adam looked to Orion. Orion smiled and nodded. Adam turned to Luke, said, "Maybe."

"What the hell does that mean? The way you speak of the Reeze, they are everywhere. They are in the wind. They follow Moon's path as if she were in orbit. Did they see Grace or not?"

Adam did not flinch. He waited patiently for Luke to simmer down. Luke realized he was being an ass, so he closed his eyes and took a deep breath. He waited for more.

"Sha-She is like a panther, a hunter, but she's not good at hiding her trail or she don't care, so the Reeze can follow her. Reeze saw two other people, think maybe they were girls, but saw them only one time. They disappeared into the bush like two deer."

"Two?"

"Yes."

"You believe them?"

"Oh, Luke," Orion said, "being from Your world, this will come as a bit of a surprise, but the Reeze don't lie. I don't believe they even understand what a lie is."

"Grace has always been an outdoor, active person, even a black-belt in karate, but there is no way she should be able to evade the native Reeze. She's not an Indian. Maybe the girls were Adam's people or the white-heads. "

"Not that close to those mountains," Orion said. "They won't come this far, much less there."

"Maybe they are from across the mountains."

"Tomorrow we go get Sha-She," Adam said. "Maybe we find out who the other people are."

Orion lowered his head and wiped at his eyes. It was obvious he didn't want Adam to go, but it was also evident they had already settled the matter before now.

Luke was afraid to go, but he would go. He had to go. He exhaled a long breath. "We will bring them back; we will bring them both back."

Orion looked up. "You have seen strange things here, coming from where you come from. Miracles I guess we can call them. Maybe the girls turned back before they went too far —we don't know for sure, but if you have to bring them back from the land of the Nephilim—if even you and Adam come back, it will be the biggest miracle of all." He turned and went back into the cave.

Luke turned to Adam and they simply stared into each other's eyes. Luke knew what he was thinking in his own heart, in his own soul—it was a combination of fear and anticipation. Adam's thoughts were as mysterious as this world.

Chapter 11

A small herd of pronghorn fled from the waterhole when Luke and Adam topped the ridge. It could have been a waterhole on the plains of Colorado. In fact, the mountains on the horizon looked a lot like the Rocky Mountains. They were giant compared to the short mountains where Orion lived in his cave. Luke and Adam drank from the water and then Luke filled up his canteen, while Adam filled up his waterskin. There were barefoot prints around in the mud.

Adam saw Luke looking at them. "Reeze," Adam said.

Luke looked in all directions. Where were these Reeze?

It had been three days since they had left the cave, and they had come across no one, just these barefoot prints and other signs. They would find a spent campfire here—still warm, a gut pile there, and discarded scraps of food—bread, dried berries, and even pieces of dried meat. It was evident these wasteful people were driving some form of animals with them—droppings were everywhere, and split-hoofed tracks were with the human tracks. The trail the Reeze followed—now the trail Luke and Adam followed—led snake-like toward the mountains. When they came upon this discard food, Adam picked it up and placed it in his bag like a pack rat. Often he would pull out a nugget and toss it in his mouth. Luke watched him several times and said nothing, but finally he could take no more. "Why do you pick up that trash like that? That stuff is scraps; it's nasty." Adam turned, pulled out a piece of meat, and chewed off a big hunk, like chewing a chaw of tobacco. He dropped the remaining back into the bag, smiled, and started back up the trail.

They made camp in a cottonwood grove along a small river as the sun settled behind the distant mountains. Adam speared a few trout as Luke started a fire. If the situation weren't so serious, this would have been like a vacation for Luke. It was like being at Yellowstone or something. The fish splashed in the smooth river as shooting stars streaked across the purple sky. The temperature was cool, but nothing a hunter like Luke could not handle; in fact, he preferred it.

A roar rolled down the river and sounded like it came from the MGM lion. Luke grabbed for his bow. Adam, putting the fish on sticks over the fire, laughed.

"What the hell is that?" Luke said as he stood and nocked an arrow. He looked down the river, but the darkness had settled in. Adam placed his hands to his mouth with his index fingers pointing down. "A walrus?" Luke said. Then he quickly realized his mistake and turned to where the sound had come. "A saber-toothed cat!"

Adam straightened the fish over the fire and laughed again.

Luke turned to face him and started to ask him what was so funny, but then he realized he was green in Adam's eyes. Hearing a saber-tooth cat here must be like hearing coyotes back home—it would scare the hell out of someone from the city. And it was pleasant to see Adam laugh; he did it so rarely. Luke put the bow down and pitched down beside Adam.

"Cat is scared of fire," Adam said. "He don't like being around people." He looked out the corners of his eyes. "Well, scared most of the time." He laughed again.

Luke laughed, too. "I hope this is *most of the time*."

Adam reached in his bag, pulled out a piece of bread, and bit off it.

"Why are you eating those scraps that they left on the ground?"

Adam shook his head. "Luke is foolish. I thought you were smart. Reeze left this for us."

Luke said nothing. He was, indeed, foolish. No one would have been that wasteful, not in this land. "But why do they just throw it on the ground where any animal could get it before us."

"Reeze think—'oh well, too damn bad.'" Adam laughed again.

When Luke stopped laughing too, he asked, "They are just ahead of us then?"

Adam turned the fish. "Ahead...behind." He shrugged his shoulders.

Luke heard something wading the river. He reached for his bow, but Adam grabbed his arm, said, "And here."

A strange glowing ball floated above the water, moving slowly toward them. It was greenish-yellow and resembled the glow of a gas lantern. As it floated closer, a figure emerged from the gloom of the river, a man, a tall man, holding it. He stopped at the river's edge, about forty yards away and stared at the camp. The glowing ball seemed to be some sort of ball of gas, and the man holding it wore a suit of buckskin and some type of fur hat—he could have been Daniel Boone or Davy Crockett. His clothes were more advanced than anything Luke had seen in this world. He had no weapons, no shield, just a skin bag—and that glowing ball. He stood there for a long spell and then simply said, "Adam."

Adam stood and the man came to within fifteen feet and tossed the bag to Adam. He opened it and smiled. He said something to the man and they both laughed. The man turned to leave and Adam said something else. Luke could tell it was a question. The man turned back, let go of the glowing ball, and it just floated in the air on its own. He slowly put his hands together, with only the fingertips touching, as if he were making a tent or house roof.

Luke turned to Adam. "What is this all abou—" Even in the firelight, Luke could see Adam had turned pale. "Adam? Adam, you alright?" Adam slowly nodded. What had just happened? Luke turned back to the stranger. He was gone! The glow ball was gone! What's going on? "Where did he go? What the hell was that glowing ball?"

Adam sat back down by the fire and absently turned the fish as he stared blankly into the fire. "A wisp."

Luke looked up and down the river, but the man and his fire ball were as gone as steam above a kettle. He dropped down by Adam. "What? A wisp?"

"Will-o'-the-wisp." He looked over to Luke. His color was coming back to his face. "Orion say the Reeze like Will-o'-the-wisp." Luke could see why with that strange glowing ball, appearing out of nowhere and disappearing.

"What's in the bag?" Luke said. Adam handed it to him. It had food in it, and Adam pulled out a loaf of bread like the one Orion had come in with back at the cave. He dug around in it and came out with a stick of sausage. "This is great."

Adam pulled the fish from the fire and laid them on a plank he had found by the river. "Bread be good with fish."

Luke sat the bag aside. "Why did you two laugh when you looked in the bag? What did he say?"

Adam half smiled. "He want to know if Adam was tired of picking scraps off the ground."

Luke nodded. "Oh, I get it. He has been toying with you all along, and you knew it. You know him."

Adam grinned.

"What did he mean when he made a tent with his fingers?" Luke said.

The grin disappeared. After a long pause, Adam said, "I ask where they last saw Sha-She. His fingers say at the place of the giants."

Luke looked back toward the dark river. He remembered Orion saying the Reeze do not lie.

The mountains grew closer and larger. Luke felt so much smaller. If they were not the Rocky Mountains he had seen in Colorado, they were the evil twin. The trail was well worn by the Reeze, but there were no scraps of food now. The wind blew across the prairie and the grass waved and whipped. Eagles and hawks floated above. It was paradise, but it felt more and more like hell.

Luke walked and thought—walked and thought. He didn't know what Adam was thinking, but he was thinking how the hell they were going to get the girls, or maybe one girl, and get away with their lives. What were these Nephilim? Were they killers? Did they hunt people like animals? Hell, did they have advanced weapons? For all Luke knew, they could have laser-beam guns. They could have people roasting on sticks when Luke and Adam sneaked into the city—he reckoned they were going to sneak in—he didn't know what they were going to do.

Adam stopped and pointed. "There is the road into the city." Luke saw a valley between two mountains. "We leave the road here," Adam said. He pointed to another smaller valley. "We go this way."

"Have you ever been there?"

"No."

Luke stopped. "No?"

"Orion told me to go this way if we had to come this far." Adam turned to Luke. "He said he hoped we didn't have to come this far." He rubbed his hand across his lips and started up the trail. Luke followed—he had no other choice.

The valley was not really a valley at all; it was a cut in the side of the mountain, an animal trail. It was a good trail; they didn't have to do any climbing with their hands, but it was steep. It was obvious that people occasionally used the trail too. Luke figured the Reeze, but he had no idea why they didn't just use the main road, which was much easier to travel he was sure.

After about thirty minutes of climbing and about half way to the top, Adam stopped and pointed off the trail. There was a skeleton hanging from a gnarled tree. "Maybe they are trying to tell us something."

"Yeah, but we are too stupid to pay attention."

When they reached the rim, Luke was literally in for the surprise of his life. Down below was a city for sure, and it didn't appear primitive. There were giant stone buildings and walls and temples. It was right out of Indiana Jones. However, the most prominent thing of all was a giant pyramid. It was ivory-white with the capstone the color of gold—it could have been gold. There were inscriptions and designs covering it, sunrays and lightning bolts. It had to be twice as big as the biggest one in Egypt. But it didn't look like anything Egyptian or Mayan, for that matter. It was shiny and radiant. It was... new.

Adam pointed. "Look." Electrical charges sparked from the point of the pyramid like Tesla's ball. The charge would jump and fly around like crazy lightning and then disappear.

Luke whispered, "Is this what the Egyptian pyramids once looked like?" It was not old and crumbly. It was shiny and majestic and active. This was not a tomb. This was some kind of...machine.

Adam held his hands up with the fingers touching, forming a tent. "Luke see now what Reeze talked about."

"Of course." Luke tried to take it all in, but it was too much to process. He was no archaeologist. He was just a redneck from the backwoods of Arkansas—no dummy, but no scholar either.

Remembering his binoculars, he pulled them from his bag. He was more in awe than before. The streets were paved with bricks. Water flowed through troughs all over the city—they weren't pipes, but they served the same purpose, and he could see all of it clearly from the high vantage point. People pulled carts—yes, carts with wooden wheels. The people reminded him of Ancient Greeks or Romans, but on their heads they wore large plumes of feathers, more like Mayans. They all had different color hair like people back home, not all red or all white. As he was looking at a market with fruits and vegetables, a figure stepped out of a huge building adjacent to it. The people bowed at the figure. Luke jerked the binoculars from his eyes and swallowed. He slowly put them back to his eyes and searched for the figure again. He was a giant, every bit of four feet taller than the others were. "Nephilim."

Adam tapped Luke on the shoulder. "Can I see?" Adam moved the binoculars slowly as he looked. Luke saw the instant when he spotted the giant. Adam turned to Luke, "Orion was right."

"Has he ever been here?" Luke took the binoculars back. He found more giants standing close to the pyramid.

"Orion said he had when he first come to this world. He will not talk much about it, only say to stay away. He sa…"

"He said what?" Luke turned. He found that they had been surrounded by the "Greeks." There were about ten of them with spears. And these spears were tipped with metal. Luke and Adam had been careless.

Adam reached for his own spear. One of them jabbed his hand with the metal spear. Adam grabbed his now bleeding hand and backed off. Luke tried to get to Adam, but the others moved in close with those shiny spears.

"Are you okay?" Luke said.

"Luke, don't fight! We fight later." He looked at his hand. "I be alright. Not too deep."

One of them poked Adam in the back, urging him down the hill and toward the city. Adam looked at Luke, winked, and started down the trail. Four more fell in behind him. Luke started to follow, but they stopped him. Adam tried to stop, but they kept prodding him with those sharp spears. "Luke!"

Luke didn't understand what they had in mind, but it was surely bad.

They pushed him back down the hill and away from the city and Adam. One of them picked up his bow, inspected it, and threw it back on the ground beside his bag. They marched him for a distance, laughing and pointing at him. Finally, one of them pulled a rope from a bag and formed it into a loop. Luke remembered the skeleton as they turned off the trail.

Chapter 12

As the soldiers grew closer, the woman slid in behind the rocks and brush as a blackwidow spider backs into the darkest part of her web. The last thing she needed was for one of them to spot her. Her muscles grew tighter, like rubber bands being twisted. Her breathing was shorter now and pumping like a piston. They came on, pushing Luke ahead of them with those long spears. Her muscles burned and tightened even more, the rubber bands about to break. Closer. Closer. Closer. She let Luke walk past. She pounced for the nearest soldier. She drove her spear into his neck. It hung there so she took his. She whirled and ran it into the chest of the next closest soldier. One of the soldiers lunged his spear at her. She kicked it away, grabbed him, and flipped him over her back. She turned to jump him, but Luke was already straddling him and pounding his face with a stone. She turned for the other two, but her friend had finished them.

Luke stood. "Grace?"

"Luke!" She ran to him and squeezed him around the neck. She had thought he was Luke, but she wasn't sure. She only knew for sure he was someone from her world—the clothes. Tears ran like water. "Oh, Luke, is it really you?"

After a long embrace, Luke pushed her out to arm's length.

"Look at you. You look like Jane."

She knew she was a sight with the deerskins wrapped around her. She had done whatever it took to survive in this strange land—even kill.

Her friend came to her, and Grace turned and smiled at her.

"Who is this?" Luke said.

Grace said. "This is Wak'o."

Luke hugged her. "Hello, Wak'o." He looked her over. "She looks like an Indian from our world."

Grace grabbed Luke's arm. "Where are we, Luke? Where is Tyler?"

Luke sighed and said, "We've come through a portal into another dimension."

Grace heard him, but it didn't quite register. "What do you mean?"

"We're not in Arkansas anymore."

"Ark-an-sa?" Wak'o said.

Grace turned to her. "You know that word? *Arkansas.*"

"Grace." Luke said softly.

She turned back to him. He had a hard look about him, not the same soft Luke she had always known.

"I'm afraid I don't know how to get us back home."

She and her friend had just killed five men. They had killed before. Her karate training was worth more than gold here in this place. Her physical abilities had given her the ability to survive. She had almost become an animal as she traveled this wild place trying to get home, trying to make sense of it all. She had been strong beyond anything she could have ever dreamed of. But now it suddenly became too much, and she folded into Luke's arms. "I want to go home. I want my family. I want Tyler." She sobbed. "Oh, Luke, I want to go home."

Wak'o moved to her and rubbed her back. The tall, buckskin-clad woman had been there for Grace since she had saved her from those blond murderers. She had taught Grace how to live off the land, how to survive in the wilderness, where to find water, where to find food, how to build a fire, how to evade pursuers—man or animal, and how to kill—animals for food or people to survive. She was not only a friend; she had become everything. She was the only person she knew in this strange place—until Luke.

Grace recovered, turned to Wak'o and pointed back up the trail. Wak'o nodded, picked up a spear, and ran back the direction from which they had marched Luke.

"Where is she going?" Luke said.

"She's going to ambush any more that may try for us."

Luke pulled Grace to a big rock shaded by a ledge, and they sat. "Grace, do you remember what happened when you went through the portal?"

Oh, yes, she remembered it all too clearly. "I had heard drums and started toward the sound. Tyler called to me but I was just going to walk a little farther." She stopped. She should have listened to Tyler. She grabbed Luke's arm. "Where is he? Is he all right? I didn't see him when they threw the net over me."

"He's fine. He's in jail. They think he killed you. That's how I got here. I came looking for you and found the portal."

"Killed me?"

"He's safe for now."

She hoped he was safe until they could somehow get back. She had worried so. She had no idea what had happened to him.

"Did they beat you, Grace?"

"A little. They were stripping me of my clothes when I remembered my karate training. I kicked their asses and ran. Oh Luke, I was so scared. I didn't know what was happening."

Luke patted her arm. "I know. How did you evade them?"

"Wak'o found me drinking water from a stream. One of those blond demons had sneaked upon me fixin' to spear me, and she came out of the bush like a wild cat and cut his throat. It was so horrific." She sighed and looked at Luke. "But I've seen much worse since." She looked down at the ground. "I've done worse since then."

"We do what we have to do to survive." He took her hands into his. "And it looks like you have survived well."

It felt good to have Luke beside her. He was Tyler's cousin and a very dear friend. He was a good hunter and had always made bows, arrows, and stone tools. That would be a great advantage here.

A few minutes later, Wak'o came back down the hill. She shook her head and Grace knew it meant the coast was clear. She had not learned to talk to Wak'o, yet, but they had learned to communicate fairly well by gesture.

"Wak'o," Luke said. "That sounds familiar."

Wak'o pointed at herself, said, "Wak'o." She pointed at Luke and said, "Nikka."

Luke jumped to his feet. "I be damn!"

"What is it, Luke?" Grace said.

Luke ignored her and addressed Wak'o. "Ni-U-Ko'n-Ska."

Wak'o perked and nodded. She suddenly spoke a lot more words that Grace couldn't understand. "You can speak her language, Luke?"

"She's Osage."

"Can you speak to her?"

"I'm afraid not. I only know a few words." Luke shook his head. "Damn. I wish I had learned more. My great-grand mother was Osage, and I was curious and found a few words on the Internet. I don't think anyone speaks it anymore."

That didn't make good sense, Grace thought. "Wak'o speaks it."

"You don't understand, Grace. She must have come through the portal at another time in history."

"But she would be extremely old."

"Not necessarily. The portal can pluck someone from history, but it would be now for them." Luke turned to Grace. "Does that make sense?"

Grace was trying to understand, but it wasn't coming together.

"Wak'o could have been in that very spot where we came

through the portal, but at another time."

"Like a time machine."

"Exactly."

Luke pointed to Wak'o and said, "*Wak'o* means woman, and *Nikka* means man."

Wak'o smiled.

Grace suddenly remembered something. "When I first met her, she tried to talk to me, and I think she was speaking French, but I can't speak it."

"Of course!" Luke said. "The French were the first white people to encounter the Osage." Luke turned to Wak'o and said, "Bonjour."

Wak'o smiled and perked up. "Bonjour."

"Parlez-vous anglais?" Luke said.

Wak'o shook her head and said, "Je ne peux parler français?"

Luke exhaled a long breath. He shook his head. "Pas français."

Tears started down Wak'o's face, and she turned and walked away.

"What did you say to her?" Grace said. "I've never seen her cry."

"I don't know enough French to even talk to her."

Grace went to Wak'o and hugged her. She turned back to Luke. "I wish I had taken French in high school."

Luke looked toward the ridge and back up the road. "When it gets dark, I'm going down there and get my friends out of that place." He turned to Grace. "One of them is a woman, and I bet she can speak French and many other languages."

Grace knew the woman he was speaking about. They had seen her. They had stalked her, trying to find out who she was and what she was about. Grace knew she was not of this land. But Grace had a strange feeling about the woman. She had a feeling that the woman always knew they were there, even though they were well hidden. Grace never tried to approach her; something told her she could not trust her. She was like a bad dog. Sometimes you can just tell. Sometimes you know if they will bite.

Dark found them at the ridge looking down on the city. It was sprinkled with candlelight, like fireflies over a marsh. It was not like cities back in Luke's world; there were no streetlights, no neon signs, only the candles and small fires. There were plenty of shadows to hide in. And Luke knew they would need that. They didn't know the area so they would need all the help they could find.

The point of the pyramid crackled and sparks shot out of it into the black night. It somehow seemed out of place. Luke sure would like to know what was going on with that pyramid. Maybe he could just go down there and tap one of the giants on the shoulder. "Excuse me, Mr. Giant. What is up with the electric pyramid?"

"We sure didn't learn about any such pyramids in school," Grace said. "Maybe aliens are in it."

"There are no ali…", Luke began, but hell, who knew what was in that thing.

"Where do you think they took your friend?" Grace said.

"I don't know, but I'm going to find out." Luke handed Grace his bag. "If I'm not back by sunup, you and Wak'o head out of here."

"I'm going down there with you."

"No. You stay here. There is no need both of us putting ourselves in danger."

"Well, do you have a plan?"

Luke had no plan. He was going to play it by ear.

"Luke, you know we can handle ourselves quite well," Grace said. "I think we've proved that."

He looked at her, admired her. She was beautiful—it was easy to see how Tyler had fallen for her. But she wasn't the innocent girl that he thought he knew. She had proven to be resourceful and brave. In fact, the two girls were probably better suited for the mission than Luke was. But the whole purpose of his even being here was to search for her, and there was no way he was going to let her risk her life anymore than she had already. "Grace, please promise you will wait here. I will need help on the escape."

She raked her hair from over her left eye. "I can't—I won't promise that to you. But we will stay put for a time."

He realized there was no need to debate the issue with her—he didn't have the time, and he would lose. "Fair enough, but please give me some time."

She smiled. "Good luck, Luke."

He made his way down the dark trail; this time he was more cautious. He slowed his pace. He was the hunter, just like back home in the Ozarks. All his senses were at their peak. His tomahawk was in his belt, and his bow was strung and ready for service. He stayed to the shadows; it was easy with the dim lighting. And he had heard no dogs to give him away, no alarms, or security cameras either.

As he moved in the shadows of the streets, he soon realized many of these buildings weren't homes. He looked into one of the buildings and found it to contain grain and implements. Another had pottery and baskets, and so it went. It was as if the place was a city of storage with a giant pyramid in the middle.

A door opened across the street. He slid behind some kind of cart. A man stepped out the door. He was extremely tall—one of the giants. Luke felt his breathing stop. The giant had a long pointy head, but otherwise he just appeared to be a very big man. The giant moved down the street in the direction of the pyramid, reminded Luke of a clown walking on stilts.

Luke saw other doors opening and giants coming out. They all went toward the pyramid. He followed, slipping from one shadow to the next.

The giants all congregated in a large plaza at the base of the pyramid. Luke found a tree large enough to hold him, and he shimmied up it. He surveyed the situation with his binoculars. He figured there to be about fifty or so of the giants and about that many more of the regular-sized people. The giants were all seated in the plaza facing a stage in front of the pyramid. The stage looked like a large slab of polished granite with two large white columns protruding from it like white tusks. The short people were around the perimeter—they were guards. The giants were all talking and laughing. Luke looked around to make sure he had not been spotted—he appeared to be safe.

A door opened at the base of the pyramid, and another giant stepped out and went to the stage. He was dressed in white and clad in gold and jewels. The talking and murmuring stopped, and they all turned to face him. He started up with a speech or sermon that would rival any preacher on television. The acoustics were so good, that he didn't need an amplifier. He went on and on and on and on. The crowd would cheer at the appropriate pause, and he would start up again. Luke was waiting for someone to come around with the collection plate when they all suddenly turned toward the back. A half dozen of the guards led someone through the crowd at spear-point—it was Adam.

Adam held his head high and chest out, his long auburn hair splayed on his shoulders like a cape. They marched him to one of the white columns. They backed him to it and tied his hands behind him and to it. As the guards marched away from the stage, the preacher pointed toward him and started in with the preaching again. Adam looked defiant. He was a man's man, indeed. The speech went on for about thirty minutes, and then the preacher stopped and went back into the pyramid. All at once it was as quiet as a wake, except for the sparkle and static at the point of the pyramid, and it dragged on like that painfully for a time.

Then the large door opened again, and the preacher came out, followed by two even larger giants—they had to be fifteen feet tall, and they both had large flat swords. Luke felt his heart drop. Adam saw what was happening and began to struggle at the column, but it was no use. The two giants moved to Adam and raised their swords, but froze with them high in the air like baseball players ready to swing. The preacher pointed and preached. The other giants were on their feet, chanting in a low murmur.

Luke squeezed the bow in his hand, but it was too far for a sure shot—they were at least eighty yards from his tree. Maybe he could get lucky—at least disrupt the proceedings.

The preacher grew louder. The crowd chanted faster.

Luke pulled the arrow to his cheek. He concentrated on the preacher.

The chanting increased.

Luke knew something bad was going to happen when the chanting hit a certain rhythm—he had to get the shot off. But he had to concentrate totally on the shot or it was no good.

The crowd began stomping and chanting faster.

Luke found a gold medallion hanging on the preacher's chest. He concentrated on it. The feather of the arrow touched his nose. His middle finger settled between his lips. He zeroed in on the medallion—there was nothing else in the world but the medallion. His muscles began to relax. His concentration was totally on the—

"Stop!"

Luke lost his concentration, but quickly tried to regain it for the shot. The preacher and the crowd all turned toward the rear of the plaza. Luke bore down on the medallion again. He anchored the arrow.

"May I approach the Great Shevay?"

Luke lowered the bow. It was English. It was a woman's voice.

The two giants with the swords stepped to the side of the preacher, and he raised his hands and said, "You may approach."

How the hell did this giant know English. Luke lowered the bow and raised his binoculars. The woman came out of the darkness. It was Moon. A few of the guards moved toward her, but the preacher yelled something and they halted.

Moon moved up the aisle between the giants; they watched her come as if she were a bride or maybe a monster.

The preacher pointed and yelled, "What do you want here?"

Moon raised her hands into the air. She had large stones in each hand. Luke quickly realized they were the diamond-like stones she had hunted for—and killed to get. There was no way he would not recognize them. Suddenly, the crackling at the top of the pyramid intensified, and Luke felt an electric charge in the air. His hair rose all over his body. He saw Adams long hair begin to rise, when all of a sudden lightning bolts shot from the top of the pyramid and streamed to the rocks in Moon's hands. Her hair whipped as if caught in a gale, and she glowed bright white and blue. Electricity and sparks danced around her in blue blazes. Luke knew she would die from this. She lowered the stones and the stream of electricity reversed itself back to the pyramid top in a zap.

All the giants immediately went to their knees and bowed their long pointed heads.

The preacher spread his long arms. "Who are you?"

Moon continued up the aisle. "I am Sha-She. I am from the great lands beyond." She pointed one of the rocks toward Adam. "He is not to be sacrificed."

Shevay said, "I am the one to say who is to be—"

Moon raised the stones and the pyramid came alive again, and she was immediately charged with the blue and white flashes. She lowered the stones. "I have not come to challenge the Great Shevay, but I will be heard."

Shevay pointed to Adam and the two sword giants cut him loose. Adam was visibly shaken by it all, but he held his composure.

"How is it that you know the secret of the pyramid?" Shevay said.

Moon continued up the aisle until she was just below Shevay. "Glen Turner."

Shevay simply stared at Moon for a long time, and then he addressed the crowd. There was low murmuring, and they departed. He turned to the sword men and spoke a few words to them. They went into the pyramid and left him alone with

Moon and Adam.

Moon climbed the steps to the stage and knelt on one knee. "I come with respect and reverence for the Great Shevay."

He motioned for her to rise. "Why do you come?"

She stood. "I've come to warn you of bad things to happen." Adam moved beside her. She continued, "Other people will come from beyond and their intentions will be evil."

"That is a matter of perspective," came a voice from the pyramid door, and out stepped a man in a gray military uniform holding a pistol. Moon slowly moved for her pistol in her waistband. The man with the pistol said, "I wouldn't do that, Fraulein." He went to her and took her weapon. He pointed to Adam. "You get down on your knees." Adam didn't move.

Moon said, "Do it, Adam." He did.

The man addressed Moon, "Who are you?" She said nothing. "You're an American."

"And you are a damn Nazi."

"I am a German soldier. My name is Karl Rineman, and we have a lot to talk about." He motioned her toward the pyramid door with his Luger.

"What about my friend?" She nodded toward Adam.

"You have to ask the Great Shevay."

Shevay said something toward the door and the two sword men came and escorted Adam through the door as Shevay followed.

Moon held both rocks in one hand, and she slowly began to raise it.

"I want to talk to you, but I will put a bullet in your pretty head if you force me to," the German said in perfect English, as he aimed the pistol at Moon's face. "Drop the stones." They fell with a clatter. "Now, move." They went into the pyramid.

Everything was quiet, and Luke saw no one, not a single person or giant or German or anyone. Now what?

Luke dropped down from the tree. He tried to make sense of what had just happened, but this place was beyond any reason. An English-speaking World War II German had just captured Moon and Adam, along with a ten-foot, tall king, and went inside of an Egyptian-type pyramid that shot sparks from its peak. Yeah, Luke was ready to wake up from the dream at any minute.

He heard talking so he slid in behind a large barrel. Two giants walked past and continued down the street. He looked over the barrel and waited to see if more came. He smelled something in the barrel, so he removed the top and looked inside. It was wine. He cupped his hand and took a few sips. It was good, but he didn't know what the wine was made of—didn't taste like grape.

He went to the stage and spotted the stones on the floor. He picked them up and dropped them into his pack, hoping the pyramid didn't shoot an arc at him. He looked in all directions —still clear. He went to the big door of the pyramid. It was fifteen feet high and eight feet wide, solid stone. He knew he wouldn't be able to open it—way too heavy. He pushed on it. It moved. It moved so easily that a child could have opened it.

He pulled his tomahawk from his belt. He had expected it to be dark inside, but it was light enough to read by. He looked up to see some type of mirrors on the ceiling. They were reflecting light from somewhere. He eased along, listening as he went. There were drawings and paintings on the wall, somewhat like Egyptian, but yet different. This was not Egypt.

He stopped. He heard Moon's voice. He kept moving down a long hall. Her voice grew louder as he moved closer. There were steps that went up to some sort of balcony over the room where Moon's voice was coming from. As he sneaked up the steps, he saw more mirrors; they spiraled up the walls. He reckoned they were picking light up from somewhere high and progressively reflecting it all the way down to the ground floor. From the balcony he could see a room below. Shevay was sitting on a throne, and the German was standing beside him with that damn Luger pointed at Moon.

"Did I hear you say your name was Sha-She?" Karl said.

141

Moon said nothing. "You will talk."

"I don't have anything to say to you."

Karl pointed the Luger at Adam and shot him in the arm. The room echoed from the loud report. Adam reeled, but regained himself. Blood trickled between his fingers as he pressed his hand against his wound.

Moon went to Adam and moved his hand. "Let me see." She inspected it, tore the tail of her shirt, and wrapped it. She turned back to Karl. "You Nazi pig, the war ended over seventy years ago."

Karl stood silent for a time and then said, "How did it end?"

"You lost."

"I believe you," he said, as he ran his fingers through his hair. "Seventy years?"

"That's right. Germany is now at peace with the world. That piece of crap Hitler killed himself."

Karl seemed to ignore Moon, or didn't care about it. "So where have I traveled to? Where is this place?"

"You are in another dimension."

"Verdammt!" Karl pumped his fist. "He was right."

"Who was right?" Moon said.

"General Kammler's man."

"Die Glocke," Moon said.

Karl cut his eyes toward her. "How do you know that?"

"I told you, you ass. That was seventy years ago. I know about the bell. I know about you, Captain. You got into the damn Nazi time machine and disappeared, and now here you are. You know what? You never came back."

Karl said nothing as he stared at Moon.

"You never will go back either," Moon said.

Karl aimed the pistol at Moon. Luke had had enough. He pulled the arrow to his cheek. Karl had his side toward Luke, so Luke concentrated on a spot right under the shoulder. The arrow went high and hit Karl in the shoulder. He dropped the gun and Moon came up with it, aiming it at Karl.

Blood poured down Karl's arm as it hung by his side with

the arrow protruding from it.

Shevay stood and shouted something and then turned to Moon. "This nonsense has gone on long enough." The place quickly filled up with soldiers—they weren't giants. They were like the one who had jumped Adam and Luke. They seemed to come through the cracks of the walls. In fact, they came from small doors that appeared to be everywhere, even behind Luke. He was surrounded with spears only inches away.

They escorted Luke down with the rest of them. When he got down to the others, Moon was tying a bandage around Karl's arm. She had torn more of her shirt and now her navel was showing. Adam was holding his arrow. "Good shot or bad shot?" Adam said as he handed the arrow to Luke. One of the soldiers snatched it from Luke.

"Bad shot." Luke said.

"Well, Constable, here to make an arrest?" Moon said with that beautiful smile Luke had grown so fond of.

Karl shook his head. "Cowboys and Indians just like Hollywood. And you Americans really won the war?"

Shevay waved his hand. "Enough!" He pointed toward the exit and said something. Immediately there was a spear poking Luke's back. The others fared no better.

"Everyone listen to me and do what I say, and maybe we will survive this," Moon said. "Adam, don't try to fight them."

Karl turned to Shevay. "I told you my Fuhrur will give you powers you can only dream of." Shevay ignored him.

"You don't hear too good, Mann Herr," Moon said. "Hitler has been dead over seventy years, and that damn bell will never leave this place."

It hit Luke—so that is why she is here. She is here because of the German. Luke didn't understand what was happening, but be believed he was onto something.

Shevay took the Luger from one of his guards and handed it to Karl. "Take your strange weapon."

"Danke," Karl said.

"You remember you are my guest, but that could change,"

Shevay said.

"Give me my gun back," Moon said.

Shevay ignored her.

"His kind are evil. They murdered millions," Moon said.

Shevay looked down on Moon. "So have we. Soon it will be three more."

Karl moved beside Shevay as the soldiers pushed the other three before them and out of the pyramid.

Chapter 13

Luke looked down from the cage they had thrown them in. It reminded him of a bird cage, a bird cage atop a tall building. "One thing about it," Luke said. "We can see the entire city from here."

Adam snatched and jerked at the bamboo bars. "Save your strength, Adam. We will need you later," Moon said, as she sat with her back against the bars. "How's the arm?"

Adam seemed not to hear her or simply ignored her.

Luke sat beside Moon. "If you cut your shirt again, you won't be decent." She blushed just a little. Luke pointed at her. "Aha. I know how you feel."

She patted his knee. "What an adventure, eh, Constable."

Luke turned and squared himself with her. "Okay Moon, why don't you finally level with me? What exactly is your mission here?"

"I've already told you—"

"Fine then." Luke shook his head. "I guess I can just quit."

"Okay, Luke…okay." Moon pulled down on the front of her shirt, but her navel was still revealed. "I owe you the total truth." She gave him a forced smile. "I really am Special Agent Moon Serling, and everything else I told you is true, mostly. The reason I am here is to stop that German from returning to our world."

"How did you even know he was here?"

"You know about Die Glocke?"

"Yeah. Well, I think so." Luke said. "I saw it on TV. It was a machine that looked like a bell that the Nazis built during the war, one of their super weapons."

"It was more than that. It was built for time travel."

"You know, if we weren't sitting right here in another world, I would say you are crazy. When I saw it on TV, I thought it was a crock of crap."

"No, it was real, and it is here somewhere."

"How could you have possibly known it would be here?"

"A man named Glen Turner escaped from here back to our world and informed the agency."

"How did he escape?" Luke felt hope. "It could be our ticket out of this crazy place."

Moon stood. Luke's eye went to her navel. She pulled on her shirt, and he felt embarrassed. "Now who's red?" Moon said.

"Come on, Moon, keep talking." He pulled her back down.

"Luke, this is hard to follow."

Luke cut his eyes at her. "You think? Give me a try. I'm getting good at this *other world* stuff."

"Okay, you've met Orion, and you know how he came from the 1800's, yet is, what, about eighty or so?"

"Yeah, about that," Luke said.

"With time travel through these traversable wormholes, we know when the rat goes in, but we don't know the time in history he comes out."

"I think I follow."

"Glen Turner was a CIA agent in the sixty's. In 1965, the agency had heard of a strange hole in the side of a mountain in Tibet that the monks were using in their worship. A long story short, he found the hole and went in. The agent with him said as soon as he went in, the hole disappeared, and so did Turner."

"Sounds familiar," Luke said.

"That's how Shevay can speak English. Turner was here for

ten years or so."

"Where is he now?"

"He escaped back through a portal three months ago, and found his way back to the agency."

"The hole opened back up in Tibet?"

"No. He was spit out in a cave in West Virginia." She put her hand up. "We can't find a portal or anything in the cave. We used all the latest technology, but nothing."

Luke tried to get it all straight in his head, but it was beginning to jumble. "You said he was here in this place for ten years, but your math is wrong. From 1965 to now is over fifty years."

"He went into the hole a thirty-year-old man; he came out a forty-year-old man. He first tried to go home before reporting back to the CIA. It didn't work. His wife was dead, and his ten-year-old son, who he expected to be twenty, was a sixty-year-old grandfather."

Luke shivered. What if he did find a way back to Arkansas; would he find the same thing Glen Turner did?

"When Turner first arrived here, he was taken to Shevay to be sacrificed."

"The Scrains took him?"

"This is what I don't understand," Moon said. "Turner described a different race of people other than what I know about." She stopped talking for a time, thinking. She resumed, "Never mind that right now. The point is he was taken to Shevay, and somehow they became friends. Turner eventually had the run of the place."

"Doesn't sound like the Shevay we fondly know."

"One day Turner was out on the prairie hunting with the Reeze," Moon said. "He said he enjoyed hunting buffalo with the Reeze. He had befriended them and was then able to keep the Giants off the Lessers, as he called them. While hunting, there was an explosion—a sonic boom, and this bell object suddenly appeared on the prairie. He said he instantly knew it was Nazi, because the portal was swirling and all manner of debris came in with the bell, and there was a large, red banner with a swastika on it. He figured the bell came from his world, so he went for the portal before it could close."

"Why didn't Turner land back in 1940's Germany? That's where the bell came from."

"I don't have an answer."

"Maybe the portal is still open."

Moon turned away for a time and then turned back more composed. "No, Luke, it closed. One of the Reeze, a woman friend to Glen, jumped through the hole with him. Only…"

"What?"

"Only it closed on her." She paused for a time before continuing. "She melded into a stone. It was horrible and Turner had to put her out of her misery. He had to kill her with a rock."

"Damn!" Luke felt as if he had been hit with a bat.

Moon took a deep breath. "Anyway, Turner saw the bell, and he knew exactly what it was, and the Nazi banner confirmed it."

"So you are here to make sure this damn German doesn't change the course of history. Your agency knew you were from here, so they reckoned you were the best one to get the job done."

"No, Luke, I volunteered."

"How long have you been searching for a portal?"

"A few months now, since he came back."

"How did you even know you would come back at the right time in history?"

"I didn't. But we hoped there was a chance. When Turner spoke of Shevay, I knew Shevay was the ruler of the giants when I was a girl. We gambled I would hit it close."

Luke stood. "This is so hard to believe, but I know it's all real. I mean, look at me. I'm here." He dropped back down by Moon. "Why risk your life to come back here? What could that German possibly take back to our world that would change anything? You don't even know what year he would return to, if he's even able to return."

"There are powers here that you don't know about, Luke. There is much more here than I even know about because we stayed away from the giants, and they are the ones with the technology."

"Hell, Moon, I admit that pyramid is pretty awesome, but Tesla could make electricity do that. They don't have cars here or planes or trains. Crap, they don't even have horses and wagons."

Moon closed her eyes for a few minutes. When she opened them, she looked straight into Luke's eyes. "How well do you know history?"

"What does that hav—?"

"You know nothing about history. You think the Egyptian pyramids are ancient, don't you?"

"Aren't they?"

"It depends on what you compare them to. What about the lost Mayan Empire?"

"Moon, I don't know what you're getting at."

"There were civilizations thousands of years before them—thousands." She got up, walked to the bars, and stood by Adam. "This civilization is one of those older civilizations."

Luke shook his head. "You've lost me. Remember, I'm a simple man from the backwoods of Arkansas."

"Archaeologists are just scratching the surface of the ancients. Every time they think they have the first civilization discovered, they find something older. They say the Egyptian civilization began around 3000 B.C. They also believe Stonehenge was built about that time. Pretty old, right? Well, now they have discovered a temple in Turkey, Gobeklitepe, from about 10,000 B.C. It was preserved because the builders covered it with sand when they abandoned it. The weathering on the Sphinx in Egypt is from rain erosion. The last time it rained enough to cause that was over ten thousand years ago. Historians had originally declared man was living in caves then and existing like animals. They were wrong. They are still wrong. These giants here prove it."

"What do you mean?"

"The Nephilim were on earth in the ancient times."

"Yeah," Luke said. "They are in the Bible."

"They are here now. This is the ancient time."

"Wait a minute." Luke stood and brushed off his pants. "You are saying we are really back home, but back in time?"

"No, Luke. We are not, but this is what it was like long before the Egyptians, even before the Sumerians. The portals were used to travel between the worlds. Something happened to stop the portals—earthquakes maybe, magnetic storms, perhaps—but now they may be beginning to open again and neither civilization is prepared for the reunion. In this civilization maybe only a few decades have passed, but in your world thousands of years have gone by, and they know nothing about the portals."

"You led me to believe the portal we came in through was just an oddity that the Florians had found. Now you are telling me portals were used like subways by ancient people. When in hell are you finally going to tell me the truth?"

"I'm sorry, Luke." She took his hands. "In my job, deception is how I stay alive. I haven't meant to be so dishonest with you. I just haven't told you everything. But if these portals begin opening again to your world, it will be devastating for both worlds."

"And you are here to stop it from happening."

Moon squeezed Luke's hands. "That's right, Constable. And now you are going to help me."

Everyone fell asleep except for Luke. He had never been more tired, but his brain was in a race after Moon's civilization mumbo jumbo. Luke had always been simple, not much into deep thought. He was no dummy and he liked to read occasionally, but he was not into deep study. He would much rather take his bow and arrow to the woods and hunt. He liked the primitive stuff, but now he didn't even know what primitive was anymore. Everything he thought he knew wasn't true…or was it? Hell, it was all so confusing. Somehow, he finally drifted off and got a few hours of needed sleep.

The guards came at dawn and woke them up. Luke couldn't see any difference in the guards than "regular" people. He wondered why they served the giants. They snatched Moon from the cage. She didn't resist.

"Where are you taking her?" Luke said as he and Adam started for them. One of them stuck Luke in the leg, just enough to bring blood.

"Stay back," Moon said. "I want them to take me." She smiled. "I have a mission and I'm a big girl."

Luke held his wound, but he still managed a smile. "You're only five feet tall."

As they escorted her from the cage, she said, "Concentrated power in a small package."

He watched her go and worried for her life as she went out of sight.

Luke dropped his pants and studied his wound—it wasn't bad, just a nick. He shook his head. He had to be more careful. The next poke may be serious.

"Luke," Adam said.

He looked to see Adam silhouetted against the pink eastern sky. He was laughing. "What's so funny? We are penned up like chickens and they just took Moon. I don't see much to laugh about." He went to the bars next to Adam and looked toward where he was looking. It was just dawning, but he could see one of the guards below their building. All at once the guard fell. Adam laughed again. Then Luke saw the guard being dragged. It was Grace.

"There are two," Adam said. "I have watched as they moved up."

At first, Luke thought the girls had knocked the guard unconscious, but he watched Wak'o cut another guard's throat. They meant business. Grace threw a rope up, climbed up the building, and soon was at the gate sawing her obsidian knife on the big rope that held the gate.

"I told you not to come here," Luke said.

She cut the last strand and Wak'o pulled the gate open. "I never was much on doing what I was told," Grace said.

"Thank you, Grace," Adam said.

"Welcome," Grace said.

Luke pointed to Adam. "This is Adam." He pointed to the girls. "Grace and Wak'o."

Adam moved past the girls. "We go now." He slid down the rope and grabbed a spear from one of the dead guards. The others followed, and Luke picked up a spear and found his and Moon's packs.

They managed to get out of town without being seen. It appeared to Luke that the locals were late sleepers.

Grace had a hideout set up on the side of the mountain. She had food and water stored there.

"I knew you were into athletic stuff and karate, but I didn't know you were a survivalist," Luke said as he inspected the cache in the little cave.

"I'm afraid I'm not. That's Wak'o's department."

Luke turned to Wak'o, "Merci beaucoup."

She smiled and handed Luke a waterskin. "Well…come."

"She's learning a little," Grace said.

Wak'o pulled a stick of bread from a basket and handed it to Adam. He took it with a smile. She blushed.

Grace looked at Luke and winked. "He's a hunk and I think Wak'o thinks so too."

Luke motioned for Grace to follow him, and they went to the other side of the cave. "Well, Miss, that's the second time you've rescued me, and I thought I was here to save you." She only smiled. Luke shook his head. "Grace, you are so pretty. I see why Tyler is so crazy about you." She kept smiling, but wasn't the least bit embarrassed. "I promise you I'm going to get us home somehow," Luke said. "I'm going to reunite you and Tyler."

"There has got to be some way to get home," Grace said.

Luke drank from the skin. "You remember the other girl here I told you about?"

"I remember," Grace said as she took the skin from Luke. "She's a little short thing, reminds me of Cat Woman. Like I said, we stayed clear of her. She looked like she was dangerous."

Luke shrugged his shoulders and said, "Okay. Well, I think Cat Woman knows the way home—maybe. We have to rescue her."

Grace smiled. "That will be fun, another adventure. But when I watched her on the prairie, I had the feeling she could take care of herself. I saw her kill a little animal. She ate the heart and liver raw. We were close and hid well, but I think Cat Woman knew we were there."

"She is formidable."

Grace pointed to the other side of the cave. Wak'o was tending Adam's wounds. "Look at her blushing." Luke could relate to that.

Adam said, "Thank you." Wak'o looked up briefly from the work and smiled.

"That's so cute," Grace said.

Luke thought it was touching, but then he thought of the horrors they had seen, and he turned back to Grace. "How are you holding up? I mean we have seen a lot of horrible stuff here—we've done a lot of horrible stuff here."

The smile ran away from Grace's face. "I try not to think about it, Luke. All my life I've always stepped up to do what needed to be done to win. I just do the same thing here."

"This is not softball or karate. This is...this is killing."

Grace slowly nodded. "Your brother was in the Special Forces, wasn't he?"

"Yeah."

"Imagine what he must have seen and had to do. We do what we have to do to win. And to win is to get home. I plan to win."

Luke had always admired this pretty girl—now he admired her more. "Then we will win."

Adam came to Luke. "I have to get Sha-She."

"Why don't we rest and see if we can come up with a plan," Luke said.

"I go alone." Adam looked at the two women. "These are brave women, but you help them get back to Orion. I will go after Sha-She." Luke said nothing—he was surprised by this. "I will be more careful this time," Adam said. "They won't get me again."

"What's your plan?" Grace said.

Adam grabbed his spear. "Plan is to kill Shevay."

"Why kill him?" Luke said.

"The giants have killed many of my people, and we have always been afraid. I will cut off the head of the snake."

"There are too many guards for you to get close enough," Luke said.

Adam started out the cave and turned back. "May not have to get close." With that, he was gone.

Luke watched Adam go and he was torn on what to do next. He had come after Grace—he had Grace with him. Adam could survive in this land better than he could. In fact, to tell the truth, Luke was probably an impediment to Adam. If Luke were to follow him, he would probably get Adam in more trouble instead of being any help.

And what about Moon? She was a government agent. What could he do to help her? What could he add with his hickory bow? Moon was the expert. Moon was the government killer—she had shown she was a professional at it too. Sure, he had held up pretty good considering he was just a do-nothing constable, and he had contributed more than he took.

Maybe the portal he came in on was the key. He and the two girls could strike out in the morning. Maybe they could figure a way to get back through it. Maybe Orion knew how to help. He had lived here for a long time, and he probably had answers. No, he would be concerned for Adam.

"What are you thinking about?" Grace said as she sat beside him. She was perky. Luke wished he had the confidence of Grace.

"Wondering what to do next," he said.

"Why, Luke, that's easy."

He smiled. She looked like a school girl ready for a softball game or something, all flushed and excited. But oh how wrong was that impression. "Okay, Gracie, how is it easy?"

"Me and Wak'o have seen a lot of this land now, and I have been keeping mental notes." She brushed a wild lock of hair from her eyes. "This place has an order about it."

"An order?"

"Yeah. Everyone knows their place and pretty much does their own thing."

"I don't know about that, Sweetie. The first two tribes—"

"Luke, cut it out with the little girl stuff. I'm a big girl now, if you haven't noticed."

He smiled and thought of Tyler, waiting. "You are right, Grace; I'm sorry. What I was saying is the tribes where we first came here have had wars among themselves in the past."

"That may be, and I'm sure my theory is not perfect, but from what I've seen, there is a class system here with the giants being at the top."

"Okay, I follow you on that, but how does that make everything easy?"

"The people on the prairie have it figured out."

"They are called the Reeze. How do they have it figured out?"

"They know who has the power—the giants—and they make sure they have something they need."

Luke grinned. "Go on."

"They roam the prairie and beyond and bring the giants stuff."

"Yeah, but they could have slaves and make them get them *stuff.*"

"But a slave would only bring the bare minimum to please

his master. The Reeze know the better job they do for the giants, the more the giants will leave them alone."

Luke stood and looked down at Grace. "Okay, so what does that have to do with us?"

"We please the giants. We bring them *stuff*."

"I think we've already shot a hole in that plan. Hell, we're on the run from them now. They have Moon captured. Adam is on the way to do who knows what to them."

Grace stood too. Luke noticed she was a little taller than he. He followed her to the opening of the cave. A hawk swooped down and caught some type of pigeon. "We have knowledge—knowledge that they don't have."

"Like what? What knowledge do we have that they need? They don't need to know how to get on the Internet or make a phone call."

The hawk took flight with the dead pigeon in its talons.

Grace nodded. "They don't know how to fly. I bet they would think it was some sort of magic."

Luke pondered it for a time. He watched the hawk fly out of sight with its prey. "We don't have a plane, and if we did, we don't know how to fly one."

"I have an idea, but I'm still working on it," Grace said. "You go catch up to that hunk before he does more damage than we can repair. I have to retrieve something on the prairie for my plan. I will meet you back here tonight."

"You going to tell me your plan?"

"A woman likes to keep a man guessing."

He didn't want to let Grace out of his sight, but he simply said, "Okay, Grace. We will try your plan."

Chapter 14

Luke caught up with Adam at the hanging tree. He had hidden behind a boulder, waiting for Luke to approach. Luke realized what he was up to and slipped around to the other side and tapped his shoulder. "You're slipping, Adam. I could have taken you."

Adam turned and stood. "Luke is getting better." He squeezed Luke's arm, pointed to a large rock at the summit of the ridge, "Let's get to there and see what we need to do."

The climb was steep, but it kept them off the road and out of sight. They made it to the top, and Luke fished in his pack for his binoculars. He saw Moon's pack crammed in the bottom of his. A sudden yearning and worry came over him at the same time. He must have stared at it for a time because Adam nudged him and pointed for him to look with his binoculars.

Luke scanned the city. The pyramid was still sparking and arcing, buzzing like angry bees. Below the hill men were milling around the wall. He moved the binoculars and found about fifty more men in a semicircle. They wore robes made of orange feathers. He remembered seeing those robes somewhere before, but he could not recall where. They appeared to be some sort of primitive orchestra. But they all had the same type of instrument—extremely long horns. They reminded Luke of something from the Alps of Switzerland. The deep, low tone of the horns drifted up to him, making his whole body vibrate. The men appeared to be blowing at a giant stone like a snake charmer would blow at a cobra. A large arc shot from the pyramid, struck the stone, and stayed attached to it like an electric snake, slithering and snapping. The stone began to rise, and the horn-blowers kept their instruments aimed at it as it rose. It had to weigh ten tons if it weighed an ounce. It levitated in the air as if a magician had control of it.

Adam snatched the binoculars. "I have to see."

Luke fumbled in Moon's pack and came out with a monocular. He couldn't believe it. The stone slowly rose. The electricity beamed a constant stream to the stone. The horns continued. How did the blowers not run out of breath? The stone rose higher, higher, until it was about eighty feet in the air, and then it began to drift backwards and over the wall. Slowly, it began to descend to the top of the wall. As it settled onto the top stones, like the top brick on a wall, electricity fanned out over the entire structure. Stones, tons and tons, began to settle from the weight of the descending stone, as if they were marshmallows. They squished and conformed to each other until there were no open cracks between them. "How in the hell?"

"Orion told me of this," Adam said. He never let the binoculars down. "The horn blowers with the orange feathers are priests."

Luke reached over and grabbed the binoculars from Adam and tossed him the monocular. The electricity drew back to the pyramid and the horns stopped. Luke watched a man climb the wall and inspect the job. "Unbelievable!"

"There Sha-She," Adam said.

"Where?" But Luke found her in his binoculars. There was a group of giants standing under some type of awning watching the show. She was beside them with her hands bound behind her, with a guard on either side. The German was there, too.

Adam started to rise. "Hold it, Adam. Let's scope it out first.

We can't do her any good if we get caught or killed." Adam nodded and settled back down with his monocular.

Luke found the German again. He had moved to the stone wall with Shevay. They were pointing at the wall and Karl was nodding. Then Luke thought what would happen if the Germans got hold of this power. If these primitive people can use it to lift giant stones, what would the Nazis do with it? The Giants may only be using a small part of the potential. The Nazis were brilliant with technology—they would get the most from it. Moon was absolutely right—Karl must not leave this world.

"What are we going to do?" Adam said.

Luke wondered what Karl had done for them to side with him over Moon. If Shevay was fond of Glen Turner, why now turn on Moon? Karl had something that Shevay wanted—what that was Luke didn't know. But that had to be it because Moon was bound and Karl was free.

Suddenly, Moon kicked one of the guards. Her hands were free. She knocked the other to the ground with her fist. "Adam, Moon is fighting them!"

Adam jumped to his feet. "We must help!"

"We can't get down there from here. We have to take the road down," Luke said.

Adam slid down from the edge and started for the road. Luke grabbed the bags. He stopped as he remembered and looked into Moon's bag—three more grenades. He plucked one as he looked back down and saw Moon kicking ass, and then she ran behind the pyramid with more guards chasing her. Luke stuffed the grenade in his pocket and followed after Adam.

They struck the road and sprinted down it—no time to be cautious. Luke caught Adam. "You get her and I will make a diversion."

"Make what?"

"You just get her out of there."

When they hit the first street, Adam almost plowed into Moon as she was trying to escape. Two guards were right on her tail. Moon turned and kicked one in the face. Adam almost knocked the other one's head off with his fist.

Luke pointed up the road from where they had come. "That way!" He sprinted past them and toward the pyramid.

"What are you doing, Luke?" Moon said. "They will kill you."

Luke raised a grenade. "I will slow them down."

"No. Don't kill them. We will never stir them away from the German. You don't understand."

Luke had not thought about it, but she was right. "I do understand. Now go! Adam, get her out of here."

Adam grabbed her by the arm, but she pulled against him and looked after Luke. "You run or I carry you," Adam said. Moon hesitated, started to speak, but Adam was a man of his word. He threw her over his shoulder and started up the hill.

"Okay, let me down." He did and they raced up the hill.

One of the guards ran out of a side alley, and Luke drew his tomahawk from his belt. The guard lunged with his spear. Luke went down and kicked the man's legs from under him. He went down, but he was back up before Luke could react. He swung the spear around like a baseball bat. Luke blocked it with his tomahawk, and the spear cracked in two. The guard raised the short piece of spear over his head, intending to drive it down on Luke. Luke was prepared for this and hit the man in the head with the flat of the tomahawk. He was out.

Luke turned and found a dozen or more guards were racing toward him. He saw a couple of giants behind. He pulled the pin on the grenade. He would let them get closer and toss it in front of them. That should scare the hell out of them and let him escape.

The man on the ground shot back to his feet. He hit Luke's arm and the grenade tumbled to the ground. "Oh, shit!" Luke whirled and sprinted up the road, the guard right behind, reaching, trying to grab him. The grenade exploded, knocking the guard into Luke's back. Luke rolled him off and straddled him. He pounded the man's face with his fist a few times until he didn't move. He looked back. The guards had stopped. "Yes!" Luke said. Two came from behind the others and ran for him. "No!" Luke shot to his feet and raced up the road.

He turned back. It was no use. These two would catch him. He tried to run faster, but he had no more. Adam and Moon jumped out from behind some rocks, and they made quick work of the two unfortunate men.

Luke bent over to catch his breath. "That was too close."

"Let's go before it gets closer," Adam said.

Moon took her pack from Luke. "Thank you, Constable, for coming for me, but let me have my bag before you blow the world up."

"You can have it. I'm not cut out for this,'" Luke said. She smiled. But at that moment he really couldn't appreciate it—he began shivering. He was afraid. It hadn't registered when the confrontation was going on, but now he believed he would cry if Moon wasn't there. After all he'd been through, why this feeling now? Why not before?

Her smile faded and she put her arms around him. "Luke, you're a brave man. It takes a lot to do what you have been doing in this world."

Luke wiped his eyes. Her arms felt so good, but the attention made his emotions simmer to the top.

"We must go now," Adam said. "They will be coming."

Luke composed himself. "You're right. Let's go to Grace's cave."

Moon squeezed Luke's arm. "You found her?"

"She found me."

Adam dug a bunch of large grubs out of a rotten tree and brought them to the cave for lunch. Luke hesitated at first, but his hunger got the best of him. He bit into the grub and it popped in his mouth—he thought he would vomit. However, the grub was actually delicious. Moon ate them without a word. They just as well had been popcorn.

Moon inspected the contents of her bag as she chewed on

the grub. "I need an army, but I only have two grenades left, and I need them for something besides a battle."

"What do you need them for?" Luke said.

She ignored his question. "That damn German made them take my gun. When I go back, I'm gonna kick—"

"Sha-She not going back," Adam said as he stood at the cave entrance, his back to her, looking out over the prairie.

Moon closed her pack and ignored him.

He turned. His face was hard and his eyes bore down on Moon. "We leave tonight for home."

"I have something I have to do here first."

"We leave tonight."

"Look, Adam, this is important, and you don't understand."

There was a long silence and then Adam spoke. "I have been outcast from my people—your people—all my life. They called my mother a whore because of Orion. They hate Orion because he is smart and different. But none of that matters. I keep going to the village because they are my people. Orion has always taught Adam to do the right thing. And bringing you home to them is the right thing."

Moon stood. "Adam, I have been gone all of these years. They have been without me that long. They don't need me now."

"You are back now. Everything is for a reason. The king will not be with us much longer."

Moon placed her hands on her hips. "I have to do what I have to do."

Adams voice grew deep and firm. "I will do what I have to do. You are Kayeeya. You made that clear to me back at the diamonds. You will be queen and our people will need you. We go tonight." He turned and walked out of the cave.

Moon turned to Luke. "He doesn't understand how important this is to the world. He is simple."

"I think he understands how important you are to *his* world. He has risked his life to save yours. No, Moon, he's not simple. In my world, he'd be a damned hero."

Moon lowered her head. "You're right, Luke." She looked back up to Luke. "But I have to stop that German; you know that."

Adam stepped back into the cave. "Girls coming."

Grace and Wak'o arrived carrying bamboo poles. Luke went down to meet them. "What have you here?"

"A frame," Grace said.

"For what?"

"A secret weapon."

Moon came down with her hand extended. "So you're Grace. The constable has searched high and low for you. I'm Moon."

Grace shook her hand and said dryly, "We know each other."

"I don't understand."

"We saw you on the prairie. We hid well, but I know you knew we were there."

Moon nodded. "Well, now we know each other's name."

Luke was uncomfortable with the exchange so he stepped up. "What is your secret weapon?"

"I guess we don't need it now." Grace looked at Moon.

"What is it, Grace?" Moon said. "We may need it."

"I have the stuff to make a glider. We would jump off the top of that mountain and fly over the city. I thought that should impress them enough to want the technology, want to be our friends."

Moon looked to Luke for an explanation. "We figured if we had technology to impress them, we may be able to work a deal to get you back," Luke said.

"Okay, I understand," Moon said.

Luke didn't believe she was too impressed with the idea. "I think they have more advanced technology than we believed, especially since they can levitate those heavy boulders."

"What?" Grace said.

"Yeah," Luke said. "They just stood around the giant stones and blew horns at them until they rose up in the air, and then they set them on top of a giant wall. When the stone settled on top, it pressed into the other stones like they were made of clay.

Hell, with that technology they could build a starship."

"That technology is ancient," Moon said. "It was used in your world in ancient times. Those huge stones at Cuzco, Peru were set in place that way, as well as Stonehenge. Many cultures did this, but the archaeologists won't admit it. The people used harmonics and the earth's magnetic field. It's simple technology, but you have to understand how to do it. Our historians are too arrogant to admit that the ancients were smarter than just using ropes and slaves."

"It didn't look simple to me," Luke said. "I'm sure you don't want the Nazis to understand it."

"You're right. It is simple, but it is also extremely powerful. Didn't I tell you, Luke, there were powers here?" Moon turned to Grace. "Your glider is an excellent idea. These people know nothing about the power of flight or gliding or balloons for that matter. They will think it is something from the gods. They know about things that appear like magic to us, such as the portals, but that is just nature to them, just like the levitation."

"Moon, you are guessing at what they don't know," Luke said.

"I'm gambling at what they don't know. There is nothing else to do."

Grace and Wak'o laid the bamboo poles out on the ground. "This is the frame. I saw this done on YouTube."

"What do you have for the skin?" Moon said.

Grace reached into her skin bag and drew out a large red cloth. Wak'o took one end and Grace took the other, and they spread it open. It was a giant Nazi banner, red with a white circle in the middle. In that circle was a black swastika.

"Damn," Luke said. "Where did that come from? Are there more Germans here other than Karl?"

"We found it out on the prairie. Someone had partially buried it under some rocks. There were large skid marks in the dirt close by, like someone had moved something huge and heavy," Grace said.

"It must have been draped over the bell," Moon said. "I

guess when it energized, the banner came with it."

"Makes sense," Luke said.

"Bell?" Grace said.

"I will tell you about it later," Luke said. "It's a good story."

"Guys, I think you are on to something with this glider idea," Moon said. "I have an idea too." She turned to Grace. "Can I contribute to your plan?"

"Sure, but I have a condition."

"You are not in any plan," Adam said. "We leave tonight."

"Adam, how would you feel if the giants destroyed all of Frelonna in a day?" Moon said. "If that man gets back to his world—Luke and Grace's world— with the Nephilim's knowledge, that is what will happen. He will destroy their village and many more."

Adam turned to Luke. Luke nodded and said, "It is true."

After thinking for a time, Adam said, "Luke is my friend. We will do this one last thing."

Moon turned to Grace. "Now, what is your condition?"

Luke found it hard to believe he was back in the Giant's city in the dark, sneaking through the alleys like a cat, but he damn sure was. And it was his idea—that's the strangest part of it all. Moon had wanted to come alone, but the plan needed two people.

Luke watched Moon—admired Moon—as she went ahead around the buildings. There was a bright full moon, so they stayed to the shadows. She was in commando mode again, and she was good at it. Luke followed when she motioned him forward. There was no doubt who was in command of this sortie. She had a club in her hand and was ready to bring it to action at any second. Luke had suggested a tomahawk would be better. She had said killing one of them would ambush the plan —they had to get back on good terms with Shevay. Luke hoped if it was needed, the club would be enough.

They went past the pyramid with its electric peak. Moon had told Luke the Giants had learned how to harness the earth's

magnetic field as the ancients in his own world had done it—
just science, nothing so special. Luke wondered if it wasn't so
special, why wasn't it done on every skyscraper in New York.
He meant to ask her more about it when they finished the
mission—if they finished the mission.

Moon motioned Luke to come to her behind a statue of a
mammoth. "See it?" She pointed to a large courtyard beyond. It
was the bell. The moon bathed it in eerie silver. It looked like
something from a science fiction movie—maybe something
from the twilight zone.

"What is that damn thing?" Luke said.

"We weren't really sure until now. We had suspected the bell
was some sort of time machine, but we weren't sure." Moon
stood, peeped around the statue, and then settled back in
behind it and next to Luke. "It works by a magnetic field." She
pointed to the pyramid's peak. "It can get that from there."

"What does it have, a lightning rod on it or something?"
Luke said.

"I don't know, Luke. If it does, it could go any time."

"We can try to get close and see what it has." Luke pulled his
binoculars. "There are guards all around it though."

"I suspected it." She took his binoculars and looked. "That is
why when we get close, we destroy it."

"What is it Karl will take back to Germany?" Luke said. "I
guess one of those horns they used to lift the stone."

She handed the binoculars back to him. She smiled and Luke
found it beautiful, but condescending. "What?" Luke said.

"I'm sorry, Luke. You don't know what I know, and I'm just
being an ass. You remember the stones I picked up on the
prairie, the ones I used to pull the lightning from the pyramid?"

"How could I not remember them?"

"They are from a meteorite, I think, but not for sure. I don't
know what they are. If I find the way back, I will take them for
analysis. But they are like some sort of magnet. If you can find
a way to get a magnetic field moving, they will concentrate it
like a laser. Those people use harmonics and magnetic fields to

166

move and shape those boulders. Those long horns and those diamond-looking rocks are the instruments that help them do that."

"So if Karl takes those rocks back with him..."

"And if that bell can come and go at will, the Nazis will easily take over the world," Moon said.

"But you said ancients in my world used harmonics to lift giant stone. The technology is already there."

"It was in ancient times. We believe the ancients freely went through the portals and were able to harvest these meteorite stones. And that is why you are going to put a grenade in that bell."

She got up and moved down the street to a clump of bushes and waved Luke forward. "We will hide here until morning."

"Hell, let's blow it up now while it is dark," Luke said.

"If we do that, the Nephilim will wipe out my people. No. I must convince them I am the friend and Karl is the enemy."

"This plan of yours seems way far fetched to me," Luke said.

"I heard them talking, and I know Karl will be here in the morning to charm Shevay. I don't know what tricks he will use. I don't know what he has in that bell. But I do know if Shevay can find an advantage with Karl, he will take it. The Nephilim are highly intelligent, but they have no idea what our world has become."

"What's to keep him from taking advantage of you?"

"That's why we can't let him know we are the ones who destroyed the bell. You must not be caught."

The weight grew much heavier on Luke.

"I hope your friend Grace is as resourceful and cunning as you say."

Luke looked up at the moon and an anxious breath escaped his lips. Oh, how he wished he were in the Ozark Mountains right now looking at them and not here in this weird place. "When we get back, I would like to take you walking along this beautiful stream I know close to home. It would be beautiful in the moonlight." He surprised himself saying that. He felt that old familiar flush come over his face like warm wax.

Moon smiled. Luke felt it more than he saw it. "I will take you up on that, Luke. It sounds lovely. But now, get some rest. Tomorrow will be busy."

Luke settled in under a bush. He felt his chest flutter. If he hadn't fallen in love with Moon, it damn sure was something like it.

"Luke," Moon said softly.

"Yes."

"Is Grace really as athletic and resourceful as you say?"

Grace's pretty face came to Luke's mind. She wasn't the Grace he had known—or thought he had known—back home in Arkansas. She really was a machine. He felt himself smile. "She's what I reckon you were like as a teenager. She will be there when we need her."

After a long pause, Moon said, "Will you be there when I need you?"

Luke didn't know how she meant that. It didn't matter; the answer would be the same. He said, "Count on it."

"Wake up, Moon. It's breaking light and something's happening," Luke said as he nudged her. Her hair was wild and Luke loved it—it fit her.

She reached and Luke handed her the binoculars. "What's happening?" she said.

"I'm not sure, but more guards are gathering around the bell, and I've seen a few of those giants milling around over there, too."

"It's too early," she said. "Grace will be late."

Luke studied Moon as she worked the binoculars. She did not miss a detail as she swept the glasses slowly in all directions. He didn't trust many people, but now he had to trust her. She was the pro here. She was cool and calculating.

"There's Karl," she said.

"What's he doing?" Luke said, but she didn't answer.

"I don't see Shevay."

The dawn was growing and the gray was fading. The peak of the pyramid made a loud crack and then it settled back down to its normal crackle. Luke let out a loud gasp.

Moon giggled a little, but didn't take her eyes from the binoculars. "Just the magnetic field shifting. We don't have to worry about ancient spacemen."

Luke smiled, but said nothing. He saw a glow coming close to them. It was three guards coming with glowing spheres in their hands. They walked close, but didn't have a clue that Luke and Moon were in the grove of bushes. One of the glowing balls disintegrated into thousands of tiny lights and then disappeared. The other two guards walked slowly, carrying the green balls as if they were explosives. They went to the bell and handed them to Karl one at a time, and he set them inside the bell. It made the bell glow green.

"What are those things?" Luke said. "A Reeze had one on the prairie."

Moon turned and handed Luke the binoculars. She sat and rubbed her eyes. "I remember them when I was a girl, but I can't remember what they are called. My people think they are spirits. Sometimes they float on their own around swamps."

"Adam said Orion called them Will-o'-the-wisp."

Moon jerked the binoculars from Luke and looked again at the bell. "The serum."

"What?"

"Die Glocke was said to run off some kind of green, glowing serum." Moon turned back around. "What does this mean?"

"You're asking me?" Luke said as he took the binoculars. "Maybe the bell is powered by those globes. Hey, Karl is going back toward the pyramid."

"Good. They said they would all meet at the bell at sunup. That's not long from now. Let's hope Grace will be ready."

No one could say the giants were not punctual. As soon as the orange of the sun peaked over the top of the eastern buildings, Shevay and his entourage paraded toward the bell with Karl in their wake—he was smart and knew his place.

"Look at him," Moon said. "I'm going to take him down a few notches."

Luke had retrieved Moons monocular and he studied the situation. There were guards all around the bell. He didn't see how in the world Moon was going to even get close, much less talk to Shevay.

Moon turned to Luke. "Are you ready for show time, Constable?"

Luke felt the jitters, but he composed himself. "I'm ready, Special Agent."

Moon smiled and nodded. "If this goes badly, Luke, it's no one's fault. Understand?"

He took a deep breath, but didn't answer.

"It is simply a mission. But, hey, I have all the confidence in the world this one will succeed."

He knew she had doubts, but he played along. What else was there to do?

"Are they up there?" Moon said.

Luke looked up to the north ridge—the same place he and Adam had been when they scoped the city. He saw Adam and Wak'o crouched down by the big boulder. "Yeah. They are in position."

She started out of the hiding spot, but turned. "Luke, you will have to get close to what you must do. If you are wounded, you must continue. This is bigger than any of us. The mission comes first. Do you understand?"

He had already come to terms with that, and he was as prepared as he could possibly be. He had thought of his brother in the Special Forces. "I do understand."

"God Speed," she said.

"God Speed," Luke said as Moon jogged toward the bell.

Chapter 15

Grace inspected the craft for the tenth time. She wasn't much on the idea of securing everything with vines and leather, but Adam and Wak'o had assured her they would hold. The skin of the craft was as tight as they could stretch it—it was no drum, but she believed it was good enough. The bamboo was strong. The pieces were mostly tan and dry, but there were a few green stalks here and there. Again, the others had assured her the structure would not fail.

She exhaled a long breath. This was like preparing for a karate match or her turn at bat. Well, no, it really was not—this was for keeps. This was really life or death. This was the ultimate game. There would be no "we will get them next time." This was it.

Adam and Wak'o crouched behind the rock, looking down at the bell. They were communicating with hand gestures. If all this worked out, she would insist Moon help with her French so she and the rest could talk with Wak'o. Hand gestures could only take you so far. Grace would love to be able to just chat with Wak'o, her new best friend.

Adam stared at Grace. He looked back down below and then walked to her. "I should be the one to do this," he said.

"Men are all the same no matter where they are," she said.

"Adam, I am the right weight for this. You are not. This thing will do better with less weight. You are heavier." Adam shook his head, but he had no reply, and she knew he meant well. She placed her hand on his thick arm. "It will be fine," she said. "I am really good at this." That sounded so good to her that she almost believed it herself.

Wak'o stood by Adam and looked the craft over. If she had come from the time of the French Explorers in America, the most advanced vehicle she would have been familiar with was the flatboat. But she was not ignorant; she knew the plan. Grace had communicated it the best she could with hand signs, and Grace believed she trusted her to pull it off. Wak'o smiled at Grace as she made fists and crossed her wrists in front of her chest. Grace believed this was the sign for love or friend. Grace did the same.

"Grace, get ready," Adam said.

Adam raised the craft and Grace stepped under and secured herself to it. She looked across to the hills on the other side of the city and said a quick prayer. The wind wasn't quite right, but it could have been worse. Adam held his position while Wak'o went back to the edge of the cliff. Grace started her mantra that she always went through before any competition or event: "I am in control. I can do this. I am in control. I can do this…" She continued as she waited for the signal.

Moon made it almost to the bell before she allowed the guards to catch her. Through binoculars, Luke watched her struggle just a little. He had seen her in action—she could have kicked their asses coming and going if she had wanted, but that was not the plan. They took her straight away to Shevay. Perfect.

Luke looked up and there was Wak'o hidden at her post on the edge of the cliff. "Please, God, let this go right," he prayed.

Luke turned back just in time to see Karl slap Moon across the face. It was all Luke could do to restrain himself from running over there to stomp that Nazi in the ground. But if

Moon could restrain—and she was a better ass-stomper than he ever was—he had to stick with the plan. Shevay reached down and picked Karl up by the collar with little effort—the giant wasn't only tall, but strong—and then he lowered Karl back down. Luke reckoned he got the message because he laid off Moon.

Moon started in with her pitch with a lot of hand gestures and drama. Karl was not to be outdone; he became animated with his, pointing at the bell often. From that distance they appeared to be salesmen, trying to make the sale of a lifetime. In fact, they were. Other giants gathered close, and they too began gesturing.

Luke looked back up. Wak'o was on her feet.

He looked back to Moon. Her hand went to her coat pocket. Wak'o was gone from the cliff edge.

Luke got to his feet. He squeezed the grenade in his hand. "Only one chance, Luke," he said to himself. "Only one chance, just like loosing an arrow."

Moon pulled her hand from her pocket and brought out a stone. Immediately a streak of lightning flew to it from the pyramid peak. She staggered a bit, but regained her footing.

Luke looked up just as the bright red triangle cleared the cliff edge. It swooped down a little, but then Grace gained control and it arced back skyward.

Moon was pointing and shouting as Luke looked back toward her. All were looking at it—a large, red triangle with a big, white circle enclosing a swastika in the middle of it. A girl hung from the middle of it with her long blond hair whipping wildly in the wind. Moon ran to the edge of the hills pointing with all following her, and Karl protesting.

This was Luke's cue. He bolted from the cover of the bushes and ran faster than a frightened buck. All were looking up. He tried to get more speed as he closed the distance. It was better than they had even hoped for—no one noticed him. Moon had carried them too far away, and they were mesmerized by Grace and her Nazi glider—the bright red was perfect. Luke slid in

173

behind the bell, and no one had seen him. He slid around the side of it. He pulled the pin and prepared to throw it through the hatch. He stopped at the last second. There was Karl's damn Reeze standing at the door looking up at the red glider. Luke backed away from the hatch.

Moon must have held the rock up again because the charge went off again.

Luke had to think fast. He had pulled the pin, so he squeezed the hell out of the trigger, praying it didn't go off and blow him back to his dimension. The plan would be no good if anyone was killed, so said Moon. He grabbed his club from his belt and eased around the craft. He conked the man on the head and he fell like a deflated dummy. Luke tossed the grenade into the bell, grabbed the man by a leg, and raced away from the bell like a wolf dragging a moose leg. A good distance away, he dropped the man and dove behind a pre-planned boulder as the bell exploded.

Everyone turned to look. Luke was safe—scared as hell, but safe. The bell was tender and the explosion had ripped holes all over the thing. Green sparks fluttered from it like fireflies.

Luke looked across to the other side of the city to see Grace had barely cleared the cliff edge, but she did clear it. She would be long gone by the time the guards got to the glider.

Moon was not fairing as well. The guards had her in tow as they went to the bell. Karl was trying to get to her, but the guards had him as well.

Luke knew the plan, but this part was hard to follow. He watched Moon carefully through his binoculars. If he could find a way, he would try to save her. Subtly, she raised her hand and pointed toward the east. She was telling him to escape and follow the plan they had agreed to. He snorted, "Damn it." He had promised her he would escape and not harm anyone in the city. There was no way he could get to her and not be captured himself without killing a guard or two. He had promised. Everything had gone as planned so far. They all knew there was a chance she would not get out of it alive. The bell was destroyed and that German couldn't get back to Hitler. The mission was a success. But such a success was bittersweet. This wasn't over and he would regroup. He turned and made his way out of the city to meet back up with the others.

When Luke looked up to the cave, Adam was standing there. As he climbed toward him, he saw the disappointment on Adam's face. He was no more disappointed than Luke, but Luke knew there was no point in saying that. The girls stepped up behind Adam. The three were a sight—Adam, the paperback cover, red-haired caveman; Wak'o, the beautiful Indian maiden; and Grace, the blond movie star. Luke did not fit this group, the lowly, country constable who had never made an arrest in his life. Barney Fife had done more.

Grace bopped down the hill to meet him. "Is Moon okay?"

Luke answered her, but looked at Adam. "She appeared to be good, but they have her captured again."

Adam turned and went back into the cave. They all watched him go.

"It's not your fault," Grace said. "She wouldn't have it any other way. Moon said we had to destroy that bell."

"I know that."

They didn't know what else to say, so they went up to the cave. Adam was sitting on a rock sharpening his spear.

"We will figure something out," Luke said.

Adam continued to sharpen his spear. "Your world is safe now?"

"I believe it is for now," Luke said. "We destroyed that time machine or whatever the crap it was."

Adam stood. "My world is back there in that city. She is to be our next ruler." He jabbed the spear into the ground. "Is Luke satisfied?"

"She chose it, damn it!"

"No! She did it for you and your world." Adam pointed his finger at Luke. "What about Frelonna? What about my people? This is your fault."

175

"You stupid simpleton. She came back to this world to do this. If she had not come for that purpose, you would not have even known she was alive."

Grace and Wak'o stepped between them. Grace pulled Luke one way and Wak'o pulled Adam the other. "This won't win the ballgame here," Grace said. "We have to remain a team."

Wak'o crossed her arms and said, "Team!" Luke doubted she knew what it meant, but she was proud of it.

"Look at what we just pulled off," Grace said. "Did you not see me flying over the city like an eagle?"

"Well, I was a little busy," Luke said.

"That's right," Grace said. "Look what you did—you blew up that bell, just as Moon said you would. We planned it, and we pulled it off—a team."

"I don't know what is *team*, but Sha-She is still there," Adam said.

"And we will get her back," Luke said.

"She made us promise not to do that," Grace said. "She said give her two days, and if she wasn't back here by then, head back to Frelonna without her."

"I'm not going to do that," Luke said.

"We go get her, Luke?" Adam said.

"Hold up," Grace said. "We were awake all last night. Let's sleep, and when we are fresh, we will be able to think more clearly. Besides, it would be better after dark if we go."

"You're right," Luke said.

Adam nodded and sat against a rock.

Wak'o brought her hands to her eyes, and with the index fingers, she pointed away from her eyes. "Good idea," Grace said. "You stand guard and I will relieve you later." Wak'o went to the cave entrance and rested on a rock.

"She didn't know what you just said," Luke said.

"No, but she knew what I meant."

Luke and Grace sat beside each other and leaned on the cave wall.

"This is all crazy, isn't it, Luke?" Grace said.

Luke ran his fingers through his hair. "I guess I should have paid more attention in science class. Maybe I would be up on these wormholes."

"Will we ever get home?" Grace said. She put her hand over her mouth. She was trying to hold it together, but failing.

Luke put his arm around her. She was a tough nut, but everyone had a limit. "I'm sure we will."

She wiped her eyes and tried to regain control. "Maybe we should have tried to save that bell. It could have been our ticket out of here."

He had thought the same thing, but Moon had convinced him that the only option was to destroy it. Now he didn't know which way to go to get home, but what he did know was Moon was the key. She was the one with the knowledge, and they would have to rescue her. But his heart told him that wasn't the only reason he wanted to rescue her.

"Luke," Grace said.

"Yeah."

"Thanks for coming after me. I've gotten you in a horrible predicament. If I had only stopped like Tyler said, this would have never happened."

"What? We would have missed all of this. Where can you go and see real live mammoths and beautiful, historic Osage girls and real live red-haired cavemen?"

Grace grinned. "You have a point."

Grace had proven to be more than Luke had any idea— strong, smart, resourceful, brave, and beautiful. Now, in the cave, she was tired and homesick. Luke knew she would rebound, but now she just needed some downtime, that's all. "Grace, do you know the story about Orion, the man that disappeared into thin air off his farm in 1854?"

"No, I don't think I do."

"Well, let me tell it to you. But I have to warn you, it's a little hard to believe."

"Wake up, Luke," Grace said, shaking him. Luke came out

177

of a dream and found Grace kneeling beside him. "Moon is coming."

Luke sat up, collected himself. "Is she alone?"

"Yeah."

Luke got to his feet. Adam and Wak'o were at the cave entrance looking out. "Is anyone following her?" Grace shook her head. Luke saw her coming across the prairie in the wide opening, not a care in the world. It did not look right, did not feel right, may be a trap, a deception to lure them out. He saw the expression on Adam; he had the same apprehension and he retrieved his spear. "What do you think, Adam?"

"I'm going to meet her," Adam said. "If it is wrong, I will raise my spear." He moved down the side of the hill like a goat. He wasted no time.

"Y'all grab your stuff in case we have to bolt," Luke said as he threw his pack onto his back. "I can't believe they would have just let her go. That damn German may have a rifle on her or something."

Grace made a hand sign and Wak'o gathered her things into her bag. "If they know where we are, we don't have a chance. You do realize that, don't you, Luke?" He knew it. "But I don't think she would have brought them here even if Karl did have a rifle on her," she said. Luke believed that too.

Adam ran to Moon. Luke studied them in his binoculars. Everything appeared to be good. Adam looked in all directions, but he never raised his spear. Luke scanned every inch of the horizon and the hilltop, but his binoculars didn't spot anything that would suggest trouble, and then he put them back on Moon as she grew near. He felt her in his chest—a flutter. He watched her get closer and he grew anxious. "They're not following her," he said. "They let her go."

"How do you know that?" Grace said.

"She has her pack." He lowered the binoculars and turned to Grace. "Her pistol is in her waistband."

Grace took the binoculars. "You're right. Maybe she kicked all their asses and took them."

Luke dropped his pack, reached in, and pulled out a tube of matches. "I've been saving these, but I'm fixin' to make a fire with one now." They already had the wood piled and ready but had never lit it, not wanting to be discovered.

"They will know where we are," Grace said.

"They probably already know. And if they don't, it doesn't matter or Moon wouldn't be coming here in the wide open like that."

"Why do we need a fire anyway?" Grace said.

"There are big fish in that stream down below—I saw them, and we will eat good for a change." Luke started the fire with the first match. As he nursed it, he said, "Beside that, Sweetie, a fire is a tonic, and we need that. It will be soothing as Moon tells us her tale."

Soon Moon came through the entrance. Luke wanted to run and hug her. He wanted to squeeze her so tight, but he did not. "Thank God you are safe."

She smiled as she looked at each one. "Team, you were amazing. Grace, that was perfect. That Nazi glider was perfect."

"Thanks," Grace said. "It was a rush."

Moon turned to Luke, "Constable, excellent job."

"Tell us what happened after we pulled out," Luke said.

"You will see for yourself," Moon said. "We are going back tonight."

"Sha-She has lost her mind," Adam said.

"We have been invited. If we want to keep peace in this world, we must go." Moon pulled from her pack one of the stones that attracted the lightning and held it up. "You're gonna want to see this."

Chapter 16

The city was lit up with all its splendor. Torches lined the streets, candles twinkled in the windows, music seemed to drift from every direction, and the pyramid sparked and zapped. Luke and the group walked down the street with no interference—people just looked on and nodded as they walked past. Yes, they were expected. Luke hoped it was not a trap. He knew Adam was suspicious as well and did not want to come.

"Relax," Moon said. "It's either going to turn out good or it's going to turn out bad. Either way, we have no choice. We would have never crossed the prairie alive if they wanted to harm us."

Luke figured she was right; no need to worry now. They had no weapons—Moon insisted they leave them behind. That was a sticking point for Luke and Adam. Moon won out.

There were a lot more people in the city than they had previously seen—more giants, too. It appeared to be some sort of festival, and the way everyone was looking at them, they must be the guests of honor.

"Look," Grace said, pointing to a group of men standing on a stone platform. They had clothes made entirely of feathers, bright and shiny, red feathers like huge parrots. They looked somewhat like the horn blowers, but they weren't orange nor giants.

"What's going on here, Moon?" Luke said.

"I don't know exactly what it is, but there is something special for them in the sky tonight. And guess what gang? We are just in time to see it."

Luke looked up at the sky. It was speckled with a billion stars. "Oh, joy, we are so fortunate. If we are lucky enough, they may cut our hearts out and throw them from the pyramid."

Shevay was perched on an ivory throne at the top of a fifty-foot, stone stairway like some Mayan god. Torches were strategically placed to reflect flickering light off his body and jewels. Guards came and escorted the group up the steep stairs.

"It appears we are, indeed, the guests of honor," Luke said.

Shevay smiled and nodded as the group sat on the stone benches beside him.

Next, the guards brought the red-feathered men up the stairs and sat them beside Luke and the group.

Below, a procession of women came and sat on benches below the steps. They were tall women, yet a little shorter than the giants. They were clad in gold and jewels. No doubt, they were royalty.

Music drifted through the city, low and soothing. There were horns, drums, and strings. Luke could not figure where it originated; it was like stereo.

A troop of children came up the steps carrying feathered head dressings that looked like the ones the red-feathered men were wearing. They placed one on Luke's head and then the rest. Luke felt ridiculous, but Moon and Grace smiled. Each child bowed toward Shevay as each descended the steps.

A short man, a dwarf, ran to the area immediately below the steps. He began turning flips and dancing. The crowd laughed and cheered. Shevay clapped his hands and laughed. Next, a magician came as the dwarf left. He juggled three balls and then made them disappear. Then he brought in a pretty woman. He made her levitate. The group roared with approval. This went on for a time, one show after the next: a man and a bear,

181

four women dancing, a man and his flute, and on and on.

Moon leaned toward Luke and whispered, "I don't see Karl."

Luke looked around. "I reckon he didn't get tickets."

The music stopped, and it all grew quiet. Everyone looked up at the starry sky.

"What are they doing?" Luke said.

"I'm not sure," Moon said.

Two men came up the steps carrying a large wooden table. It was more like a chopping block. Another man brought up a large flat, bronze or gold, knife and placed it on the table, and the three men left back down the steps.

Two men began beating on drums below. Luke hadn't even known they were there before. The sound was exactly like the sound he had heard before he and Moon went through the portal. Moon and Luke looked at each other.

"Kapow!" The top of the pyramid exploded into activity. The crowd moaned. The charge from the peak danced and crackled more than Luke had previously seen. A blue-white beam shot from the pyramid and streaked up into the night sky. The peak crackled again and beams went horizontal in six different directions. The beams did not waver; they were like laser beams, steady, brilliant. In the distance beams rose from other far off places. The beams aimed at the same place in the sky.

"Orion's belt," Moon said. Luke looked up and saw all the beams from the ground were merging in that direction.

"That is correct, Sha-She," Shevay said. "You call it Orion. It is the place of our God. It is where we come from."

"Where are the six horizontal beams going?" Luke said.

"Other cities. They are pointing to their pyramids many distances away. This is the night when our God lines up with the stars. We worship and sacrifice at the exact same time."

"Sacrifice?" Grace said.

Shevay stood and two giants came up the steps. One stood at the wooden table and picked up the large knife. The other took hold of one of the feathered men. The feathered man howled and jerked from the giant, but it was useless. The giants bent the man over the table. One of the giants brought the large knife high in the air. Luke covered his eyes; no way could he look. He heard the knife whack into the wood. The crowd cheered. Through his fingers he saw the feathered headdress tumbled down the steps. Luke remembered they were wearing the same headdresses. The next feathered man started screaming and yelling more than the first. After another whack the screaming stopped and the second headdress tumbled down the steps. Luke knew the best thing to do was run. He lowered his hands and made ready to pull Moon to her feet. That is when he saw the two men standing to the side with their heads bare, but still very much attached to their shoulders. The next man was pulled to the block screaming. It was all symbolic. When the knife came down, the man threw his headdress down the steps.

Luke wiped sweat from his eyes. He took slow breaths and tried to relax himself. He looked over the crowd. He inspected the beams. Is this what happened on his earth in ancient times?

Luke was last, and when he was pulled from his seat, he howled and jerked like the others. He cringed when the knife hit the block, but he tossed his headdress down the steps as the rest had. "Bravo, Constable," Moon said.

Eventually the beams weakened and went out. Shevay stood and gave a speech. The crowd cheered. More torches were lit. Food was brought in on carts. The festival continued.

Moon took Luke's hand as they made their way to a food cart. Luke felt his face grow red, but he didn't think about it because he was too confused and worried about what would come next.

The festivities went on for hours. Luke didn't understand it all, but it appeared to him the event was a holiday like Christmas back home—a big deal. There was more and more about this world Luke did not understand. What was the deal with all those beams and the pyramid? What about the levitation of the stones? What about the precision of everything—the pyramid, the buildings and columns, the gold jewelry, the cobblestone streets? This part of this world was not a primitive society, not by a long shot.

Guards took them into a giant room in the pyramid to spend the night—big as a high school gym, with painted murals on the wall; the ceiling was painted black with shiny stars—looked real; a large bath with running water—big enough for all of them to bathe at the same time; beds with soft mattresses. There was gold everywhere.

Luke and Moon sat on a marble bench as the others explored and marveled at the room. "I bet you think different of your ancient history now," Moon said.

Luke didn't take his gaze from the starry ceiling. "What does this have to do with our history? We're in another world."

"Etoiles." Luke turned to see Grace pointing at the starry ceiling. "Stars," she said. Moon had given her a few French words to work on translation with Wak'o.

"Stars," Wak'o repeated.

Moon grinned and turned back to Luke. "Like I told you, ancients moved between the portals from this world to yours."

"She is right." Luke turned around to see Shevay coming through the grand door. This time he was alone. The giant, with all his majesty, sat down beside Luke and Moon. "As I got to know Glen Turner, as we told each other of our worlds, I realized his world is the same world our portals once went to."

"Do you go there anymore?" Luke said.

"The portals, as you call them, stopped working many years ago. One may blink open every now and then, but they are dangerous to use. However, when I was young, we journeyed through them. There were great cities there: Clearvoy, Pumapunku, Atlantis, Ponkari, and others."

Luke felt a chill. "Atlantis?"

"Yes."

"Were the people there like you?" Moon said.

"Like me?" Shevay shrugged his great shoulders. "There

were some Nephilim."

"But now you are cut off from them," Moon said.

"For now. Maybe the portals will open later."

"I wish they would open right now and get us back home," Luke said.

"There are the odd events that happen," Shevay said. "Glen Turner is one of them."

"Yeah, I guess we are the odd event too," Luke said, "and Orion."

"Yes," Shevay said, "but not Orion."

"You know about Orion?" Luke said.

"Of course." Shevay smiled. "I knew about all of you."

"Then you know about the portal we came through with those damn white-headed people," Luke said.

"Yes. It is the only continuously active portal that I am aware of."

"But you said they were all closed except for one blinking open now and then," Moon said.

"I said the ones that did open are dangerous. We have hidden the portals from the other peoples of this world, except for that one. The Florians found it. They do not really understand what it is. They sacrifice the odd animal that comes through it."

"And people," Luke said.

Shevay ignored the *people* part. "If the Florians didn't have something to sacrifice at times, I believe they would destroy the portal. They are a mean and crude people."

"Can you control the portals? Can you open and close them?" Moon said.

"Yeah," Luke said. "You can send us back to our world."

Shevay hesitated, but then said, "No. Years ago we could, but not anymore. The last time we controlled the portals, we sent a party through the portal that you came in through, but they did not come back."

"You sent Nephilim into it?" Moon said.

"Of course not. We sent guards."

Moon stood and approached Shevay. "Did any of these

185

guards have special knowledge or at least knowledge of how this civilization works?"

Shevay bowed his great, long head. "Two did. One was my grandson. The other was the key keeper."

"You said—" Luke started.

"My grandson was only quarter Nephilim."

"What was the key keeper?" Moon said.

"He was the wizard that opened the return portals with his special key. He was descended from key keepers as far back as time."

"And they never returned?" Moon said as she sat back down.

"The key keeper was young and a rogue. For some unknown reason, the key keeper abandoned my grandson and the party. He didn't want to return back to our world. My priests, Raceseyers, found him, but he closed the portal with his key before they could retrieve him. Years later they found him again and pulled him through a portal before he could close it."

"Why didn't he take the key and escape?" Luke said.

"The key doesn't work that way. It only opens the portal from the outside world. He could move from portal to portal in that world only. Once he was back here, only the Raceseyers could open a portal. Excuse me—once could open a portal."

"How did your priests find him, but can't find your grandson?" Luke asked.

"My priests could follow the force of the key. It is like a beacon."

"My guess is you killed the key keeper," Moon said.

"I cannot. My religion will not let me kill the wizard."

"Did he tell you where your grandson was?" Luke said.

"He would not."

"So you don't know where he went?" Luke said.

"I didn't for years, but now I do."

"How do you know now?" Moon said.

"The party took things with them. My grandson carried a small, star sphere," Shevay said.

"Will-o'-the-wisp!" Luke said.

Shevay smiled. "Yes. That's what Glen Turner called it."

"But what does that have to do with anything?" Moon said.

"When Karl appeared with his bell, there was a container of the green liquid from a star sphere in the bell."

"Xerum 525," Moon said.

"What?" Luke said.

"It was the stuff that powered the bell," Moon said. "They probably used up all the small sphere to propel the bell back to here. If Karl were to bring more spheres back to his time—"

"The Germans will win the war," Luke said. "But wait a minute. There are legends of Will-o'-the-wisps in my world."

"They must be different. They have to be or the Germans would have used them." Moon got up and paced. "Where is Karl now?"

"He left for the Florian portal," Shevay said.

Moon stopped pacing. "Why didn't you stop him?"

Shevay stood. His great height dwarfed Moon. "He said he would bring my grandson back to me."

"He's lying," Moon said. "You didn't give him that key, did you?"

"The key is lost and only descendants from the key keepers can use it anyway. Karl was going to bring my grandson back with the bell, but for some reason it exploded," Shevay said. His tone grew angry.

"Great Shevay, Karl and his people were horrible killers. They killed millions. We must stop him from going into the portal," Moon said.

"Can you bring me back my grandson?"

"Shevay, your grandson didn't survive the big war in that world, or I would have known about him," Moon said.

Shevay started for the door and guards appeared on both sides of it.

"Shevay, I'm sorry, but it is true," Moon said. "Karl and his people did horrible things."

Shevay turned back. "Haven't we all?" He turned and went through the door. The guards closed it behind him.

Luke pulled Moon back down to the bench. "What does this all mean?"

Moon stared at the door that Shevay had gone through. "If Karl makes it back, the world will be very different."

Luke held her hands in his. "Shevay said the portal is unstable. Who knows where Karl will go if he gets out through the portal."

"I'm not convinced Shevay doesn't still control the portals," Moon said. "Even if he doesn't, Karl is still a Nazi with knowledge that is too dangerous. There is still a Nazi movement in your time, waiting for the right opportunity to rise. He must not leave this world."

Luke didn't know how she planned on stopping him, but he believed she meant what she said.

Moon got up from the bench and paced. She stopped at the wall and looked at one of the murals. She walked along the wall looking as if she were reading the story the pictures portrayed.

Luke went to it. There was an army—it appeared to be Greeks or Romans, and some of the soldiers with long spears were killing giants. There was also some type of big swirl between the army and other giants. One of the giants on the safe side of the swirl was Shevay.

"That looks like Alexander and his army," Moon said.

"Alexander?" Luke said.

"Alexander the Great."

"You don't know that."

Moon pointed to the clothing and weapons. "It looks like it." She placed her hand on the swirl. "This is a portal. The painting shows the Nephilum escaping through it."

"Wait a minute." Luke laughed. "You're saying Alexander's army chased the Nephilum from my world?"

"I'm not saying it. This painting is. Alexander conquered everything he attempted to conquer. He had the greatest army ever."

Luke stepped back and took in the whole work of art. It sure looked like Alexander. "When I learned about Alexander in school, I don't remember the teacher saying anything about any giants."

"Maybe the giants were already gone from your world, but tried to go back for some reason and ran into Alexander's army," Moon said. "Maybe the historians in your world didn't record it, but the giants here did."

It made as much sense as anything else in this world. "I reckon they just happened to catch a portal open and clashed with Alexander or someone like him."

"Perhaps," Moon said, "or perhaps Shevay opened it."

Luke ran his hand across the mural. One of Alexander's soldiers had something in his hand that appeared to be a little, stone animal with a glowing, bright red "X" on it. "What do you think that is?"

"I don't have a clue," Moon said.

"It looks like an elephant." Luke turned to face Moon. "Or a mammoth."

"Amis. Friends," Grace said, pointing to another mural on the wall.

Wak'o repeated. "Friends."

The next morning the guards led the group into a large dining area. There were ten giants seated at a long table, and they watched the group come in. The guards sat the group at the same table. The giants with their elongated heads were intimidating, and Luke studied the room for an escape route. The giants smiled and appeared to welcome them.

Shevay came in and addressed the giants in their language. He then turned to Luke's group. "We welcome you here to have breakfast with us before your journey."

"Journey to where?" Grace whispered to Luke.

He whispered back, "I reckon we will find out soon."

The guards brought in smoked meat—appeared to be ham —and rough-looking bread. There were no eating utensils to eat with, just marble troughs from which to eat. It was the best meal by far Luke had enjoyed since coming to this land. The rest of the group seemed to agree as they dug in.

After a time Shevay turned to Moon. "Sha-She, I thought on what you said last night. I also thought of the things Karl had spoken to me about." He waved his hand toward the other giants. "This is the Royal Council and I have asked their advice. I am afraid they believe Karl is the one to trust, and you and the rest should be put to death."

Luke hadn't spotted that escape route yet, so he searched harder. Grace, sitting next to him, squeezed his arm.

Shevay laughed. "It is a joke. I learned that from Glen Turner."

Moon was cool. "That was a very good joke, Shevay."

Shevay took Moon by the hand and she rose from her seat. "I know the caliber of your father. He is a good man."

"How does the great Shevay know so much?"

Shevay raised his head and laughed. He looked back down at Moon. "I have, as you call them, spies. I know everything about this part of the world. I must if I am to remain the Great Shevay. I know of your returning through the portal with this man." He nodded toward Luke.

"You are very wise," Moon said.

"I believe you as I believed Glen Turner. He asked for nothing and you have asked for nothing but understanding. Karl asked for many things."

"Will the Great Shevay stop Karl from making it to the portal?"

Shevay clapped his hands and guards came into the room. They had leather bundles and weapons. "The Council has spoken on the matter, and I have agreed. We will not intervene."

"But he will—" Moon started.

"It is your concern. You must stop him." Shevay pointed to the guards. "Here are supplies for your journey. Be swift and be careful."

Moon and the group went to the supplies.

"Sha-She," Shevay said. "Karl has befriended many. Some of

the Reeze are waiting, and they are formidable."

"So are we," Adam said.

Shevay went to Adam. Even though Adam was muscular and strong, he was small beside Shevay. "You are Orion's son?"

"I am."

"Give my old friend my kindest regards. Tell him I can't wait to meet with him again." Shevay smiled, and then he, the guards, and The Council left the room.

Grace took hold of Adam's arm. "How does he know your father?"

"I don't know," Adam said.

Luke saw the look on Moon's face—she didn't believe Adam.

Adam turned to leave. "We go now."

Chapter 17

They stood at the top of the hill and looked back down on the city with its shiny pyramid clad in gold and white, its beautiful columns, towering obelisks, its grand cobblestone streets, its giant precision stone walls. From the high vantage point, Luke saw the symmetry to it all—it was perfect. In fact, he had never seen any city laid out so perfectly. If he ever came back, he meant to find out how they measured, how they cut the stones, how they drilled, welded, and formed everything. He had seen the levitation, so he knew some of that, but he wanted to know much more. Yes, indeed, he was a long way from the Ozarks.

"What you doing?" Luke turned to see Adam talking to Grace. She had a phone up taking pictures. She showed him the pictures. "Magic?"

"No," she said. "It is the kind of technology we have back in our world. It is like painting or drawing, but it's done electronically." Seeing that he did not understand, she pointed to the pyramid. "Uses power like the pyramid." He smiled and nodded.

Luke thought of his own phone and fumbled in his pack for it.

"No need, Luke," Grace said. "This is yours." She extended

it to him. "It fell from your pack back at the cave, and I've been taking pictures with it. I know I should have given it back, but I believed you and Moon would not have let me take pictures for one reason or another."

She looked like a helpless child, which Luke damn well knew she wasn't. He waved her away. "Keep it, Sweetie. The service is really spotty here."

"Thanks."

"Why did you think we wouldn't want you to take pictures?" Moon said.

"I don't know. Bad karma, I guess." She looked at the phone. "Won't be able to take many more; battery's about dead."

"I have a little solar charger in my pack," Luke said, fumbling around in it. He pulled it out and tossed it to her.

"Great, I can take more pictures. I want a record for when we return to our world." She crammed the phone and charger in her bag. "I will charge it when we rest."

Luke was glad she had the attitude that they would return. He hoped so too, but every day seemed to bring a new obstacle.

"My phone was taken by those people at the portal," Grace said. "What about yours, Moon?"

"I broke it on the teeth of one of them."

Luke laughed. "What about your camera? You had a camera too."

She dropped her pack and rummaged around in it. "Here it is." She pulled it out and tried to turn it on. "The batteries are dead and they can't be charged."

"We will get batteries at the next corner store," Grace said.

Moon and Grace laughed. As the others started down the hill, Luke took a long last look at the city. He had the feeling he would, indeed, be back because he had a growing doubt he would ever see Arkansas again.

Adam had led the way all day, staying far enough ahead to spot any danger. Luke brought up the rear. The trek was uneventful. The prairie was so open that no one could sneak up on them, but that was going to change before long. They soon would be coming to river bottoms and undulating hills. It would get a little more interesting with some of the Reeze buddied up to Karl.

Luke stayed about a hundred yards behind the rest, and it gave him plenty of time to think; there was nothing else to do. Grace had been his concern from the beginning, but he had her all wrong. She was a very capable person. She could kick ass as good as anyone in the group, and better than Luke. She was more than an equal on this adventure. Wak'o was an Osage, so from her he planned to glean as much knowledge of how to live off the land as he could. The Osage had been some of the fiercest and proudest of all the Native Americans. She was definitely an asset in this world. If Adam wasn't the leader, he was at least the first sergeant. When the situation appeared bleak, he was the man of the hour. He was one of the most important of the group. Moon was the leader. She was a machine, full of fighting ability and knowledge…and mystery. Now, that left Luke. What was he to this party? He had knowledge of primitive skills, but Adam and Wak'o had him on that. He was a good hunter, but again, so were Adam and Wak'o. No matter how you cut it, he brought less to the table than the others.

Luke caught something out of the corner of his eyes. It was a man running through the grass, and he was hell bent toward Wak'o. It was a Reeze.

"Look out!" Grace screamed. She was too far ahead to help Wak'o—so was Moon.

Wak'o saw him coming and squared up to him with her club in her hand.

The Reeze was too far for Luke to shoot. Luke sprinted toward Wak'o, but there was no way he was going to get there in time.

The Reeze raised his spear as he charged Wak'o. She deflected it with her club and lowered her shoulder. The Reeze rolled over her shoulder and slammed on the ground. She turned and swung her club down toward the Reeze, but missed. He raised his spear and drove it into her middle. Immediately, Grace came up and kicked the Reeze in the face. She then wheeled around and slammed her club into his temple. He lay on the ground quivering, dead, but still holding the spear. Grace eased it from his grasp as Wak'o moaned.

Moon ran up and grabbed hold of Wak'o. "I've got you, Honey." She turned to Grace. "You will have to pull it out. Now pull fast and straight. Do it quickly."

Luke ran up to the group. "Oh, no."

Grace squared up. "Okay. Okay." She took a few deep breaths and jerked the spear straight back. Wak'o screamed and fell limp in Moon's arms.

Luke and Grace helped Moon lower her to the ground. Luke pulled his water bottle from his bag and handed it to Moon, as she talked soothingly to Wak'o in French.

Luke remembered his first-aid kit in his pack. He fished it out and offered it to Moon. "I have this."

"Luke," Moon said slowly and calmly. "Hand me two of the biggest bandages in the kit, and the tape."

"Okay." Luke fumbled with it, and Grace took it from him and assisted Moon.

Adam ran up and towered over the group. "Will she survive?"

"How far to the river?" Moon said, not answering Adam's question.

"Not far." Adam pointed to some cottonwood trees. "There."

"We must make a litter to get her there," Moon said.

"We can make one from cottonwood poles," Luke said.

Adam turned to Luke. "You were the rear. This should have been prevented."

Luke instantly knew he was right. It was his own fault. They were strung out too far from each other. If he had only been closer—

Adam backhanded Luke, sending him to the ground. "It

should have been you."

Moon snapped. "Adam, get me a litter, now!" Adam looked at Luke for a short spell and then turned and ran back toward the river.

Grace offered her hand to Luke, but he brushed it away. "He's right," Luke said.

"Shut that up," Moon said. "We are on a mission. The mission comes first. Now you two go help with that litter." Grace offered her hand again and Luke took it.

As they jogged to the river, Grace said. "You think she will be okay?"

Luke had to shake the blame from his mind; Moon was right, and it did no good. He turned to Grace. "If anyone can help her, Moon can." Grace wiped her eyes as they ran to the river.

A fingernail moon settled over the camp as Wak'o quietly moaned in the darkness from the pain. Luke couldn't help but admire her strength. If he were suffering with such a wound, he would probably be screaming.

Luke tried to stay vigilant as he stood at his post along the river, but it was no use. He wasn't much good to them tonight —he couldn't help do anything else but blame himself for what had happened. He looked across the camp to see Adam's silhouette high in a cottonwood tree. No one would get close with him up there.

Fish flounced in the darkness and owls and coyotes called from the black abyss as Luke lay his bow beside him on a log, which had been deposited there during some past flood. He turned to see the two women bent over Wak'o, silhouetted by the fire. For some reason it reminded him of the scene in *Gone With The Wind* where Scarlett and Prissy are delivering Melanie's baby. Yeah, he thought, gone with the wind just like his own world.

He reached over and picked his bow back up. He squeezed it with both hands, could feel the grain in the wood, which he hadn't been able to sand away. He felt the small knots. If he were back home, it would have been said of them, that they gave the bow character, but here, they were just knots that were on this particular piece of wood that he had used at the time. Back home the bow would have been a toy to play with. Yes, it was a weapon, but, of course, there were modern weapons that were exceptionally better to kill game with. Here on this prairie, in this world, the hickory was a state-of-the-art weapon, not a toy. He raked his finger across the stone point on his cane arrow—sharp as any metal point, very capable to kill. He sighed and looked up at the moon; it looked like it was smiling back at him with its sideways grin. Why hadn't he been closer? Why had he allowed Wak'o to be injured? The answer came back from the old moon— he was the amateur here.

Luke caught movement down the river. He nocked his arrow and stood. Green orbs floated above the river about a hundred yards downstream, will-o'-the-wisps. There were at least thirty, maybe more. If each one was held by a Reeze meant to do them harm, it was over. They moved slowly toward their camp. Luke turned to look up at Adam, but was startled to see Adam already next to him.

"With that many Reeze, we don't stand a chance," Luke said.

Adam said nothing, just moved past Luke and stood in the river.

Moon went to Luke. "What does Adam think?"

"Hell if I know."

Moon moved to the river's edge and said something to Adam in their native language. Adam replied. Moon waded out into the stream with him.

"What are y'all doing?" Luke said.

"We must catch one," she said.

"Catch one?" Luke said. "A spear is what we will catch if y'all don't get out of that river and take cover."

"Luke, these are alone," Adam said. "They are not being carried. We must catch one. You stand guard while we do it."

Luke had no idea what they were up to, but, hell, he had little idea now what was going on as a whole. He looked back to see

Grace standing over Wak'o with her arms spread, questioning. Luke returned the gesture.

The orbs floated closer and Adam was right; they were alone like a colony of giant fireflies. They were not a constant—some light green, some a deeper and darker green. One would blink out, but another would slowly form, as a person might turn up a dimmer switch. Moon tried to grab one and it came apart into a million pieces like sparks and disappeared. She tried another with the same results.

"Esva," Adam said.

"Esva?" Moon replied.

Another one drifted to Moon and she slowly took hold of it. It remained formed in her hand. "I've got it!" She turned toward the bank and it exploded silently into a million fireflies and disappeared. "Damn it."

One drifted to the edge of the river and Luke set his bow down. "I will get this one."

"No, Luke, only the dark ones," Adam said. As he said it, the orb blinked out. Luke then understood. The ones he had seen blinking out were all lighter. The dark ones stayed bright, just like the ones the Reeze had here at the river before and the ones back at the bell.

A big orb, the size of a basketball, drifted toward Adam. "Esva," Adam said softly as if he were trying to sooth a wild horse he was trying to catch. He slowly squeezed his hands around the orb as if he were plucking a giant apple from a tree. "Esva," he soothed.

"You got it," Luke said.

"Remove the bandage from her," Adam said as he turned toward the shore with the orb. Moon climbed from the water and went to Grace and Wak'o. They worked slowly and delicately to remove the bandage. Wak'o moaned through gritted teeth—she never moaned loudly, ever.

Some of other orbs appeared to stop moving in the water and just float in place. Others followed Adam out of the water. Barely a whisper now, Adam continued, "Esva."

The orbs followed Adam into the camp, emitting their green, liquid, light making everything glow—even the fire seemed to be green. Adam gingerly lowered the orb down to Wak'o's wound. The blood running from it appeared to turn green. "Esva," Adam whispered as he slowly moved his hands to the side of the orb and squeeze. The orb changed form as a round water-balloon might if you were to squeeze its sides. It elongated and began entering the wound. Wak'o gasped. The orb continued its flow into the wound like sand from an hourglass. The other orbs began undulating around the people in a slow circle like a green, dreamy carousel. Adam eased the last of the orb into the wound and held his hand over it. He slid his other hand to cover the exit wound. His hand and the area around the wound emitted a purple glow.

"What—" Grace began, but Moon put her hand over Grace's mouth.

Wak'o began to convulse. The orbs began undulating faster as they went around in the merry-go-round. "Esva," Adam said more loudly. "Esva." The orbs moved faster and faster and faster. "Esva." The orbs moved faster still until they blended into one stream of green around the people. "Esva." The orbs moved faster still. Wak'o shook violently as Moon and Grace looked to Adam for what to do. "Esva!" Adam shouted. The orbs spun like a centrifuge, drawing other orbs in from the river as a tornado draws in debris. Adam snapped his hand away from the wound. The orb slowly slid out like a snake or smoke. It was now brown, not green. It shot up erect and then straight up and out like a laser. All the other orbs melded into it as it went straight to the heavens like the beam of a spotlight.

"What the hell?" Luke said.

The beam went up and up and up until all the orbs followed it like a tail. It went up until it was just a dot like one of the many stars, and then it was gone.

Wak'o slumped and began breathing softly.

Adam brushed Wak'o's hair from her face and said, "Mieux?" He had been listening to Moon's French lessons. Luke had, too, and he knew it meant "better."

Luke watched Adam tend Wak'o, and Grace smiled at Luke. They were at the same conclusion: Adam was in love with Wak'o.

Moon stood and nodded. "Okay. Okay." She turned and went to the river.

Grace looked at Luke. "Okay what?" Luke shrugged his shoulders and went to Moon.

Moon was looking at the smiling moon. "You want to know what just happened, don't you, Luke?"

"Oh, I think I've got it figured out." Luke picked up a flat rock and skipped it across the black river. "Spacemen just sent down—"

"Don't be a smart ass."

"Okay, Moon. What just happened and what does *esva* mean?"

"You will have to ask Adam what *esva* means because I don't have a clue. I'm not exactly sure what those orbs are either." She turned to face Luke, her face picking up the red glow of the fire. "Some kind of plasma, or residue of the magnetic field, fairies: will-o'-the-wisp." She turned back to the river. "I've never seen my people do what Adam just did. I don't think my people know how to do what Adam just did."

"Your people are Adam's people."

"Only half of Adam."

"Well, the other half are my people only at another time in history."

"I'm not so sure." She turned back to Luke.

Luke was more lost for understanding than he had been when he first came through the portal. "What do you mean, Agent?"

"Remember the story I told you about the disappearance of Orion from that farm in 1854?"

"Come on, Moon, cut to it. You know I remember."

"Was he just a farmer, a slaveholder? How was he able to survive here being just a redneck farmer from 1854? Why do the Nephilim know about him? Shevay called him his old friend. My people have always been leery around Adam. I am beginning to think it's not because Orion is just different."

"What are you saying?"

"I don't know, Luke, but there is something more to Orion than we know."

Grace ran up to them pointing back to Adam and Wak'o. "Look!" Wak'o was sitting up. Adam was helping her to drink from Moon's water bottle. "Luke, Adam wants you."

The bleeding had stopped, but Wak'o was still in bad shape. Moon and Grace took over tending her as Adam grabbed up his spear.

"Luke, you have to go for Orion," Adam said.

"What can he do?" Moon said.

"She will die here," Adam said. "We have no way to carry her. We may be attacked by the Reeze at any time."

"Like she said, what can he do?" Luke said

A bird whistle came from the darkness. Adam turned in the direction from which it had come. Another bird answered. "They are here," Adam said.

"I'll put out the fire," Luke said.

"No," Adam said. He pulled Wak'o away from the firelight. "Grace, you stay with Wak'o."

"Okay," Grace said.

"Luke and I will take our posts," Moon said.

Adam nodded and slipped into the darkness.

The sliver of moon shed very little light to see by, but Luke was ready if anything came close. He had an arrow on his bow.

As the minutes passed, he was less afraid, but more anxious. From the darkness he heard a rustle and a thud. He squeezed his bow so tightly his hand hurt. He heard a whistle. It was Moon's signal that things were good. He relaxed his bow a little. She was deadly.

Luke strained to listen. Someone was wading the river. He focused his eyes with all he had, but it was so dark. Suddenly a loud splash came from the river, and then silence. Adam whistled from the river. He was also deadly.

More birdcalls came from the darkness. Luke found the situation almost humorous. It was like an old western and he was surrounded by Indians, but he was the one with the bow and arrows. A man screamed with pain. Adam whistled. Instantly the humor was gone. It was going to be a long night.

The gray light of dawn was never more welcome as it was now. Luke had not shot one arrow, had not seen one enemy. Adam and Moon had taken care of it all night. Luke believed they had killed a dozen or more. He found himself shaking and it wasn't from the cold.

He saw someone walking along the river, raised his bow; but then he heard Adam whistle. Luke exhaled the longest breath ever.

"They are gone," Adam said as he walked up.

"Or dead," Luke said.

"You must go for Orion," Adam said. "You must go without rest."

"I will. I will be fine."

"No need." Moon came up to them. "Grace has gone."

"What?" Luke looked back toward the coals of the fire. "How do you know she went for Orion?"

"Wak'o told me. She left about an hour ago."

"I will catch her," Luke said and started.

"Luke," Moon said. He turned. "You can't catch her."

"Damn it!" Luke threw his bow to the ground. He felt guilty. It was all his fault. "She will be killed."

Moon shook her head. "Do you really think you are more qualified for the mission than she is?"

Luke picked up his bow and walked by Moon to the coals of the fire. He placed a few twigs on it and fanned to get it started, and then put bigger pieces of wood on. Of course, Moon was right. He was the least qualified for the mission. The only reason Adam had suggested it was because he needed Grace here to help protect Wak'o.

Adam and Moon moved Wak'o back to the fire. She was still alive thanks to the orb, but she was still critical. Luke knew it was his fault. And now Grace was on the race of her life because she knew Luke wasn't the man for the job. He had come to save her, but look at him now.

Moon put a large stick on the fire. "Grace will be fine; she is so athletic. They will never catch her."

Luke turned to go to the river. "I will get fish for the fire."

Moon followed him. "Luke, you can't blame yourself for this —not for any of this. You are not a trained soldier. You're not a trained law—" Moon lowered her head. "I'm sorry."

"No, Agent. You are right. I'm not trained, nor qualified to be here. I've only survived this long because of you and Adam." He looked off in the distance. "And now, Grace."

"I think you have made a good accounting for yourself. There are few less Scrain because of you."

"Oh, yeah. I'm a regular one man army. Just leave me alone. At least I can hunt and fish so let me go do that." Luke turned from Moon and went to the river. She didn't follow, and for that, he was grateful. He waded into the river to wait for a fish to swim by, and he thought and worried about Grace.

Chapter 18

Grace ran like an animal. She was afraid, but not afraid of the Reeze chasing her. She was afraid her leather sandals would fly off her feet. She had outdistanced the man, but he wouldn't give up. She probably could outlast him, but she didn't want to burn up all her precious energy right off the bat, miles to go before she reached the mountains and Orion—if she could even find him.

She had to force her machinelike legs to slow the pace. It wasn't an easy thing to do—they wanted to go. Instinct told her body to pour it on—get away as best as you can. She looked back—he was gaining. She talked to herself, "You can do this. You can do this." As he drew closer, she slipped her leather top down, revealing one of her breasts—all is fair in love and war, and this was most definitely war. He grew closer until he was only fifty yards or so behind her. She tripped and fell, and then stumbled back to her feet. She hoped it looked real as she turned to face him with fright and self-pity dripping from her face. The man ran up to her with his spear raised, but he hesitated and his eyes found her exposed breast. Bingo! He never saw the club until it was inches from his head, way too late. Too bad there is no Internet here Grace thought. The man's wife back at the hut could really use www.find-me-new-caveman.ugg.

She looked back the way they had come and saw no one else. She breathed a sigh of relief as she looked down at the bludgeoned man. No need wasting the man's death. She took his waterskin, found a little jerky on him, and picked up his spear. He didn't have anything else worth taking.

She jogged along for another mile, came over a rise, and almost ran into a camp of six or seven Reeze. She skidded to a stop. They were skinning an animal—antelope maybe—and all stood as she stopped. She was caught off guard and was calculating whether to run back or forward when one of them motioned for her to pass. She made a wide circle and went on. She remembered Adam saying not all Reeze were in with the German, but there was no doubt they knew who she was. They watched her go and then went back to the job of cleaning the animal.

As she ran, she kept looking back and didn't dare stop to rest, hoping they didn't change their minds and come after her. The prairie soon gave way to trees and bushes. She worried anything could be hiding behind any one of them.

The water was soon gone. She knew she should not have eaten the salty jerky. Now water was on her mind, right behind wondering if her going after Orion was such a good idea. Yeah, she was better fit for running than Luke was. Yeah, she was the most athletic. She, with the help of Wak'o, had been surviving just fine. She probably could defend herself better than Luke could. Those were the pros. But there were the cons as well. First, she wasn't exactly sure how to find Orion. She had listened to Luke and Adam describe the place, but now she wasn't so sure. She would just keep heading east and hope she found him. Second, she was not even sure she could lead Orion back to the party. Third, Luke had made a mistake back there and had let the Reeze get to Wak'o, but had he really made the mistake, or had Adam just expected too much and blamed Luke. Luke was a hunter—the best hunter she knew. He was a true survivalist, not just some armchair want-to-be. He wasn't a warrior, but neither was she. However, both were quickly becoming warriors. Now that she really studied on it, and if it was on a scale, Luke probably was more qualified for this journey. She shook her head and slapped her face. No need to second guess now. She was here now and she was going to do it right, somehow. But right now, she needed water.

The ground in front of her fell off into a slow grade ravine with a river below. Yeah, Baby, just what she was looking for. She skidded down the long slope to the water. She threw her bag and tools aside and fell to the water's edge and drank and drank and drank. Oh, what a relief. The river was as clear as purified water. All the water in this land was good and sweet, nothing like back home.

She scooted back onto her butt and admired the babbling river. This was paradise. This must have been what the Garden of Eden looked like. She had always loved hiking in the wild. She loved camping and just enjoying nature. The Ozarks were beautiful, but they even fell short to this place.

She reached around to get her waterskin to fill for the rest of the journey. Six Reeze were there, spears raised. Too late and too many for the naked breast maneuver. Yeah, Luke should have been the one for this mission.

Luke looked out at the vast prairie and wondered how Grace was making out. It was getting dark and she would have had to make good time to arrive at Orion's cave by now. Luke was relieved that the day before he had described the mountain range where Orion lived. It was easy—it looked so much like the Ozarks where he and Grace were from. But it was a big area, and if she didn't remember Luke's details, or if he had gotten the description wrong, she could get lost. And if she had to spend the night alone on the prairie—

"Luke." Moon put her hand on his shoulder. "It's no use worrying. It's out of your hands."

Luke turned. She was right, but being right didn't stop him from worrying or blaming himself.

"She will make it," Moon said.

"How's Wak'o?"

"The bleeding hasn't started back, but she is weak. She would probably be dead if not for the orbs."

Luke nodded. "And we are sitting ducks here." He kicked at a weed. "The Reeze were friends with Orion and Adam. How could that Nazi sway them?"

"Only some of them."

Luke took both of Moon's hands and looked into her eyes. "What can Orion do? Why does Adam want him here?"

"I told you; there is more to Orion than we know."

Luke dropped her hands and turned back toward the prairie. "You don't know that."

"Luke…" She didn't finish.

"Back home I know the wild like I know the inside of my cabin. I can eat off the land. I can build a fire in the rain. I can make my own clothes from nature." He turned back toward Moon. "I can survive there. But there the spirits are in the wild, the spirits of nature. They are not tangible. They are…just out of sight. You believe they are real, but you have no proof. It's like God. It's like the Indian spirits. We believe in them. It's faith. But here you see things. Here you have real magic, like those orbs. This is more than I can comprehend. This is more than I understand."

"Those orbs are a mystery, indeed, but no more of a mystery than you have in your world."

"There are no damn floating orbs in my world."

Moon smiled. "People have been reporting those will-o'-the-wisps since recorded history and you know that."

"Those are just fairytales."

"Are they really?" She took Luke's hands again. "Here's a mystery then: how do the geese find their way when they migrate? How do they even know to migrate? Hmm? How about this: when armadillos want to die, how do they know where the highway is?"

Luke admired her smiling face. She was more beautiful every

time he looked at her. But her smile fell and she looked past him. He turned to see a good many Reeze silhouetted on the prairie by the fading purple sky, reminded him of Indians in a western.

"We're in trouble," Moon said.

"I didn't make enough arrows," Luke said.

"Take your position!" Moon said as she ran toward the fire. "Adam, they're coming."

Luke jumped behind the breastwork they had fashioned from driftwood. Everything was ready. Clubs were there, extra arrows, rocks, and spears. Adam carried Wak'o in his arms and placed her in the prepared bed they had made for her. Adam handed her a spear.

Adam turned to Luke. "You ready?"

"I'm ready." He was as ready as he could be, but was it enough?

The little fort was on the highest point in the area, and they had a commanding view of the prairie and river below. They had cut down anything close that would give the attackers something to hide behind. It was about as good as they could do.

Moon placed wood on the fire about thirty yards away. They hoped it would draw the attacker's attention to that, and if they attacked towards it, they would be easy pickings.

Moon slid into the fort. The three were situated like quails, their backs to each other. "We can't let them get in here with us. We don't have room to fight. I know it's a small target, but we must hit them in the head."

"In the head?" Luke said. "You don't ask for much."

"Luke is right," Adam said. "That will be hard."

Moon laid her pistol in front of her. "A spear or arrow to the chest may not stop them right off—more than likely it won't—and they will be among us." She turned to Luke. "I must conserve my bullets. If at all possible, you shoot first with that bow. You should be able to stop them before they get to us. We will finish what gets through."

208

"You must think I'm Robin Hood." Luke felt a heavy responsibility settle on him like a boulder.

"I know how well you shoot," Moon said. "Don't think about what if you miss; think about how many you can stop."

"Here they come!" Adam said.

Two sprinted across the prairie toward the fire with their clubs high in the air. They stopped at the fire and searched frantically for someone to club. Luke shot one in the temple and he collapsed. The other finally saw the fort, but before he could take a step, Luke put an arrow in his throat. He dropped his club and grabbed for the arrow, but the blood spewed and he sank to the ground.

"You were a little low on that last shot," Moon said.

"I will do better on the next one," Luke said as he placed another arrow on the bow.

"Here come four more," Moon said.

They zeroed in on the fort this time, coming in single file again, screaming as they came. Luke shot the first one in the head. The second one tripped over him. When he got back to his feet, Luke shot him in the head, as well. Before Luke could get another arrow ready, the other two were at the fort. Moon dropped both of them with her pistol.

Luke heard a loud shrill behind him. He turned to see a Reeze on the end of Adam's spear. Moon whirled and hit the man in the face with a club. Adam threw the dead man away from the fort.

Luke looked back out across the prairie. More Reeze had appeared there. "Adam, how many Reeze are in the tribe?"

Adam looked to where Luke was looking. "It appears Karl has fooled many of them."

Moon pulled out Luke's binoculars and surveyed the men. "There are more than fifty."

"Are they getting ready to attack?" Luke said.

"No. It appears they are settling in for a wait. Some are circling around down river."

"They will wait until it is completely dark," Adam said.

"I won't be able to shoot before they are upon us," Luke said.

"We can't leave," Moon said. "They have us circled."

"Now I know how Custer felt," Luke said.

Adam stood and raised his spear. The Reeze across the prairie raised theirs in reply. Adam looked down at Luke and Moon. "If they don't leave, they will all be dead."

Moon dropped the binoculars back into Luke's bag. "You have magic that I'm not aware of, Adam?"

"Orion will come," Adam said. "He will come."

Luke looked at Adam's face. He really believed Orion would save the day. But how was that old man going to get them out of this fix?

"Orion will come. You will see."

Moon sat down beside Luke and smiled. "We need some of that real magic now." She winked.

Luke looked up at Adam. He slowly nodded. "Maybe we will get it."

Grace's wrists burned when the man tied the straps around them. She should have been more on guard, but it was way too late to think about that now. Now was the time to plan what to do next.

They shoved her along, one man leading her from a rope around her neck like she was a horse—ass is more like it. They followed the river, going to who knows where. She wanted to cry, but she wouldn't give the heathens the satisfaction. In fact, the first chance she got, she was going to put a foot up beside one of their heads.

As they walked, she saw mountains rise up in the east. Her heart leaped. They looked just like the Ozarks back home. She recognized the hill top she was supposed to be looking for, the one Luke and Adam described. But they weren't going that direction. They were walking south. She was close. Why hadn't she been more careful?

After about an hour, the men stopped to drink and eat. One

of the men who had been in the rear and away from her walked up to her with a cheesy grin on his face. She knew this wasn't going to be good. He tried to pull her breast from her top. She kneed him in the groin and when he yelled and bent, she kneed him in the face, flipping him to the ground. He rolled on the ground moaning. She stomped his head. The man holding the leash jerked her to the ground. She felt as if her head was being yanked off.

"Aagoo!" The man with the leash said, placing a spear to her belly. He said more garbage that she barely heard, but she got the message.

The other men shook the man on the ground. He didn't move. From the odd position of his head and neck, she knew he was dead. All the men began pulling at their hair and chanting more gibberish.

The man with the spear yanked on the rope, hauling Grace to her feet. He pulled a large bone knife from his belt and raised it high. Grace wanted to shield herself from it, but her hands were lashed behind her.

The man with the knife shrieked. There was an arrow stuck through his hand and the knife fell. The cane arrow was almost perfectly halfway. It had a stone point on one end and feathers on the other.

They all turned to see a man standing on the rise above the river. Grace thought him to look like Moses.

All the men raised their hands at the same time and said, "Orion!"

"Orion," Grace said under her breath.

Orion raised his bow over his head and yelled something down to the men. They immediately ran down the river like scared deer. The one appeared odd, running with the arrow swinging from his hand.

Orion descended the rise slowly, but deliberately. Grace thought the river would surely part before him. She closed her eyes and thanked God for sending an angel at just the right time.

Orion started across the river from his direction, and Grace started from hers. They met almost in the middle. They were next to each other before they even spoke a word.

"You must be Grace," Orion said as he pulled a stone knife and cut the straps from her wrist.

Grace pulled the leash from her neck. "And you are Orion."

Orion looked across the river. "You are alone?"

"Yes."

"Where are the others? Where is Adam?"

Yes, he looked like Moses, but he wasn't Moses. He was just an old man. How in the world was he going to help get Wak'o off the prairie? How was he going to rescue the others?

The purple sky was mostly gone when the Reeze began building campfires on the prairie. Adam warned it was just a diversion to mask the coming attack. The fires were just something to hold Luke and the group's attention while the Reeze eased in for the kill. Luke could still make out their silhouettes, but it would soon be too dark for even that. He knew they would attack then. He looked down at his hands—they were trembling. His teeth were even chattering.

"This will be close quarters fighting," Moon said. "They will be right on us before we see them. Your bow will be no good, so get a club."

Wak'o whispered something in French and Moon replied.

"What did she say?" Luke said.

"She wants us to leave her and take to the river."

"We will fight right here," Adam said.

"Yeah, that's what I told her."

"Listen!" Adam said as he cupped his ear.

"They're in the river," Luke said.

Adam started over the barricade. "I will get them first."

"No!" Moon said. "That's what they want. They want to split us up. We stay together."

Adam backed down and nodded. "Yes, Kayeeya, I will stay."

Luke grasped his tomahawk so tightly his hand hurt. His

inside was just a jumble of hard knots—he hated the dark anyway. At the same time, it was the highest rush he had ever known. His hobby back home was living and hunting primitive. He had never thought about primitive war, but it was on him now, and it was an adrenaline overload.

He looked over at Moon in the fading light. She was as focused and coiled as a lion ready to strike. Her pistol was ready and a club set by her feet. She had closed her eyes—she was listening. She had all her faculties focused on the sounds around her. Luke had done that very thing while hunting back home.

Luke turned to Adam. He was standing with a spear in his hand, and he smiled down and nodded at Luke. Luke smiled back. There was no one better to have on your side than Adam. He was simple and true. He did things with a purpose. He meant what he said, and he backed up what he said with action.

Wak'o sat below Adam, bundled in a robe. She was still very sick. They had stopped the bleeding with the orbs, but she was still in rough shape. She still held a stone knife in her hand. The scene made Luke think of Bowie at the Alamo. If all went bad, she would go out fighting. Luke turned back to the prairie and prayed this didn't turn out like the Alamo.

The fires were all that could be seen now—darkness was complete. Luke could still see his own companions up close, but that was all he could make out in the draping darkness. The Reeze would be com—

"Yaa!" A man jumped over the barricade. Luke swung the tomahawk like a tennis racket and rolled the man back over the logs. It was purely instinctive, like shooting when a covey of quails explodes in front of you. He heard a yell and thud behind him. He whirled to see Adam pulling his spear from a wide-eyed man's chest. Then it was over and quietness settled back in.

"They were probably just seeing if we were still here," Moon said.

"Now they will come in force, right?" Luke said.

Moon turned to him and with a faint smile said, "I think they will."

Luke looked at her for a long spell, but she said nothing else, just smiled. The weak smile said it all—they didn't stand a chance. It was the Alamo.

Luke heard a screech. He turned with his tomahawk in time to see a red streak fly across the sky and land among the Reeze's fires. After a short pause, there was a small explosion. Then another came across the sky. It looked like a giant bottle rocket. It exploded just before it hit the ground.

"What is it?" Luke said.

"I don't know," Moon said.

Another *bottle rocket* streaked across the sky, and exploded close to the fire. There were screams. It must have hit some of the Reeze. More rockets came, one after the other. They had found their mark as the screams and yells intensified.

"They are rockets or mortars," Moon said.

"In this world?" Luke said.

Adam began laughing.

Moon turned to him. "You know what it is?"

The river became alive with splashing and churning.

"They are running!" Moon said. "They are leaving."

A streak ran across to the river and exploded. Luke could plainly see the Reeze in a panic in the river from the flash of the explosion.

Moon said, "Look," as she pointed toward the campfires. Luke looked that way to see a big silhouette between them and the fire. A rocket zoomed from the silhouette and landed on the other side of the river, hastening the Reeze retreat.

Adam laughed harder.

"What is it, Adam?" Luke said.

"Orion."

Slowly the silhouette grew closer. It was Orion and Grace sitting atop of a mammoth.

When they approached, Grace slid from the beast and ran to the barricade. Holding something in her hand, she ran to her friends. "Are y'all okay?" When she was sure everyone was good, she said, "Check this out!" She held up a giant bottle rocket. It was made of bamboo. "Scared the hell out of them."

Luke scrambled across the barricade and squeezed Grace. "Thank God you are safe."

"Yeah, and thank Mr. Orion."

Orion slid from the giant beast. Moon hugged him. "Glad to finally meet you. You arrived just in time."

Luke took the rocket from Grace and turned to Orion. "Where did you get the gun powder to make this?"

"I made it, simplest thing in the world."

"The Reeze didn't think it so simple," Moon said, as she took the rocket from Luke and inspected it.

"I don't know why they have turned bad," Orion said. "I have always gotten along good with them."

"They have fallen in with bad company," Adam said as he climbed across the barricade with Wak'o in his muscular arms. "We must get her home."

Orion squeezed one of Adam's arms. "My brave son."

"You were right," Adam said. "We should always stay away from the giants."

"This time you were the one who was right, Adam. You did what you had to do as I always have." Orion inspected the girl, turned to the giant mammoth and patted him on the trunk. The large animal went down on its knees like a circus elephant, and Adam climbed on its back with Wak'o.

Orion was like Moses and Tarzan all wrapped up in one Luke thought—a hell of a good man to know.

Luke built up the fire as Adam placed Wak'o on the bed, and Orion concocted some sort of medicine or potion. This was the first time Luke had felt safe in quite a long time. All the natives were afraid of the mammoths down below the cave, so he wasn't worried about an attack.

Luke saw Moon sitting at the cave opening, watching the sun barely casting its first glow in the east. He sat beside her. "My second most favorite time of the day."

She kept her eyes on the pink sky and said, "What is your favorite?"

"When you see this same glow in the west."

Moon turned and took both Luke's hands in hers. "Do you still want to go home?"

Luke wanted to say, "Of course," but it didn't come out. He found he wasn't sure—strange. But was it really? After all, he had always dreamed of this life. This was paradise.

Moon smiled and squeezed his hands. "I thought as much." She turned back to the east and the smile slowly fell.

Luke admired her face; the pink light of the sun accented it better than any makeup, her auburn hair wild, yet perfect.

"He has made it to the portal by now," she said. "He was smart by befriending and fooling the Reeze. They bought him time."

"Maybe not." Luke said it, but didn't believe that. She was right; he had plenty of time to get there.

She turned back to him. "Yes. If he was going to make it, he has made it by now. And if, indeed, that is the case, I have failed my mission."

"He could have been hurt or killed by those white-headed heathens."

She looked down at the animals on the prairie. "You know why the mammoths are still here and not extinct as they are in your world?" She didn't wait for an answer. "The people here are afraid of them. It may be just because they are so big, or it may be for religious reasons. I don't know. In your world they were hunted, and that may be why they went extinct—we will never know for sure." She turned to Luke and looked squarely into his eyes. "All those portals between the two worlds were closed from this side by the giants to keep this world from being contaminated or invaded. The Germans have the bell and they will return and screw it up."

"Shevay made it sound like the portals were broken," Luke said.

"I don't believe that for a second. When I saw that mural of Alexander, I knew for sure then that Shevay controls the portals. He can open them and he can shut them when he wants."

Luke thought on it. "But if that were the case, why did he let Karl go? He sure as hell will contaminate this world."

"Maybe his grandson really was lost through the portal and he believes Karl can bring him back."

"So you believe Shevay and the giants control the portals and can open and close them at will? I don't know if I believe that, Moon."

"Yes, I believe the giants can." Moon hesitated. "Others."

"Others? What others?"

She stood. "I'm not sure."

Luke stood and took her by the shoulders. "What does that mean?"

"Maybe not of this world."

"You mean aliens—spacemen?"

She ran her fingers through her hair. "I'm not sure—we're not sure." She looked back toward Orion. "But we know things that suggest there are others."

Luke saw she was looking at Orion. He turned her back toward him. "Moon, what are you talking about?"

"You now know about the Nephilim. There were others. We have found proof, but it is held close to the vest by the government. Atlantis was real. The Inca didn't build all that stuff in South America—at least, not alone. The Egyptians had help."

"What evidence of this do you have?"

"Advanced tools. Advanced weapons. Things found among ancient artifacts."

"I never read that in a book or saw that on TV."

"The archaeologists found themselves dead."

"Come on, Moon, you expect me to believe…?" But he saw it in her eyes. She was telling the hard truth.

"Luke, if you get back, that knowledge can't get out. It

would be like a gold rush. That technology would be hunted for as nothing else ever has. Governments would spend all their treasuries to find it. Your civilization cannot handle it. And more than that, we don't know what else is to be discovered."

Luke turned and looked back out over the prairie. "I don't know what to believe out of you. You have told me so many lies. You have misled me. I don't know who or what you are."

"I told you. I am—"

Luke turned toward her. "Don't!" He put his hand up. "No more. I don't want to hear any more."

"I understand."

"I will help you stop that German because I've seen and believe that much, but then I am finished with it."

"Okay, Luke. I don't blame you. Maybe we can get Adam and Orion to help us."

"Help do what?"

Luke turned to see Orion approaching. Luke cleared his throat. "Mr. Orion, it appears someone else has come from our world, a German."

"Prussian," Moon said.

"Well, what about this Prussian?" Orion said. "Let's invite him here. Maybe he has knowledge to get us home again."

"Orion, he has knowledge of the Nephilim that he wants to take back to his evil government. He will try to go through the Florians' portal."

"They will kill him," Orion said.

"He is resourceful," Luke said. "He has already manipulated some of the Reeze as you well know. He may do the same with the white-headed people."

"If he makes it back, he will have the knowledge to travel freely between the two worlds," Moon said. "He will come back to conquer."

"As did Alexander," Orion said.

Luke wondered where that came from.

A buckskin clad Reeze started up the entrance to the cave. Luke ran for his bow.

"No, Luke!" Adam said as he wrestled the bow from Luke. "He is a friend."

The man handed Orion two loaves of bread and they spoke in the Reeze's language. The man had a lot of hand gestures as he described something. Orion handed him a small leather pouch and the man left back down the trail.

Adam smiled. "That is good, very good."

"It appears the Prussian did not persuade the Reeze king," Orion said. "He was captured. The followers were executed."

"But there were many," Luke said.

"They defied the king and now they are all dead," Orion said.

"Did he kill the Prussian?" Moon said.

"No."

"Then we must go there. He must be eliminated."

"He escaped along with three or four others a few hours ago."

Moon turned to Luke. "I must go now. He is heading for the portal."

"Alone?" Luke said. "I will go too."

Grace rose from tending Wak'o. "I am coming too."

"No," Moon said. "I must do this alone. I don't want to put any of you in any more danger."

Luke ignored her and gathered his things, as did Grace, and they stood at the entrance.

Moon smiled. "Okay then." She turned to Adam. "Please stay and tend Wak'o."

Adam grabbed up his bag and spear. "I was once suspicious of you. I thought you were like a panther in the dark. I was wrong. You will be Kayeeya. Adam will protect Kayeeya."

Moon took hold of Adams strong shoulders. "Adam, I am not your Kayeeya. I come from a far away place—"

"Don't talk down to him," Grace said. "He knows who and what you are. I think you are the one confused."

Moon turned to Grace, but said nothing. She slowly nodded and then started out of the cave. Grace hugged Wak'o and then followed Moon.

Adam said something to Orion in his own language and Orion nodded. Adam went back to Wak'o and gave her a kiss on the forehead and then left the cave also. Luke waved bye to Wak'o and she waved back and smiled. He took Orion's hand. He wanted to say something, but nothing came.

"Be careful," Orion said. "And if somehow you get back to our world, remember to give the carving to my daughter."

Luke nodded and left out of the cave and thought if Orion was more than just a farmer from 1854, he certainly knew nothing of the future.

Chapter 19

The group stopped to take a break by a small stream. They had been traveling—running—for miles, and Luke needed the water more than treasure. When he had his fill, he sat back on his butt for the needed break. The stream was orange with the reflection of the setting sun. Its beauty almost made Luke forget the dangerous mission—almost.

Moon piled down beside him and handed him a strip of jerky. "We may get lucky and actually beat Karl there. We may even be fortunate and the Scrain have already killed him."

He watched her tear a strip of the jerky with her perfect teeth. She savored it as she sat. He didn't know her now any better than he did in the beginning. But now he was in love with her whether he wanted to be or not.

"We will make a plan before we get there," she said. "I will scout it out first and then we will take him out."

"And then what?" Luke said.

She stopped chewing and looked at Luke for a long spell before finishing the jerky, but she didn't answer.

"When he is all good and dead, then what happens?"

"What do you mean, Luke?"

"Your mission is complete, right? I mean, that's what you came here for, right?"

She said nothing, just stared off into the distance.

Luke stood. "Well, my mission was to find Grace, and now I have. I'm taking her back through the portal."

She got to her feet. "Luke, I think that will land you in Nazi Germany."

"You don't know where it goes."

"If Shevay does, indeed, have control over the portal, he has it set for Karl to find his grandson in World War II Germany."

"That is not what you believed before. You told me Shevay believed the portals open at different locations, but at the same time period in our ancient world. To him that is now. And if that is what he thinks, he is wrong."

"I thought that, but now I'm not so sure." Moon stroked hair from Luke's face.

"We know it was open to our time," Luke said. "Grace came through it and days later you and I came through it, so I believe we will go back to that time."

"But look what happened to Turner."

"Turner didn't go through one of the portals. He jumped in the hole the bell made."

Moon began to speak, but just sighed.

Luke believed he knew exactly what she was thinking. It was all so complicated and the bottom line was—this world was more of a mystery than when he first arrived.

Grace walked up. "Luke, this place is so pretty."

Luke fumbled his attention to her and smiled. "Grace, I was just thinking the same thing. We will remember it when we get back to Arkansas."

Grace looked to Luke and then to Moon. "Is that even possible?"

Moon managed a slight smile, picked up her bag, and went to where Adam was sitting.

Grace turned back to Luke. "I don't understand."

"Honey, if we can, we are going back through the portal that brought us here."

"We will have to fight our way to it, won't we?" she said. "Is there any alternative?"

"Stay in this world."

Adam and Moon came up. "Let's move," Adam said as he started across the stream.

Moon followed Adam, but turned when she crossed the stream. "Grace, anything is possible." She turned back and fell in behind Adam.

Grace watched Adam and Moon go for a time before turning back to Luke. "Luke, I will do whatever you say. I trust you. I want to go home."

That heavy weight settled on his soul again. Hadn't he come to rescue her after all? Well, dammit, that's what he was going to do.

They moved down the dark trail like alert deer as the evening settled over the wild land. Adam was up ahead somewhere and out of sight. There was no way the group would be ambushed with him running point. Moon had her nine pulled and was in full commando mode. If she had to shoot, the surprise was over and the game would be up as they ran for their lives. Luke squeezed the bow in his hand as he brought up the rear. He expected a Scrain behind every bush and in every tree.

As they made their way down the trail, Moon pointed to bare feet sticking from the bushes. Adam had twisted the neck on one of the Scrain and had thrown him off the trail. Luke remembered when he had first met Adam. Luke had figured him to be a simple, big and dumb native—wrong.

Moon put her hand up and stopped the little group. She turned and pointed forward. There were several columns of smoke rising in the distance. Moon mouthed softly, "The village."

Luke's heart raced. This was it. For the last little while, he had been praying to God for strength and guidance. He needed all of his wilderness training brought to the ready. He prayed that the Almighty would keep his "buck fever" at bay. Luke would now need all his faculties brought to the top.

Luke caught movement behind him. He whirled and drew the bow at the same motion. But his inner brakes locked—it was Adam.

"If I had been a Scrain, you would have killed me for sure," Adam said.

Luke lowered the bow and took a deep, cleansing breath.

Moon came back to them. She said nothing, only waited for Adam to report.

"Many are out on the hunt and are to return tonight," Adam said. "They are building fires in preparation for the cleaning of the kill and a great feast."

"What about Karl?" Moon said.

"He is wandering around the village freely."

"Why?" Moon shook her head. "I don't understand. They kill everything. Why not him?"

"He's not alone."

"What do you mean, Adam? Come on out with it."

"The feathered Raceseyers are here."

Moon just stood there and said nothing.

"Why are they with him?" Luke said.

"Do you think Karl is taking them through the portal with him?" Grace said.

"Crap! I remember now," Luke said. "The Raceseyers were here when we came through the portal. I knew I had seen them somewhere, but I just couldn't remember." He looked to Grace and Moon. "Didn't y'all see them?"

"I was so scared." Grace shook her head.

Moon said, "No. There was too much going on when I went through the portal. My attention was on escaping. But it all makes sense now. They are the ones who open it. They use those horns for the harmonics, just like when they lift the heavy stones." Moon dropped to her butt. "The Nephilim control this portal and any other portal that may be in this world; that's how Shevay knew we were here."

"Shevay said he left this portal for the Florians to play with, so they would not destroy it," Luke said.

Moon picked up a stone and threw it into the darkness. "Oh, they leave it for them to play with alright. They come and open it like you would keep a piece of machinery working so it doesn't seize up. They levitate that giant rock for the portal to even work. These simple Florians come to it like animals come at feeding time. The giants let them have whatever sucks in to keep them appeased."

"But why do the giants want to keep it working?" Grace said as she dropped down next to Moon. "If they don't use it themselves, why do they even bother with it?"

"I thought Shevay understood we needed to stop Karl," Luke said. "He gave us weapons and told us to be swift to catch up to Karl. I don't understand. Is this a game for him?"

"I don't know," Moon said. "Something isn't right here. He made sure Karl made it here, and he made sure we arrived here too."

Adam reached down and hauled Moon to her feet. "My Kayeeya, we must leave here now."

Moon pulled from his grip. "What are you talking about?"

Adam turned to Luke. "Luke, you stay here and I will return for you, but I must get Kayeeya away from here and I must be swift."

"Adam, I have to stop Karl," Moon said. "I'm not going anywhere."

"Sha-She, they are waiting for us," Adam said. "This is a trap."

Moon stood just looking at Adam. It was clear to Luke she didn't understand, but now he did. "Go with him, Moon."

"I'm not going—" Moon started. Adam hit her with his big fist and caught her before she collapsed. He threw her over his shoulder.

"Why did you do that?" Grace said.

Adam ignored her. "Luke, if they open the portal, you two go for it. You will probably be killed anyway, so it is your only chance. I have to get my Kayeeya back to safety." He squeezed Luke's shoulder. "You are a brave warrior." He looked down at

Grace. "You both are. I am sorry to leave you alone but I need no tail."

"Go," Luke said. Adam whirled and sprinted down the trail and out of sight.

"Luke, what's going on here?" Grace said.

"The Nephilim open the portal and let the Florians have what comes in to appease them, a sacrifice to keep them under control so they don't bother the portal. If the portal didn't give up something every now and then, they would probably destroy it. This time the portal will not be letting anything in, only out. Something will have to be given to the savages for sacrifice."

Grace looked down at the ground. "And we are the something."

Luke hugged her. "That's right, Honey. Shevay had it planned well. He believes Karl will bring his son back, so he planned to sacrifice us."

Grace collected herself and stood straight. "But we are going to screw up his plans."

Luke smiled and tapped her on the face with a mock punch. "We dang sure are and we are going through that portal." Luke picked up his bow and bag. "Now, let us go see how we're going to do it." Grace followed him as they sneaked toward the portal.

Shadows danced like distorted demons as the Florians lit bonfires and torches around the plaza. The purple sky loomed ominous over the village as more and more people gathered at the carnival-like activity, at least a hundred already, their white hair changing from orange, yellow, and red with the reflections of the fires. A massive wooden cross loomed high in the center of the plaza as if waiting for Jesus himself to be brought forward. Luke wondered if they would actually crucify someone. Clubs, stones, and spears were piled neatly around it. Luke was reminded of the short story *The Lottery*. He now had a good understanding of how this was supposed to be played out if they were caught. At least Moon was safe with Adam. He hoped the punch from Adam wasn't too severe. He smiled to himself. She had it coming for hitting him with the pistol butt.

Luke had found skins to cover their clothes. Grace only needed to cover her hair—she already looked like a cave girl. Earlier they had hidden under a fallen tree close to the fire, waiting like lions to pounce when the opportunity presented itself. Luke didn't know what that opportunity would look like. As more people gathered, he was beginning to feel more like a deer than a lion, but he believed he was ready. If they opened that portal, he was going to cover for Grace; and then he was going to follow her into that wormhole and hope and pray they landed back in Arkansas at the exact, right time.

Grace squeezed Luke's arm and whispered, "I'm more scared than I have ever been, but I'm ready."

Luke turned to her, smiled, and winked. She was such a beauty. She was strong. So was Moon, but he had to keep his mind on this situation now and not her. He wanted to escape this place but he didn't want to leave Moon. The forces were almost the same.

The plan for now was simple: Luke didn't have one—not really. But he was shooting for two objectives. The most important was to stop Karl from going through the portal, and that more than likely meant killing him. Luke had never killed anyone before coming to this world, but he had only killed here in self-defense. Killing Karl would be different—it would have been planned in advance. That was a different bear altogether. The second objective was to escape through that portal. An arrow could take care of Karl, but he didn't have any idea how he was going to get them through the wormhole.

Luke watched Karl pace all over the plaza. It was easy to tell he was not a patient man. More than once he addressed the orange-feathered guys and pointed to the side of the hill where the portal had spit Luke from Arkansas. No doubt he wanted them to go ahead and get the show on the road, but they paid him little attention. These men were dedicated to Shevay, and they would follow his wishes only.

Once when Karl came within twenty yards of Luke's hiding blind Luke thought about putting an arrow in his brain, but suppressed the thought. If he did that, there would be no reason for them to open the portal. There would be nothing to distract all the Florians, and they would be on them like flies on a hot t—

"Luke, look!" Grace said.

He looked where Grace was looking. One of the Raceseyers was placing stones on a pedestal about forty yards in front of the mountainside. Luke raised his binoculars. All at once sparks and electrical charges crackled over the stones. "What the hell?"

Grace reached for the binoculars. "What are they?"

They were the same type stones Moon had collected in that valley, the same ones she used to pull lighting from the pyramids.

"I think that may be the key that opens the portal to get out of here." Luke turned to Grace. "The Raceseyers had those rocks when they raised those giant stones. Moon used them to direct the electricity at the pyramid."

The drumming started. Luke found the drummers, four of them beating on skin-covered logs.

"It's the same sound I heard when I was brought here," Grace said. "I think it's beginning."

Luke took the binoculars and crammed them into his bag. "Let's be ready. We don't know how this is going to go down." Luke dropped his bag and the little mammoth carving fell out.

"What is this?" Grace said.

"Orion asked me to give this to his daughter if I returned to our world. I guessed I would give it to one of his descendants."

Grace picked it up from the ground. All at once a red "X" appeared on its side and began glowing. "Look, Luke!"

Luke took it. The "X" glowed and then went dim. A memory flashed in Luke's brain. Orion had said: "Give this to my daughter. If not her, maybe a grandchild—some descendant. Tell them it is the key."

"What is that thing, Luke?"

"Of course. Of course." Luke shook the carving in his hand. "Shevay had said the key keeper had abandon his grandson. His priests, the Raceseyers, tried to bring the key keeper back, but he kept closing the portals with his key. This is that key."

"What are you talking about?"

"Remember that painting with Alexander's men? One of the soldiers had this little mammoth carving with the "X" on it.

"I don't understand."

"I knew there was something special about him. Grace, Orion is a wizard—the key keeper. That was Orion with Alexander. That's what that painting was portraying. They tried to get him back, but he escaped again. The Raceseyers finally caught up with him in 1854 in Alabama."

"Are you talking about the story you told me about Orion Williamson?"

"Yes. They pulled him back into this world when he stepped off that porch and started across that field."

"Then this key can get us home."

"No, Grace. Shevay said it only opens the portal into this world, not out of it." He crammed the carving into her bag.

"Why are you putting it in my bag?"

"Grace, Honey, if something happens to me, you go for the portal and don't look back." She bit her lip and slowly nodded. Luke continued, "If you see you can't make it, you run like the Ozark wind to Orion's cave. There you will be with good friends, good people. Okay?"

Tears started down Grace's face. "Luke, I will do what you say." She wiped at the tears, but they continued. "I don't know how to thank you for coming after me. This is all my fault."

"No, Sweetie. It's not your..." Luke saw a nightmare unfolding in front of him on the plaza. The Raceseyers were pulling Moon by a rope tied around her neck. She was blindfolded, her hands bound behind her back.

Grace turned to see what Luke was looking at. "Oh, no!" She scanned all around. "Where is Adam?"

Luke felt his very soul sink. He squeezed his bow in his hand

and nocked an arrow.

Karl marched up to Moon and said something, but he was too far for Luke to hear, and then Karl slapped her so hard she fell to the ground and her blindfold fell off.

"Damn it!" Luke said. But he could do nothing. He had to wait.

One of the Raceseyers shoved Karl aside, as the others hauled Moon to her feet. They marched her to the cross.

"They are going to tie her to the cross," Grace said. "Oh, my God. Where is Adam?"

One of the Raceseyers pulled a long, copper spike and a hammer from a bag.

"No. No. No." Grace whispered.

Luke felt the blood race through his body. He raised the bow and took aim. He hesitated, torn. If he shot, they would all be killed and the German would escape through the portal. But inside, his very heart screamed for him to shoot.

Two of the Raceseyers held Moon to the cross as another placed the spike against Moon's hand. Karl ran up and jerked the hammer from his hand. Even he couldn't stand it. Another Raceseyer grabbed him and hauled him away. Moon kicked and jerked, but it was no use. She snapped her head side to side, but said nothing as the hammer came down on the spike. But with the second blow, she lost the battle of will and screamed. The darkness was complete now and the bright fire painted evil, crawling shadows over a tortured Special Agent Moon Serling. The Florians cheered.

Luke lowered the bow and looked away. There was nothing he could do. The screams pierced his soul, but he had to bear it. Grace moved to him, buried her face in his side and wept.

The Raceseyers gathered around the stones and another brought horns for them. They slowly began to blow, softly at first, and slowly the lonely note grew louder. They did not move or sway—they were in a trance. Moon had stopped screaming. She had collected herself as well as she could and stared at the twinkling night sky. Luke looked to where she was staring. Orion's belt shown bright—it always draws your attention. The Florians slowly approached the cross, picking up the stones and clubs and spears. The drums beat louder. The horns grew louder. Luke's hair began to rise as a charge filled the air, and a vacuum began pulling leaves and sticks toward the hillside. It was beginning.

Moon withstood the first two stones that hit her body, but screamed with pain as the last one slammed into her shin. She collected herself and looked back toward the starry sky in defiance as the white-heads took turns picking up the weapons to hurl at her.

Luke watched as they picked up each stone, but forced himself not to shoot. He kept looking at the mountainside as things were drawn into the portal. It started small and slowly grew. He could see through it as surely as if it were a window. The Florians chanted and sang some crazy song as it grew larger.

"Oh, no!" Grace said.

Luke turned to see a big man pick up the largest club from the ground. The crowd screamed and cheered. Moon did not look away from the sky. Out of no where Karl bulldogged the man to the ground, but others came and pulled him off. The man stood back in front of Moon with his club, and Karl looked down and turned away. He looked back at Moon one more time, then started for the growing portal. Karl was the enemy, but he clearly didn't want Moon tortured.

Moon turned toward Karl and yelled, "Stop him!" At the same instant, the big man raised the club like a major league batter.

Luke had to stop Karl—it was the mission. It is what Moon demanded. He eased the bow up before him and drew all his focus on a tiny spot on his target. He had done this thousands of times. It was all primal now, all controlled by the subconscious like an inner autopilot. He bore a hole into that very spot with all of his mind and being. At that very instant, at that very place, there was nothing else in the world but that tiny spot. His breathing was slow, his body solid and unmoving as a stone. He drew the bow back in a slow and fluid motion until his hand found the magic anchor spot on his face. This all happened without him thinking of it or controlling it. All he knew of the world was the spot he was focused on. Focus. Focus. Focus. The arrow drilled into the big Florian's temple and he collapsed in half swing of his club. The world came back to Luke in a rush. He reached for another arrow, but a Florian came out of nowhere and drove him to the ground. Grace rammed her knife into the man's brain. Luke knew it was too late now, and Karl would escape.

An explosion rung Luke's ears as he climbed to his feet. Karl dropped to his knees just before the portal and folded to the ground. His bag dropped from his side and a green glow shown through the folds. Luke whirled to see Adam holding Moon's pistol. Adam was bleeding from a wound to the head, and a broken spear was lodged in his shoulder.

"Here Luke," Adam said as he tossed the pistol to Luke.

Luke caught it and turned with it in time to stop two Florians as they ran to Moon.

Adam took Grace's knife and ran for Moon. He was bloody and battered, but he sprinted all the same. He yelled, "Kayeeya." He dodged two spears. When he ran to Moon, he realized she wasn't tied to the cross, but nailed. He turned to fight and protect his princess.

Luke emptied the pistol. He turned for his bow, but saw that Adam had dropped Moon's bag. He grabbed it up. There was one grenade left. He saw the portal closing. He turned to Grace. "Honey, go for the portal!"

"But what about you? What about Adam and Moon?"

Luke handed Grace the grenade. "You know how this works?"

She quickly examined it. "Yes, I think so."

"You pull that pin when you start running, and you toss that thing like a softball at those horn blowers and that pedestal of rocks."

"But Luke—"

"Grace, you have to save Tyler." Luke turned to see the portal shrinking. "I'm so proud of you." He gave her a quick smile, and then said, "Go!"

She kissed him quickly on the cheek, snatched the pin out, and raced for the portal. Two Florians jumped in front of her. She kicked one in the groin, and Luke put an arrow in the other. She tossed the grenade and it landed in the middle of the stones. She dove through the portal as it closed and disappeared. The grenade exploded. Orange feathers and chunks blew in all directions. The side of the hill where the portal was located shot electric sparks and arcs and crumbled into a pile of rubble.

The Florians were confused from the blast, but they soon rallied. Luke shot his last arrow and ran to Adam and Moon. He picked up a spear and stood with his back to Adam.

"I'm sorry, Luke," Moon said.

Luke turned and kissed her. "I'm where I want to be." He turned back in time to run his spear into an attacker. He knew it was hopeless as the enemy closed in.

The first attacker caught an arrow through his body and dropped to the ground. Two more had a similar problem. Luke searched for the source of the arrows and found Wak'o atop the tallest hut. She was astraddle it and slinging arrows. It was Orion's bow. Then there was a loud trumpet and the Florians scattered in all directions like roaches. Rockets started flying and exploding, lighting up the village. It was Orion on a mammoth. Yes, there really was something unique about the man.

Moon fainted and Adam held her as Luke carved the wood away from the spikes with his knife. It was a slow process, and he believed it hurt his heart as much as it hurt Moon's hands. He finally broke the last one free, and Adam laid her on an animal skin that Wak'o had found and brought up. Luke pulled the bloody spikes from her hand. Moon awoke and gritted her teeth, but it could not stop the scream.

Adam retrieved the bag from Karl's body. He slowly extracted the green orb. "Esva."

Orion placed Moon's hands atop of each other and aligned the punctures. He then took the orb from Adam and lowered it to the nail wounds. He squeezed it into the top wound, and Luke could see the glow between her hands as it also went into the other wound.

"Orion, save some of it," Luke said.

Orion concentrating on his task, didn't look up, but said. "Pull it out of him."

Adam and Luke were both kneeling beside Moon, and they stood. Wak'o took Adam's hand as Luke grabbed hold of the spear stub sticking from Adam's shoulder.

"I'm going to pull fast," Luke said.

Adam looked into Wak'o's eyes and smiled. "Pull."

Luke jerked so fast that when the spear came free, he hit the ground.

Orion stood with a much smaller orb and placed it into the wound. They watched as it oozed in. After a short time, the orbs came out of Moon's and Adam's wounds brown and tired looking. They slowly flew in a circle around them. They began undulating as they picked up speed, faster and faster, until they became one blur. Just as they had at the river's edge, the brown orbs shot into the sky, and out of sight.

Luke helped Moon to her feet, and she slowly wrapped her arms around his neck. Wak'o did the same to Adam.

Orion made a gesture with his hand and the mammoth came toward him.

Luke surveyed the destruction and death. "Shevay will not stand for this."

Orion rubbed the great mammoth's trunk. With his white hair reflecting the firelight, he now appeared to be the wizard he truly was. "I will deal with Shevay. We go way back, and I know his weakness."

Luke smiled at Orion and nodded.

Moon squeezed Luke. "Looks like you are stuck with me in my world."

Luke admired her pretty, but exhausted face. "You know, I've always dreamed of a world like this." He kissed her long and slow. It was like a drink of refreshing water after a very long thirst.

"Adam, place Wak'o and Moon on this beast and let's go home before the savages return," Orion said.

Luke went over to retrieve his bow and bag. He looked down and saw Grace's footprints where she had scuffed the ground as she started for the portal. He looked toward the heap of rubble where the portal once was. "Have a good life, Grace...in your world." He turned toward a smiling Moon. "I intend to have one in mine."

Chapter 20

Grace landed on her face. It was suddenly daylight. She rolled over and looked back toward the portal. There was only the trail she had last seen when she and Tyler were hiking, no portal or other world. She sat and wrapped her arms around her knees. "Oh, Luke," she whispered. She just sat there for a long time looking down the trail, not knowing what to do next. It was surreal. "Moon," she said to no one, "Karl didn't make it out. We don't have to worry about that anymore." She thought of Moon on the cross and began to weep. Grace figured she would never know what happened to her friends and was sure the grenade had closed the portal forever.

Ding! Ding! Ding... The dinging continued about twenty times. She reached in her bag. It was Luke's phone. There were three bars and the text messages were catching up. She was really home! She looked at the date—it was exactly a week later from the time she went through the portal. "Yes!" She got to her feet. "Yes!"

A shadow fell over her. It was the eagle. She danced around in a circle for a time. She crammed the phone in her bag and started down the hill. She almost stepped on a box turtle with its orange-spotted neck stretched, surveying the immediate world. Grace pointed back up the hill. "I wouldn't go that way.

You could get lost up there." She laughed, extended her arms, and turned another circle.

The truck was there right where it was supposed to be, and the key was hidden under the spare tire just as Luke had said it would be. She started the truck and the radio came on. *Good News from the Graveyard* by Southern Raised filled the cab. Luke loved that Ozark band, she remembered. She looked at her animal skin clothes and laughed. They were going to love it at the sheriff's office. She pulled the truck onto the road and headed for Tyler.

Just as the truck reached the bottom of the mountain, static buzzed and crackled from the speakers. The truck engine stopped. "What now?" The engine would not start; it would do nothing. A flash reflected in the mirrors. She looked out the window and back toward the mountain. The eagle was still circling. A strange streak of lightning zagged across the clear sky. It was almost blinding. She turned away. "What on earth…"

A red glow oozed from her bag lying on the seat. She took a few deep breaths to calm herself. She slowly reached for the bag and dumped it out. The "X" on the little mammoth was glowing again, but as she picked it up the glow slowly faded and disappeared. "Oh, boy, what next?" She shoved it and the other contents back into the bag. She didn't want to think about it right now. She just wanted to hurry to Tyler. She tried the key and the truck started. "Thank goodness." She put the truck in gear, but hesitated. Something compelled her to look back toward the mountain one last time—there was no lightning now, just a normal Ozark mountain, just another normal day. The eagle was gone.

Note from the Author

Thank you for reading *Portal to the Forgotten*. I hope you enjoyed it as much as I enjoyed creating it. If you would like to be the first to know when my next book is released, go to www.johngschwend.com and sign up for my mailing list. I promise I will never send spam or give away your email address, and you can unsubscribe at any time.

Word of mouth and reviews are crucial for any author to succeed. Without them, our work is invisible. Please consider leaving a review, tell your friends and mentioning my books on social media. Even if it is only a few words, it will be a giant help.

Please check out my other novels and short stories at www.johngschwend.com. You can email me at johngschwend@gmail.com.

Best wishes,

John Gschwend

Sample of Chase The Wild Pigeons

Darkness crawled across the overgrown graveyard. The headstones were bent and canted from neglect and shoved aside by determined bushes and saplings. A smoky fog had rolled in off the Mississippi River, floating through the cemetery like ghosts.

Joe snuggled in behind a big headstone, knowing the Yankee sergeant would be coming soon; he had learned the soldier's routine well. Joe looked over his shoulder; his partner was hid behind a square, green-furred headstone. That's right, Curtis; stay alert. We can't afford to be caught, have to complete our mission for the cause.

Joe didn't know why these Yankees had held up here in Helena instead of going on down to Vicksburg where the fighting was. It didn't matter; they were here, and he was going to do his duty.

He settled in for the wait, had to have patience. He placed his face against the stone, cold and damp. He felt the inscription with his fingers. Curious, he backed off enough to read it. There barely was enough light, but he made out:

Allen Buford
Born 1802 Died 1851
May the angels guard him for eternity.

Joe felt a shiver, thought about looking for the angels.

"Psst!"

Joe started, then whirled. Curtis was pointing. Joe turned. The big Yankee was coming down the path. In the late gloom, his uniform appeared more black than blue. It was him, Sergeant Davis of Iowa.

Joe buried behind the headstone like a tick behind a dog's

ear. Everything was automatic now. They had planned it well. They had practiced the escape. He was ready. He felt an electric screw in his chest and drumming in his ears, but he was ready.

The Yankee drifted down the dark, foggy path like a demon. He was a huge man, the biggest Yankee at Helena. He stopped at the exact place Joe had planned, slowly scanned the area, his Springfield rifle covering the area in a smooth circle, the bayonet on the end like a medieval spear.

Joe tried to melt into the back of the headstone. He knew Curtis was doing the same.

The Yankee finally seemed satisfied he was alone. He dropped a handful of leaves by a stump. There was a convenient chunk of firewood standing about eight inches beside it. The big man leaned his gun against a headstone, then unbuttoned his pants, and they fell to his ankles. He lowered his shining butt down on the stump and firewood—a homemade privy. Soon the music began—he was sputtering and spewing like a clogged flute.

Joe grinned. He had heard the soldiers call it the "Arkansas Quickstep." They had all sorts of afflictions and diseases, living in cramped quarters and not being use to the southern climate.

Curtis giggled behind him.

Sergeant Davis snapped his head in that direction. "Who's there?"

Joe turned toward Curtis, but his partner was hid well. He's going to get us shot, Joe thought. He was usually scared of his own shadow—now he's laughing.

Davis turned back, must have assumed it was the wind. The sputtering began again.

Joe got to his knees. He was going to do this right. This mission would go off perfectly. He squeezed the weapon in his hands.

Davis grunted, and his rear popped like a cork shot out of a bottle.

Curtis snickered.

Davis yelled, "Who the hell is over there? Answer me damn

it!" He reached for his musket.

Joe knew it was time. He leaped to his feet, jerked the rope in his hands. The rope snapped tight, catapulted leaves and sticks from the ground, then snatched the chunk of firewood from under Sergeant Davis's right cheek. Davis's arms fanned the air for purchase, but found none. His left cheek let go of the stump, and he landed butt-first into his own mess.

Curtis screamed laughter.

Joe struck out for the escape route. "Come on, Curtis!"

Davis tried to stand, slipped, and fell back into the shit. "Who the hell is over there?"

Joe stopped.

"No, Joe, keep going," Curtis said, "we've been lucky so far, let's don't push it."

Joe grinned. He turned toward the darkness that hid Davis and whistled "Dixie."

Davis replied instantly: "Joseph Taylor! You little runt!"

Joe cut out for home with Davis's yells fading behind him.

You can purchase *Chase The Wild Pigeons* at Amazon.com and most online bookstores. The audio version is available at Audible.com, itunes and Amazon.com. You can listen to samples at www.johngschwend.com.

Made in the USA
Coppell, TX
30 September 2021

63269179R00142